Syndicated

Aella C Grey

The Book:

"They control the narrative, they always have, and that's where their power lies for now."

Maris Sylvara came to Kharidia to report the truth. As a correspondent for the News Alliance Network, she expected danger, but nothing could prepare her for the brutal reality of war or the slow, disturbing change in her boyfriend, Rob. When an attack creates distance between them, Maris is forced to flee, sprinting right into the path of the rebellion's most feared weapon: a lethal, golden-eyed magic user cloaked in mystery.

His power is undeniable. His presence, magnetic. And despite everything she's been told, Maris can't bring herself to run from him.

While helping Kharidian civilians escape the destruction, Maris begins to see the war—and her own heart—in a new light. But as her choices grow darker and her hands far from clean, one question remains:

Will she lose herself to a monster… or will she lose herself to the war? Find out in Syndicated, book four in the Prince of Hell Series.

The Author:

Aella C Grey is an author hailing from Winnipeg, MB, Canada, currently residing in the sunny state of Florida. When she's not immersed in the world of writing, Aella indulges in her other passions, such as playing video games, diving into captivating books, and cherishing quality time with her beloved dog and supportive husband.

With a vivid imagination and a deep appreciation for storytelling, Aella brings her unique perspective to the realm of fiction. Her love for literature and interactive entertainment has fueled her creative endeavors, inspiring her to craft compelling narratives that transport readers to captivating worlds.

Aella's writing draws readers in with dynamic characters, intriguing plots, and a touch of magic. Whether she's exploring mystical realms or delving into the complexities of the human experience, her stories are infused with emotion, suspense, and a dash of the unexpected.

Stay connected with Aella C. Grey through her website to discover more about her upcoming works, behind-the-scenes insights, and to join her on thrilling literary adventures.

Syndicated

Prince of Hell IV

by

Aella C Grey

Aella C Grey - Florida, USA

1. Edition, 2025

Aella C Grey - Florida, USA

Table of Contents

Important

Much like the Unbroken, the Prince of Hell series has ties to real world problems, which some readers may find uncomfortable. As with all fictional books, the relationships are special in their own way, with characters that have their own personalities and flaws. None of my writing is meant to diminish the seriousness of what individuals have gone through in their lives, nor is my writing meant to demean religion in any way, shape or form.

Want a playlist that goes with the book?

Prince of Hell has its own Spotify playlist, created by Aella C Grey.

Trigger warnings:

Anxiety, Abusive Relationship, Alcohol, Attempted Sexual Assault (CH6-P41-42), Battle Scenes, Blood & Injury Depictions, Branding, Child Death, Cults, Death, Demons, Dismemberment, Explosions, Fire, Gore, Genocide, Gun Violence, Hostages, Hospitalization, Murder, Physical Abuse, Poverty, Profanity, Religion, Religious Trauma, Sexual Assault (CH5-P31-33) Secret Society, Sexually Explicit Scenes, Violence, War Themes

This book contains heavily sensitive and traumatic scenes depicting things that are horrendous and should never be glorified.

Read at your own risk, but know that your mental health is more important, so please do not take this lightly.

Dedication

To everyone who gas-lit themselves into thinking it was their fault.
To everyone who wondered if they could have done something
differently to change the outcome.
To the ones who years later still regret not speaking out, or those
who scream into the darkness only for it to fall upon deaf ears.
And for those whose stories have long gone untold...
I'm with you every step of the way.
Let Maris Sylvara do what we couldn't.

Glossary

There are multiple pronunciations for these words, especially given different dialects, so please see the phonetic pronunciation below as intended for this series.

Maris (Mah-ris), Sylvara (Sill-vah-rah), Sitri (Sih-t-ree)

Deliom (Dee-lee-ohm), Lennard (Leh-nar-d), Anne (Ahn-neh)

Kira (Kee-rah), Caass (Cah-ss), Caassali (Cah-sah-lee)

Arrenault (Arr-eh-n-alt), Merrick (Meh-rr-ick)

Vassago (Vah-sah-go), Greenberg (Gree-n-berg)

Daimōn (Dey-mohn), Godfrey (God-free), Barclay (Bar-clay)

Marianne (Mah-ree-ann), Janine (Jah-nee-n), Abbess (Ah-bess)

Qur'an (Qur-ahn), Ramayana (Rah-mah-yuh-nuh)

Mahabharata (Ma-hab-hara-ta), Puranas (Pu-rah-nuh)

Upanishads (Oo-pan-i-shads)

Bhagavad Gita (Buh-guh-vuh-d gee-ta)

Lemegeton (Le-meh-jeh-ton), Solomon (Sol-uh-muhn)

Grimoire (Grim-wah-r), Goetia (Go-eh-sha)

Theurgia (Thee-ur-jee-ah), Paulina (Paw-lee-nah)

Almadel (All-mah-del), Notoria (No-toh-ree-ah)

Bael (Bay-ehl), Asmodeus (Az-moe-dee-us), Purson (Per-son)

Vine (Vy-n), Beleth (Buh-leth), Paimon (Pay-mon)

Balam (Ba-lahm), Zagan (Zai-g-ahn), Belial (Bee-lie-all)

Agares (Ay-gar-es), Dantalion (Dan-tal-eon)

Amdusias (Am-do-see-as), Vapula (Vah-pool-ah)

Aym (Ay-m), Bathin (Bah-th-een), Zepar (Zeh-par)

Eligos (E-lee-gos), Gusion (Gu-sh-ion), Barbas (Bahr-bahs)

Valefor (Val-eh-four), Vepar (Veh-par), Astaroth (As-tuh-roth)

Berth (Behr-ith), and Buné (Boo-neh) Ipos (Eye-poh-s)

Gäap (Guh-ahp), Orobas (Oh-roh-bas)

Chapter 1

"Yeah, take that dick." Robert grunts between shallow thrusts, palming my breasts. He breathes hard and shudders, leaning forward as he comes. "Shit, Maris."

Two minutes.

That might be a new record.

He withdraws quickly, sucking in a breath as he crawls backward. With his weight off my chest, my steady breaths come easier. Being shorter than Rob by a few inches, and half his weight has its perks—one being that I don't need to fake breathlessness.

Suffocating under his body does that for me.

He pats my thigh twice and stands beside the bed. "Did that feel good?"

Rob's already losing inches as he softens, with a bead of come threatening to drip from the tip.

I give him a wry smile that feels more like a wince. "Uh, yeah."

If my answer satisfies him, he doesn't show it. Instead, he blows out a breath and steps across the room to the bathroom. Seconds later the shower turns on, and he slides the door half-shut. "Did you come?"

The empty feeling in my core contradicts my words as I sit up. "Uh, I think so."

I hate lying, but the last time I told him I didn't come, he threw a fit in his embarrassment, and blamed me for being too tight.

'If you weren't gripping me so hard, I'd have lasted longer.'

'Maybe next time if you don't just lay there, you'll come.'

'You always find something to blame me for. I can't even enjoy sex without you ruining it.'

When he said I was too tight, I nearly lost it. The last thing I want to explain to a grown man is that foreplay is a thing, and "tight" isn't the flex he thinks it is.

So I don't go there.

"Well, that's better than nothing," he calls out from the other room. I can almost hear the shrug in his voice before he lets out a relieved sigh. "At least I won't be so wound up for our meeting with Thornton."

His release trickles down my thigh as I walk to the bathroom. Steam fogs the shower to my left, but I slip into the separate toilet room to clean up first.

The dull anxiety knowing we have a meeting with our boss still hums at the back of my mind. "It'll be fine, I'm sure." I call out, assuming he can hear me over the shower. "He probably just wants to know how our research is going."

Ben Thornton is the third news director we've had in the past two years at News Alliance Network. He's been funding our research on the war since we got assigned to it.

Sometimes I think we only got the assignment because of our competition. The lack of resources definitely supports that theory.

The toilet flushes, and I silently thank my IUD for the unspoken work it's doing as the door to the shower opens.

Robert steps out and grabs his towel behind the door. "Maybe. It's not like we've broken anything worth substance though. All we have is what other reporters and journalists have already covered. None of it is unique."

I chew my lip as I watch him sweep the towel over his body, and I can't say I disagree.

We just aren't close enough to it, and I don't have the money to fly there on my own dime.

A ticket alone is over two thousand.

Prices skyrocketed when the conflict started, and I don't foresee it getting better anytime soon. They put a civilian travel ban in place just before we were assigned, which only made our options even harder to come by. So, unless Thornton wants to pay an arm and a leg...

Rob wraps the towel around his waist, walking into the bedroom to get dressed without another word, and I head for the shower that he left on, like usual.

I step under the scalding water with a relieved sigh. The water seeping into my long, dark locks of hair, weighing them down before the excess streams to the floor.

This has always been our routine after sex. He showers immediately to clean off and leaves it on for me. I've always thought that he assumed the gesture seemed sweet, but more and more it feels less like love and more like filth.

I've always craved to just lie in bed after for a bit; to savor the intimacy. But the one time I mentioned it, he brushed me off.

He didn't want to get come on the sheets.

He felt sticky, or sweaty.

There was always a reason he didn't want to or couldn't.

Either way, I felt stupid for asking, so this has been our ritual ever since.

Rob's voice carries from the bedroom, and I squeeze shampoo into my palm. "I mean at this point, the war will be over soon anyway, and it's not like we're involved much. This is foreign affairs. I don't even know why people are so interested."

My chest tightens as I lather shampoo through my hair.

There are rumors that the rebels are close to being wiped out, despite fighting on multiple fronts. The most prominent rumor is about the magic user they have in their ranks.

Weeks ago, a video taken by a civilian in Kharidia went viral on social media, further perpetuating the rumor.

The thirty-second clip showed an enormous fireball the size of a bus hurtled through the air and slamming into an apartment building. Screams erupted as the fire spread, and when gunfire filled the air, the recording stopped.

That was the last video uploaded by that civilian.

I can only assume they're dead.

Lathering soap over my body, I scoff. "Don't pretend you haven't seen the video, Rob."

Rob leans in and makes a face at me in the reflection of the mirror. "Give me ten minutes with a video editing program and I could make you believe anything, Maris."

I roll my eyes, and he disappears back into the bedroom.

They **could** be doctored, but it wouldn't make sense unless someone was trying to drive a wedge between humans and magic users—or servilians—as they call themselves.

Besides, it's only viral on social media, which is probably why Thornton tasked us with researching it more.

He wants a counter-narrative.

It's not even like this war is new. It's been months at least. But, people are becoming more aware of it, and how our government has been helping provide intel to one side.

Allegedly.

All of this is alleged, because without boots on the ground, there's no way we'd know for certain.

My stomach churns uncomfortably, and I shut the faucet off.

The last thing we want is for the videos to be true, and to start a war between servilians and humans. Tensions have already been high across the globe.

When magic returned to earth years ago, and the servilians reappeared out of nowhere, it polarized countries. Some welcomed them with open arms, others pushed back and hid their existence away.

Ours did the latter.

But pretending they don't exist and suppressing their livelihoods, wasn't enough. Not when they congregate around the cities where their portals are, and they can summon elements as easy as breathing.

I was ten when I met a servilian for the first time. If I'm being honest, I should have known he wasn't human because of his height and stature, but being so young, I guess it only makes sense that I overlooked that.

He cleared all the leaves on my parent's lawn with one flick of his wrist, and that's when I knew for sure he was different. That didn't stop me from trying to summon magic myself, though.

I spent weeks copying the hand movement he did without the results, and I was so frustrated that I stomped over to his house and demanded that he teach me.

Grabbing my towel, I fight the urge to smile at the memory as I dry myself off.

Young me was so upset when he said I don't have abilities that I cried. To make matters worse, the stranger apologized to me with tears in his eyes before explaining why I don't have abilities. But he spent the next hour telling me how beautiful humanity is.

That was the day I learned everything I needed to know about servilians.

When my parents found out about the stranger, they told me to stop making things up, and relied heavily on the church to set me straight.

It never worked, even if they thought it did.

A few years after, we moved to a larger city, and when they saw magic for the first time, they were forced to accept servilian's existence.

They never did say they were sorry for gas lighting me, though.

Since then, the country has been in a state of turmoil. Half of us know they exist, and the other half doesn't. Of those who know, they either accept servilians as they are, considering them ordinary people with abilities, while the others treat them like dirt.

That said, for the majority of the world, they're simply known as magic users, since most don't know their origin.

Hanging my towel, I pace out of the bedroom to find Rob tucking his polo into his pants, and I make my way past him to the closet.

If this is a servilian–magic user–helping a foreign adversary, it could spell disaster and cause even more hardship over the region. Not to mention the tension around the globe with servilians would get irrevocably worse if humanity sees a servilian fighting a human war.

Grabbing a pair of dress pants from the closet, I blow out a breath.

God, I hope the viral videos are doctored.

Chapter 2

"Ah, Mr. Paulson, Ms. Sylvara. Good morning." Thornton murmurs from behind his long black desk. His hard gaze is fixed on his screen; he clicks around a few times, and I have a feeling we are about to hear some bad news.

I don't think he'd remove both of us, but part of me knows funding *two* journalists who aren't getting anywhere with their research is just money circling the drain.

"Morning, sir." I murmur. My palms grow slick, and I press them to my dress pants.

We both ease into our seats when his gaze turns to us. "Well? How's it been going?"

Dread coils in my stomach. Even though we both have the same answer, Rob stays silent, forcing me to take the brunt of the explanation.

"We don't have many leads at the moment. Cited sources have nothing fresh to offer, and without physically being there, it's impossible to get new stories."

Thornton's jaw ticks. "So you're empty-handed."

"We need fresh sources, and civilian travel to the region has been halted. I'm not sure what you're expecting."

"Not sure what I'm expecting, Sylvara?" He pushes to his feet and slams his hand against the desk. "Channel Five News has reported on the same content for a week and is doubling our viewership. I don't give a fuck what you think I'm expecting. I want a story."

My eyes widen. "Channel Five News just had a reporter *die* to get them that story!"

Finally, Rob decides to chime in. "Besides, their viewership is inflated. Everyone knows they manipulate their numbers on purpose."

My eyes widen as I look at him.

What. The. Fuck.

*What does that have to do with **anything**?*

Somehow, it seems to work on Thornton as he nods. "Still. We can't have one journalist doing fuck all, never mind two." My teeth clench. "I sent a request last week for funding approval to send you both to the front lines. If you can't get me a story being that close to it, then don't bother coming back at all."

My eyes widen in earnest, finding Rob who just infuriatingly nods his head as if he would be just fine to lose his job–or life– because of this.

I'm aware my line of work is not always a safe one, but to be on the front lines of a foreign country's war...

"What exactly do you want from us, Thornton?" I'm aware my tone is more sharp than it should be, but if I'm going to risk my life to get this asshole his story, he can take my attitude.

Thornton's eyes narrow on me. "I want you to find out what atrocities this abomination of a magic user is committing, and anything else that will help us end this war."

I frown. "It's not our war."

He just waves me off. "We all know the effects of war impact all countries, not just the two involved. Your tickets are in your emails."

Rob nods dutifully beside me. "Yes, sir."

Thornton gestures to the door. "Now get out and don't come back unless you have something we can run with."

I can hardly give a nod as I push to my feet, feeling an odd note of bitterness toward Rob and Thornton both.

He wants a story? I'll get him one.

That's if I don't die first.

My feet carry me down the hallway, lagging behind Rob if only to keep distance between us.

I'm painfully aware of how well he plays the role of dutiful reporter, always eager to kiss the feet of our superiors, but this entire ordeal has left a sour taste in my mouth.

Maybe it has to do with this morning, and being left wanting, but even as I stare at his back, there's not a single flicker of emotion toward Rob other than disgust.

I mean, sure, I'd never felt overly attracted to him.

We just got along, and over time I'd developed something close to attraction. It's like those stories where one person would say their partner isn't their typical type, but something about their personality just clicked.

That's what I thought our relationship was.

Rob walks into the open elevator and holds his arm out, keeping it from closing before I can file inside. Awkward silence stretches between us as the doors close.

"You don't always have to take his side, you know." I grind out, feeling his attention turn to me.

"The hell does that mean?" Robert says in a low tone.

"It means you really play the golden boy well." I murmur, keeping my voice light. "You really sold it. Almost had me convinced that you moonlight as Thornton's lapdog."

In my peripherals, Rob's brow raises ever so slightly. "I was being professional and doing my job, Maris—something you could benefit learning from."

I scoff, crossing my arms over my chest. "Professional doesn't usually mean signing up to be a goddamn bullet sponge."

Rob's jaw feathers, but he doesn't respond as the elevator dings, and the doors roll open.

In fact, Rob says nothing when we get into the car and the entire drive home. When I hold the door to the apartment open for him, all I get is a curt nod before following his steps into our shared space.

I don't know what's worse. Him being this angry with me, or that I feel nothing in response.

Part of me knows what this means deep down, but I shove those thoughts away.

He disappears into the kitchen, and I head straight for the laundry room, hauling clothes from the dryer into the basket.

My mind still reels, knowing we're heading straight into a literal war zone within the next twenty-four hours.

Kharidia was once a beautiful country, its people and rich culture on display for all to see. When I was in my senior year of high school, I'd done an essay on the countries in the region, and Kharidia was one that always held a special place in my heart.

Beautiful enormous fountains near their government buildings, gorgeous landscaping that fostered local trees and flowers. They build apartment buildings to allow less foresting, respecting the space of the species of animals.

They had free healthcare, free education and were quite progressive until civil war broke out.

To this day, no one truly knows why it happened, or what caused such an acute onset of societal unraveling.

I can't imagine the devastation from the past few years.

We'll find out soon, I guess.

Losing myself to my thoughts, I go through the motions of putting away our clothes methodically. It's not until a sudden thud sounds out from the bedroom, and I lean over to see Rob standing over his suitcase.

I raise a brow, grabbing my duffel bag and walking it to the bed. He's folding his shirts carefully, flattening them before placing them into the body of his luggage.

His caution is so out of place, considering the fact that we're probably going to die in combat there, but I say nothing, tossing two shirts into the opening of my bag.

"You could do with some tact, Maris." He snaps, and my cheeks heat.

"I didn't think packing my bags for my funeral required the higher standard of professionalism you hold yourself to." I bite back.

He laughs, but there's no humor in it as he rolls a pair of socks. "You're so fucking dramatic. It's a job."

"It's a war zone, Rob. Do you know what the word 'war' means, or should I spell it out for you to look it up?"

He grasps the belt in his hands tight enough that his knuckles pale, looking like he might snap the leather in two. "There's always something with you, isn't there? Something to complain or bitch about."

My teeth grind together, and I throw a pair of pants into my bag with force. "It's my fucking life, Rob. I'm allowed to be concerned for it."

"No. What you are is un-fucking-grateful." He growls, stepping in close. "You think Thornton would have kept you on if I hadn't smoothed out your little outburst earlier?"

My eyes widen, and he gets a ghost of a smile on his face, but there's no happiness in it. "I put all this fucking work in to make us look good, and you waltz around acting high-and-mighty, expecting the applause."

I jolt when he jerks his arm, and the belt clatters into his suitcase loudly. "I'm done coddling you and your bullshit, Maris. You want to act like a fucking brat? Fine. You're not dragging me down with you."

He whirls away, storming from the room and slamming the door behind him so hard that the frame rattles. I flinch at the sound, still stunned by his sudden aggression.

Rob has had his moments of anger, but never like this.

I just can't believe he doesn't see the danger, or care.

Even if he doesn't value my life, he should sure as hell value his own.

Part of me wonders if this is a result of his denial about the magic user, or the dire state the country is in, but if he won't accept or acknowledge it, it will be too late once we're there.

I pull out my phone, glancing at the email with our flight details as trepidation washes over me.

The clatter of glass being set on the counter echoes through the closed door, and I already know Rob's pouring himself a glass of whiskey.

Releasing a ragged breath, I toss another shirt into the bag with a sense of defeat. I'm going to have to apologize tonight to keep the peace, but some part of me knows there's a good chance that this might be the first sign of the end for us.

Counting the hours before we need to drive to the base, I groan internally that we only have a few hours to pack, get essentials for travel and get to bed.

My feet carry me to the bathroom, and I sort through our travel items, recounting what we'll need for the two months we'll be there.

I can't silence or ignore the quiet voice in the back of my mind, whispering that there's a good chance we'll die before the two months are up.

Chapter 3

The hum of the plane was enough to lull me to sleep for more than half the flight, but as the cabin shudders up and down from turbulence, sleep is no longer possible.

I glance over at Rob, seeing him clutching his bible with his head tilted back. The motor of the plane drowns his snores out, and I glance over at the screen in front of me.

Forty minutes left.

I'm surprised I slept through the entire flight, but considering how little I'd slept last night after making peace with Rob, I suppose it's not that shocking.

Outside the window, a red glow on the horizon catches my eye, and I chew the inside of my cheek. Bright yellow and crimson illuminate the clouds that obscure my view of the ground from here, but I don't need to see the ground to know that's where the fighting is.

Not when constant flashes of light brighten the clouds in random areas, much like lightning.

I'm lost in thought as we descend, slowly creeping closer to restricted airspace with each passing minute. Turbulence suddenly jolts the plane, and Rob's face smacks against the wall beside him.

"Ah, shit." He clutches the side of his face as the plane jerks again.

It takes a long few minutes for us to dip below the cloud cover, and my eyes gravitate to the window. I'm hardly able to make out much as darkness still covers most of the ground, so I face forward and ignore Rob soothingly rubbing his face.

By the time we're blissfully landed and taxiing to the boarding bridge, my muscles are painfully stiff. My stomach grumbles as the seatbelt light turns off, and I release the clasp in a hurry.

Joints popping loudly as I straighten, every muscle in my body feels like it's threatening to snap with how tightly wound they are.

"Grab my carry-on, would you, babe?"

"Sure." I pop the handle and tug it down, silently thankful that nothing shifted too much with the turbulence before I haul our carry-on bags to the floor.

By the time we're in the car, I'm so hungry that I could eat enough to feed a small army. But it's not until the end of the hour and a half drive that my appetite becomes non-existent.

Concrete buildings that line either side of the road have been completely leveled. Rubble that was once a city now lay scattered in the distance. A large metal fence down the road signals the entrance to the base, but my eyes slide to the right.

It's hard to discern anything from the mounds of concrete, brick, and wood. My chest aches at the sight, and I find myself mindlessly scanning them for any sign of locals, even though I know I won't find any.

"They better have given us a room together." Rob grumbles as we pull up to the entrance of the military base.

I'm too exhausted and tired of his attitude, so I just agree. "I'm sure they did. It's not Thornton's first time."

The last time someone put us in a hotel was when Thornton first started, and we had to inform him we're competing journalists working together.

It's not for the faint of heart.

He kept us in the same rooms for all assignments after that, so I doubt this time will be any different... Though some small part of me hopes it is.

We pull up to the first enormous building, seeing military trucks coming and going, soldiers loading onto vehicles, and others traveling from building to building.

Was I wrong about this being our war?

None of the outlets said anything about us having boots on the ground.

Something inside of me twists, and I struggle to consider the possibility that everyone back home could be lied to in such a blatantly obvious way.

There has to be some explanation.

We come to a stop at the front entrance, and my heart's in my throat as we climb out. Thankfully, Rob gets our luggage and leads the way inside. The signs are English and what I assume is Kharidian, and I study the symbols as he takes us to through security to the front desk.

A man with a name tag that says Aaron stands behind the counter, glancing between us. "Name, clearance, and government IDs, please."

We pass our documents over, and after a few minutes of typing into the computer, he has us scan our fingerprints before passing us a wristband.

"Secure this tight and don't take it off. It's waterproof, so you can shower with it on."

Rob nods. "What if it breaks or something?"

Aaron levels him with a flat stare. "Then come back to the front to get a new one. We will use your biometrics in the event you lose the band, or your hand." Aaron's lips twitch before he gestures down the hall. "Your rooms are ready, but there's a note on your files saying that General Deliom wishes for you to see him at his office when you get in."

I don't miss the plural Aaron said for our rooms, but still swallow hard. Meeting with a general is already far over our pay grade.

Rob gets the details from Aaron on where the General's office is before leading the way to our rooms to drop off our luggage.

Surprisingly, he says nothing about us being in separate rooms, and I chalk it up to our new environment as we navigate through the labyrinthine barracks to where Aaron said General Deliom's office is.

We get to his door and Rob knocks twice before we step inside with my heart in my throat.

The man who I assume is General Deliom is sitting at his desk. His shaved head reflects the light from the ceiling as he looks down at a stack of papers.

He doesn't bother looking up as Rob clears his throat.

"Mr. Paulson and Ms. Sylvara reporting for duty." The grin on Rob's face is enough to make me roll my eyes, but I slide into the seat in front of the desk.

I can play the game too. It's about time he sees that.

Deliom leans back, tearing his eyes from the paper on his desk as he looks between us. "Thank you for coming. Your flight went well, I trust?"

We both nod, and he blows out a breath. "Great. You'll need to rest up tonight, then, because effective tomorrow morning, you're deploying with one of our spec ops units. They're being tasked with sweeping areas of interest for hostiles and investigating as needed."

He pauses, and, per usual, I can't keep my mouth shut. "I didn't think we had any reason to have boots on the ground."

His jaw tenses. "Not that it's any of your business, but our bases have been subjected to repeated terror attacks from the rebel groups. Besides, we are not retaliating. We're investigating."

He leans forward and clasps his hands in front of him as the oak desk groans under his weight. "Two days ago, while supporting the local government and facilitating a prisoner swap at a local encampment, we were ambushed." He turns the monitor toward us, and clicks play on a video.

The encampment shows several soldiers on high alert as a couple of what look like civilians head toward the other party. Within seconds of them reaching their destination, fire erupts from the right side of the camera angle, and everyone scatters.

Within seconds flames engulf the whole encampment, and the feed cuts off.

There's no way that was a bomb.

Fuck.

I mean, there are bad humans. Servilians can't be entirely perfect. I'm sure there are bad apples in their population, too.

The General slides what looks to be a drone surveillance photo in front of us, and I swallow hard.

The entire area's been obliterated. From their foundations to their highest points, the buildings have been destroyed by fire, leaving behind nothing but charred remains, heaps of rubble, and ash.

Whoever this is, they clearly don't give a shit about who they hurt, whether that's the prisoners, the soldiers on both sides, or the servilians that their actions will negatively affect.

General Deliom clicks his tongue and tilts his head as he assesses us. "You will be in danger the moment you leave this base–hell, maybe even on base–so stay alert and stay alive."

The way my stomach feels like a sack of stones is foreboding, and I'm in a daze still, replaying the video in my head as he tells us about the unit we're going to accompany.

Lord help us.

Chapter 4

Exhaustion weighs heavily in my body as we exit the barracks. We've hardly gotten out the doors when I see two armored military trucks sitting in front of the building.

The sand color is speckled with bullet holes, and I swallow hard.

I know I made comments about attending my funeral, but the closer we get to the conflict, the more I feel like I was right on the mark.

A man in full tactical gear walks around the front of the first truck, his stride purposeful as he comes to a stop before us. Soldiers in matching gear file in to form a line behind him.

"Mr. Paulson, Ms. Sylvara. I'm Fredrick, the commander of our special operations here in Kharidia." Fredrick reaches out to shake our hands, and I hope he doesn't feel the tremor in mine. He gestures to the first man beside him and the rest of the men. "I'll give you a moment to meet the men in our unit before we head out. You have two minutes."

Rob steps in front of me, shaking hands with each member of the unit, and giving them a curt nod. Henry, Kevin, Nick, Teddy, Daniel, and others all introduce themselves as I file away their names for later. Approaching the last member of the unit, bright blue eyes lock onto me, and I reach out to shake his hand.

"Maris Sylvara." I murmur, seeing the corners of his eyes crinkle.

"Lennard Caassali, at your service."

He winks, and my cheeks burn as I retract my hand.

Men.

"Load up!" Fredrick shouts, and both units hurry to their respective trucks. The inside leaves much to be desired in the way of comfort as we climb in after them. I plop into the hard seat, with Rob taking the spot beside me.

The truck rumbles and eases forward. Each rock of the vehicle makes my stomach lurch, and when the sandy earth around us turns to char, Fredrick pulls over onto the side of the road.

Both units file out methodically, spreading to form a perimeter, and it's not long before Fredrick gives us the go-ahead to move freely within the zone.

Snapping photos here and there, I notice a blackened bone on the ground before spotting the rest of the person it belonged to. Bile rises in my throat.

I didn't expect to be this close to death.

Spotting some odd markings near one of the destroyed buildings, I step over and snap a few photos before taking a deeper look. A large circle with a symbol drawn in the middle catches my attention first, with the darker markings tipped with white, looking like they burned hottest. The charred symbols are indented, like the symbol melted into the ground itself, and I snap a photo.

By the time I've surveyed the area, I'm nearly certain I've taken a photo of every inch, and a heavy note of sadness weighs down my steps back to the vehicle.

When I spot Rob, he's wide-eyed as he glances around. His gaze lands on me and he grins. "Isn't this awesome?!"

I can't help the frown that pulls at my brows. "What's **awesome** about people dying?"

He scoffs. "I meant the magic user."

My mouth snaps shut, and I turn to the sound of footsteps, only to see Fredrick approaching with a guarded look. "Everybody load up. We have new orders. Let's go!"

My stomach churns once more as we pile into the truck. I'm hardly seated uncomfortably before the vehicle lurches forward.

No one says anything as we drive slowly through the demolished area to wherever their new orders will take us. A minute or two into the journey, the landscape around us transforms.

Tall, worn, and weathered buildings now stand where destroyed rubble once lay on either side of the road. Tattered blankets and clothes strewn hang from the windows with deep cracks running down the walls, but there are no parts blackened by any explosions here.

My eyes sweep each window and door, looking for any sign of civilian life, even though a large part of me knows, even if they were here, they'd be hiding.

The truck engines are loud enough that even without being in a war zone, I'd shy away from them.

We pull over to the side of the road, with both units spreading out to take the perimeter. I've just moved to the side of a building when I hear gunfire in the distance.

My head snaps in the direction, my gaze meeting Fredrick's as he motions for us to follow. As he heads into the building, my pulse rages, and I quicken my pace to keep up.

It's so quiet you could hear a pin drop as he checks the first room. "Stay here. I'm going to do an exterior sweep." He says in a low tone.

We nod, and he heads out the back door, disappearing out of sight.

Without having Fredrick here, even knowing we have two full units of special operations slowly traveling the block, I still feel incredibly vulnerable here.

A long moment passes and my pulse is raging in my ears as I strain to listen for Fredrick's return. After what feels like an eternity, Rob turns to look at me with his jaw tensing.

"Let's go see what's going on."

My eyes widen, and my whisper comes out more like a hiss. "Have you lost your mind?!"

Rob just grabs my arm, tugging me painfully toward the door. "If we don't know what's coming, we're as good as dead."

Wrestling my arm from his hand, I rub the tender spot with a wince. "And if we get caught in the crossfire, we're as good as dead."

Gun fire erupts, sounding closer than before, and my heart gallops as I glance wildly between him and the exit.

"Okay, let's just take a look." I whisper, hoping to god my split decision isn't misguided. We walk out the back door where Fredrick went, keeping ourselves as close to the wall of the building as possible.

We hardly make it more than twenty feet when I see my very first dead body that isn't just charred bones. She can't have been over fifteen years old, with her stomach swollen where she lies sideways against the wall. When I spot the bugs landing on her open eyes, I fight the urge to vomit.

My gaze turns to Rob, seeing the pure disgust in his eyes as he tugs me away from the body and into an alley.

Gunfire sounds out closer than before, and we freeze in place.

What if the spec ops unit is under attack?

Rob's throat bobs, and he glances down the alley. "Wait right here. I'll be back."

I want to scream, but I slink back into the wall and nod. "Sure. I'll be right here."

He disappears around the corner, and each heartbeat feels like an eternity as I wait. When he doesn't return quickly, I slowly creep along the side of the building to look down the conjoining alley.

The gunfire stops for a breath of a moment, with my back to the wall of a building, when a soft cry fills the air.

I freeze in place, caught between wondering if I'd imagined it and running to the child that's surely terrified and alone.

Gunfire rings out again, and at the end, a small sob cuts off abruptly, as if the owner had covered their mouth.

There's no movement down either side of the alley, but a door off to my right sits slightly ajar, and I inch closer as another round of shots sounds closer than before.

By the time I'm near the door, a sniffle echoes from inside and all I can picture is a terrified child hiding from what would surely be her own death.

But if I can help her get out...

I give the alley one last glance for movement before slipping inside. Tattered cloth and various other things lie strewn along the floor of a short hallway, covered with dirt and dust. Each cautious step I take feels shattering to the tense silence, and my heart's in my throat as my gaze bounces between the stairs to my right and the doorway to my left.

With the half-closed door coming up first, I silently beg the chaotic butterflies in my core to calm and slip inside.

The moment I pass the entrance, a large pair of hands are on me, covering my mouth and securing it shut as I'm forced backward.

My aggressor's chin brushes my forehead through the dark mask covering the lower half of his face, and I grunt into his hand when my head collides with the wall.

My eyes widen as a hard body melds to mine, and I'm about to look up at him to speak when his hand squeezes my mouth hard. I'm already caught out of position. The last thing I should do is piss him off.

My survival instincts are screaming at me to listen, so I do.

An engine roars nearby, followed by gunfire, and a wave of terror washes over me, urging me to obey the stranger even more. With my heart in my throat, pounding in my ears like a war drum, I bring my gaze up to meet his, and my breath catches.

Even with the stranger's face fully obscured, his eyes are arguably unique enough that I'd be able to spot him in a crowded room full of similarly masked men.

Golden amber irises as fiery and bright as the sun peer from beneath thick, dark lashes, and they search my face for a long moment.

A vehicle engine roars closer before it cuts out, and the stranger must think I'm not a threat as he steps back. His hand over my mouth squeezes slightly once, and I hear the unspoken command loud and clear.

Stay fucking quiet.

Almost imperceptibly, I nod my head and his hand falls away as he steps back another few paces. Without him crowding my space, I could easily take in more of what he looks like, but part of me rebels against that thought. Keeping my gaze locked on his is no arduous task.

Yet in my peripheral, I take in the dark material draped around him, making him look more like an assassin from a video game. The black hood draped over his head casts his masked face in shadow, melding with the ebony robe hanging from his shoulders.

He leans over to the side of the bed, and my gut twists when he helps a little girl up before lifting her into his arms. She's covered in blood, cradling her injured arm to her chest as he pulls her securely into him. He takes three long strides to the closet as footsteps outside grow closer.

Crouching down, he slides the door shut, and his eyes are the last things I see before they disappear behind the wooden surface with a click.

The door to the room opens and Fredrick walks in with Rob in tow. "What the hell, Maris?"

Anger etches across Rob's face, and I swallow hard. "Sorry—" My mouth feels dry, like all the moisture has been sucked from the room as I lick my lips. "There was gunfire, and..."

Fredrick surprisingly nods. "It was smart to find shelter. We need to retreat." He turns to look at the door to the hallway, and I know I need to keep them away from the closet.

Rob walks over to the bed, and I hurry over to him, grabbing his hand as his head snaps toward me.

"Thank you for finding me." I whisper, and Rob leans in to place a kiss atop my head. It's all I can do to think that the stranger's chin was just there, and I swallow.

"I'm just glad we got to you before they did. They're brutal murderers Maris. The bodies, some of them, they're mutilated, it's–" He growls, his eyes hardening. "Disgusting."

The way his lip curls unsettles my stomach, and I see Fredrick glance between us. "I'll go gather the men. We leave in two minutes."

Fredrick disappears down the hall, his heavy footsteps growing more distant as Rob's jaw feathers. "You can't disappear like that again, Maris."

My eyes widen. "Me? You're the one who went to investigate and never came back!" I whisper loudly at him. "What did you expect me to do?"

A flash of anger crosses his expression, and his hand snaps out to grab my arm. With a bruising grip, he yanks me to the doorway near the hall, leaning in so that his harsh whispers stay quiet.

"I expect you to listen. If I say I'll be back, I expect you to fucking stay put like an obedient fucking girlfriend and not go off gallivanting in this fucking hellhole where these piece of shit rebels would not just kill you on sight, but they'll **torture** you, Maris."

I can hardly listen to his words as his fingers dig into my arm, feeling like they might reach the bone before he releases me abruptly and scoffs.

"If you get killed out here, Maris, just know, it's because you don't fucking *think*." He chews out, staring into my eyes with a level of rage I've only seen a handful of times.

Without another word, he walks through the doorway, and I jolt as a sudden bang fills the air from him slamming the door to the alley open.

I'm fully aware the man in the closet likely heard all of that, and part of me wants to turn around to tell him I don't think the way he does, but I don't.

If only to keep their secret just that.

With that thought, I swallow my wounded pride and push myself forward.

I always knew Rob had a mean streak, but he never aimed it at me when we started dating. He'd get pissed if someone cut him off, or at video games, but it wasn't until this year that the anger spilled over into our relationship.

He sure as shit never tried to physically hurt me until now.

I hardly get to the door when my shoulder warms. The heat quickly becomes searing, and I pause, turning to look over my shoulder as the white-hot pain intensifies. A long few seconds pass, and I lift my shirt with a gasp to look at the source, seeing angry red lines burned into my skin.

The burn is in a perfect circle, with a center that looks almost like a brand, and horror washes over me.

What the actual hell?

My gaze snags on the closet. Piercingly bright, molten-gold irises flash between two wooden panels, disappearing in the blink of an eye.

Did he do that?

I storm over to the closet and swing the doors open, expecting to see him still hunched over with the little girl in his arms, but I don't.

Standing there with the doors wide open, casting light into the shallow closet, I stare at it with a sense of newfound horror as I realize who I just stumbled upon.

I walked right into the presence of the feared magic user and left unscathed. My shoulder throbs, and I reach up to touch it through my shirt tenderly.

Well, almost.

The truck's engines rumble to life and gunfire rings out in the distance as I swallow hard, sliding the closet shut. Each step toward the others feels like a step to the gallows as I debate telling them what I saw.

They will brand me as a risk. Literally. I'll have constant eyes on me, and they won't trust me with information.

I can't tell them.

Fredrick holds the door open as I walk into the alley. "Let's go!" He shouts over the sound of the engine, and I'm climbing in when a stray bullet hits the body of the vehicle.

Fredrick ducks before slamming the door shut, and another bullet hits the top as he throws himself into the driver's seat.

We lurch forward, and when another bullet hits the armored plates, I flinch instinctively at the sound, ducking my head.

"What took so long?" Rob growls under his breath, and my pulse hikes as we turn a corner.

A bullet hits my side of the window and I gasp. "Jesus. I wanted to check something to see if there was a picture I could get, but there was too much clutter."

He shakes his head in my peripherals. "And you nearly got us killed in the meantime. Do you ever fully think through your decisions, or are you always this fucking reckless?"

My eyes are wide at the blatantly rude commentary, and Fredrick's eyes glance at us in the rearview.

As much as we're in a high stress environment, I refuse to allow a man to speak to me with such disrespect.

"You want to talk about *reckless* decisions? How about deciding to split up in a literal war when gunfire is going off? Maybe *you* shouldn't have gone to investigate to begin with!"

"Enough!" Fredrick barks, and my mouth snaps shut. "Bitch at one another when we make it back alive. For now, keep your head on a swivel and pay the fuck attention."

We fall silent as the vehicle passes a wide intersection, and I spot one of our military forty yards out with his weapon drawn. My eyes follow his line of sight to where a civilian woman stands with her palms upright in surrender.

His upper body jerks with recoil in my peripherals as she staggers back and horror rifles through me when she drops to her knees like a stone.

A building obscures my view, and I stare blankly at the window as tears roll down my cheeks.

He *just killed an unarmed civilian.*

One of our military just killed an unarmed civilian.

More bullets hit the side of our vehicle, but I'm too far gone into shock to register or worry about them as the vehicle lurches from side to side.

After seeing that, I don't know if I blame them for shooting at us.

God knows, I would be.

Chapter 5

Walking into General Deliom's room sends a wave of unease over me, and the seared brand on my shoulder throbs like a third-degree burn as we slide into the chairs before he glances up from his desk.

"Well?" He grumbles, tossing his worn glasses onto the stack of papers in front of him. "Fredrick said there was some trouble."

My mouth drops open, but snaps shut again as Rob's voice fills the air. "We ran into some trouble, but it wasn't anything our men couldn't handle."

Our men? He's talking as if he's suddenly part of the military in a country where we aren't even supposed to be actively taking part in the conflict!

Deliom nods. "Great, glad to see you're both unharmed. We lost good men today, and for what? Rebellion forces are targeting our centralized locations around the country, and we suspect it's their feeble attempt to push our presence out."

Rob nods, like it's the most sensible thing he's heard all day, but all I can think of is the woman I watched get gunned down hours earlier.

"We have orders to protect our other four encampments to the north, east and west of the region, so you'll be tagging along to get what you need for your story. However..." His eyes level on me, and I feel my blood pump harder as the brand on my shoulder throbs. "Fredrick told me there was some delay that caused undo risk. That cannot happen again. I will not risk my men for selfish journalists next time; you will be left to fend for yourselves against the murderous rebels."

I swallow and nod, knowing this is wholly directed at me.

He waves us off. "Now go. Get cleaned up, eat dinner, and be ready to leave at the same time tomorrow."

We file out of the room, and I'm lost in thought, ignoring Rob's muttered, one-sided conversation about how he's never seen anything like this before.

I'm so lost in thought that I'm hardly paying attention as we walk past my quarters, and I snap back to the present as Rob opens the door to his room.

"Oh–" I murmur, shaking my head. "I didn't realize we got here so quickly."

Rob chuckles, holding the door open. "Can we chat for a minute before you go cover your walls with handmade wallpaper?"

I huff a laugh, because he's absolutely right. The first time he'd seen evidence of me researching something was in Pennsylvania, there were a string of doctors over the course of a few years who wound up with some kind of poisoning, but when it couldn't be linked up to where they worked or lived, the trail went cold after I'd called a handful of their patients.

But I still obsessed over it for weeks until a nurse admitted to murdering her coworkers in the same manner—then shortly after, Thornton put this on my plate.

I'll never forget Rob walking into our apartment, seeing papers strung together, pins stuck in the walls and a handle laid on the floors as I tried to piece together the puzzle. Normally I'd have hid it away in my office, but I needed the space.

Perhaps I missed my calling as a detective.

"Maris?"

I blink at Rob, remembering the kind and caring side of him as he sat there looking over my disorganized chaos with a fresh perspective.

"Sure." I grin, following him inside, and he kicks his shoes off beside the door with a relieved sigh.

His room is a mirror image to mine, with a single bed in the center, a small desk near the door with a stool that fits under it. A tiny dresser lines the wall before the entrance to the bathroom, and I blow out a breath.

Not wanting to sit on the bed, I leave my shoes beside his, move to the desk and bend to pull the stool out when Rob grabs my arm. I nearly recoil, but his touch is gentle, so I let him turn me toward him.

He guides me toward the bed and gestures with one hand to it. "Here, sit."

I'm not usually one to be told what to do, but I choke down my usual sarcastic retorts.

I've done enough damage for one day.

Rob eases to the bed with me, angling himself so our knees press against one another, and he clasps my hands in his. "I wanted to apologize."

My brows shoot up, but I say nothing as he keeps his eyes trained on our hands.

"I behaved like an ass today. I never should have treated you like that."

I nod, knowing that this is the typical apology Rob gives after he's had time to think about his outbursts. Usually, though, they're not directed at me.

One of his hands drops to my knee, and he rubs along my thigh as I start to get a suspicion of what he's after. The realization leaves a bitter taste on my tongue, but I try to ignore it and assume the best in him.

Because how could you want to have sex after seeing something so atrocious? We literally saw dead bodies, for fuck's sake.

"Maris, say something."

My attention flicks to him, and he searches my face as I sigh. "I'm sorry too..." I whisper, still filtering out the truth as guilt rifles through me. "Really… I should have thought things through more and been more cautious. I'd never want to put us at risk like that."

The brand on my shoulder throbs, and I grind my molars to keep from reaching over to it.

"Oh babe, we weren't at risk." He says, leaning in to press his forehead to mine.

I want to correct him, to clarify that I meant our lives, not our relationship, but he leans in and presses his lips to mine before I can.

My eyes widen, but his are clamped shut as he hungrily moves his mouth against mine, and I try to pull back.

As I do, he takes it as an invitation, leaning his weight forward to force me further back on the bed. He grinds himself against me, and I feel the tip of his dick press against my pelvic bone as he dry humps me.

I don't know how to tell him I don't want this without offending him in the state he's in—or making him more angry than he already was.

His hand glides up my thigh, and I'm purposefully not responding to his touch to tip him off that I'm not interested, but he's just not getting it.

The man could be fucking a dead body right now, and I don't think he'd notice at this point.

My hands move to his chest to push him off, but before they make contact, he grips them firmly. The weight of him pressing me further into the bed pulls at the burn on my shoulder, and I wince as he devours my mouth.

If I don't stop him soon, he's going to be so pissed.

The memory of the pain I felt earlier when he grabbed my arm comes to the forefront of my mind, and I feel a pit form in my stomach. The pit doubles in size when I consider the fact that he's my boyfriend, and I'm seriously not interested in being intimate with him right now.

That's almost more guilt inducing than anything else, because shouldn't I want to?

He breaks our kiss and releases my hands as I debate whether I should risk his wrath by telling him no.

When he unbuttons my pants and tugs them off, the urgency around telling him to stop grows, but the anger he displayed earlier still gives me pause.

It's fine, right? I can just get it over with and pretend it's fine. It's not like he lasts long. I can do two minutes.

Two minutes with the man I've dated for years. I can do this.

I swallow my fear as he tugs his own pants down to his knees, and his dick sticks straight out as he crawls over me.

I'm painfully aware that I'm not aroused at all, so there's little chance he's going to put it in with ease, but it's not like he's more than average size for a man.

I'm not prepared when he grabs my arms again and tugs them behind my lower back with force.

"What are y–?" my words get muffled by his mouth covering mine, and he squeezes my wrists at my back in one hand.

Using his free hand, he notches himself against my dry entrance, and tries to force his way in, despite the lack of lubrication. I wince, feeling the sharp pain as he swallows my cries.

He must mistake them for something else entirely, because he withdraws and rubs his tip against my pussy, spreading pre-cum all over before shoving himself in once more. This time he gets in halfway, and moans into my mouth, but all I feel is the pain of him forcing himself deeper.

Rob withdraws to his tip and uses his hand to tug my leg over his shoulder. His hips snap against mine hard, closing the rest of the distance, and bringing his balls flush with my ass.

When I cry out, but he doesn't pause, just seizes the opportunity, to claim my mouth with his.

He slams into me again. And again. And again.

Each time he uses brutal force, and I feel hot tears stream down my cheeks until finally it's too much for me to bear.

I break our kiss with urgency as he goes to move, and jerk my head back an inch. "Rob, it hurts–"

He slams in again, and I'm nearly certain he did so harder this time. "Just relax, Maris."

Rob's voice sounds detached, cold even as he uses one hand to hold my knee bent to my chest. He stops slamming into me with sheer force as he kisses me, his tongue delving into my mouth as he thrusts as deep as he can.

He's crushed against my cervix, and the excruciating pain shooting through my core has more tears streaming down my face.

Does he not feel or see that he's hurting me?

He withdraws to the tip, panting hard as he slides back in, groaning against my tongue as he gyrates. The way he fucked me before might have been boring, but I'd easily take that instead of the pain he's enjoying dishing out to me now.

He just continues to pump into me, with each thrust shifting my place on the bed, as if he's trying to reach deeper with each one. The brand throbs at my shoulder, and I hone in on it, if only to disassociate from everything else.

This is the longest he's gone without coming, and I'm silently praying to God it ends soon because I don't know how much more I can take.

I never should have come to his room.

He pulls back and glares at me, as if my lack of response pisses him off before he withdraws and hammers into me with so much force that I cry out with each thrust. Our bodies smack together loudly, my pussy bruising at his brutal invasion.

His tongue searches my mouth as his balls slap against my skin, and each shallow breath is a pained whimper that doesn't get past his lips. He competes against himself with each thrust, and I feel like I could pass out from the agony radiating through my core.

He suddenly gets an urgency to his movements as he jerks, and pumps hard once, twice, three times before burying himself as deep as he can. His dick stiffens, and he groans loudly, biting down on my shoulder with his teeth sinking into the still healing skin.

I whimper against the pain, and the sound gets caught in my throat.

Where the fuck did all this aggression come from?

What happened to the Rob I knew?

His dick throbs, and he pulls back with a lazy grin. "Fuck, Maris. There's nothing like some good make up sex."

My wide eyes search his face. "That was make up sex?"

My words fall on deaf ears as he leans in to place a quick chaste kiss against my lips, and when he withdraws abruptly, my legs squeeze shut as the radiating pain lances down my thighs.

He says nothing, but hums to himself as he lazily disappears into the bathroom.

What the fuck.

Before he can notice, I'm tugging my underwear and pants back on, numbly eager to make my escape. I slide into my shoes and slip out the door, not bothering to announce my exit.

I know we've had some rough moments, but he really seemed like he enjoyed hurting me. What's worse is that even if that was some kink of his that he's just figuring out, he didn't bother to listen to what I was saying.

My core is in pure agony as I slip into my room, shakily locking the door behind me as the adrenaline of what I'd just gone through fades.

I'm not a weak person, and the idea that someone who should care about me could easily silence me into submission and hurt me like that...

It only serves to further my suspicion that Rob is changing, or perhaps he's simply turning into the person he always was.

Either way, I don't want to be with someone who doesn't prioritize me as much as himself. He was always bad at foreplay, but to be so rough and completely ignore me, not to mention that he was more rough when I said it hurt...

A large part of me knows I need to end this relationship, but I swallow down the growing concern that he would try to hurt me if I do.

Injuring me without repercussions would be incredibly easy in a war zone.

Feeling particularly gross, I make my way to the shower, knowing what I need to do, but not knowing how to do it without risking my life more than I already am.

Tomorrow. I'll deal with all of this tomorrow.

Chapter 6

Surprisingly, I made it to the entrance of the barracks early this morning with my camera hanging from my neck.

Sleep was elusive, and the pain in my abdomen made it uncomfortable to sleep on my side like usual, so I tossed and turned for hours.

Thornton responded late last night after I'd sent him some details I'd gathered, pushing back on the notes I'd included about members of our military having boots on the ground and any part they played in the conflict.

That would include the soldier who murdered a civilian before my eyes.

The knowledge that Thornton won't run with a story that talks about anything our soldiers are doing wrong leaves an acrid taste in my mouth, and I spent most of my restless night wondering how I can find an even-medium.

A balance.

The people deserve to know the truth, but it's nearly impossible to get the truth out when news sources produce and run one piece of syndicated media, cycling it until another comes up that matches the narrative they wish to control.

But that truth is also that there's a magic user killing people–and branding them–against their will.

My feet carry me out the front doors of the barracks to the road, and I shift my camera aside to reach the brand, feeling it beneath the material of my shirt.

Even still, it's a truth I don't want the masses to hear, simply because of the harm it could cause on servilians.

But who am I to make such important decisions about what story deserves to be told and what story doesn't?

Does that not make me just as bad as Thornton?

Fredrick steps out of the barracks with his troops in tow and looks at me. "Morning, Sylvara."

I just nod back, seeing Rob approach in my peripheral as I watch two armored trucks pull up alongside us.

"Morning, everyone."

He says it so cheerfully that I almost want to break up with him then and there, if only to drag him to the same bitter hint of rage that I'd felt all night.

But I don't.

"Load up!" Fredrick shouts, and we climb in to the uncomfortable seats. My abdomen screams in pain with each bend and twist, but I keep it quiet as Fredrick shifts into drive, looking at us in the rearview. "Today we're heading to our western base to support their efforts against the rebellion's attacks. There's been multiple sightings of the magic user's attacks in surrounding areas. A-team will secure the perimeter; B-team will escort you to the designated reporting areas."

I nod, and he glances between us before falling silent. Outside of distant explosions and gunfire, the entire drive is quiet save for sound of our gear and clothes shifting with the rocking of the truck.

With my mind free to wander, I survey the ravaged buildings on either side of the road with what feels like a fresh set of eyes.

The damage to each building—blood splatters both new and old decorating the walls. It all makes me wonder why the hell we're here.

We don't have any invested interest in Kharidia politically or financially, so **why**?

No matter how many possible reasons I consider for why we would be involved, I come up empty.

Fredrick slows our approach as gunfire goes off in the distance, and he points a gloved finger to a series of buildings up ahead. "We'll unload there, hide the trucks in the alley, and make the last twenty yards on foot."

He must notice the confusion on my face as he grins. "There's a neighborhood where the trucks can't reach–that's our base. They don't expect it because it's an enclosed, abandoned apartment building, but it's a perfect, centralized location where we've stationed troops along all the surrounding roads in and out."

Part of me wants to argue that if it's enclosed, it could also be a perfect tomb for us, but I choke down my retorts.

Not my circus, not my monkeys.

Fredrick pulls us into an alley, and we climb out, forming a straight line with A-team leading and B-team close behind us. We slowly make our way to a tall, ten-story apartment building, and I swallow hard.

Even without the pain in my core, there's no way I'm going up to the top.

Fredrick leads us inside, and A-team disperses to clear the perimeter as Rob, Fredrick, and all but one person from B-team climb the stairs. Their footsteps are loud in the tense air, and each round of gunfire in the distance nearly makes me jolt.

"Aren't you a journalist?"

I turn to the spec ops agent with wide eyes. "I am, why?"

His face mask makes it nearly impossible to see his mouth, but with the way his bright blue eyes crinkle at the corners, I'm nearly certain he's smiling.

I probably should have remembered his name, but... "Are you insinuating that I'm not doing my job, Mr.—?"

He huffs a laugh. "Lennard."

"Ah, right. Mr. Lennard."

He laughs even harder. "It's just Lennard. Should I call you Ms. Sylvara?"

I shoot him a warning look. "Only if you wish to summon my mother from her grave, and trust me, neither of us wants that."

Still, he's not wrong. I got here and was so focused on not wanting to go upstairs or be around Rob that I abandoned the entire reason I'm in Kharidia in the first place.

Turning in a circle, I spot a set of doors that lead into a courtyard, and gingerly make my way toward it. I'm about to turn the corner when Lennard halts my movements with his hand on my arm, pulling the butt of his weapon to his shoulder and surveying the area. When he's certain it's clear, he motions for me to follow.

Rob's laughter echoes through the building, and I shudder.

He's not even trying to be quiet. The sound of it haunts me, and I cut down right from the courtyard, eager to get as far away from it as I pace down a hallway that I assume leads to a garage of some sort.

It's not well furnished, and almost looks as if it were a maintenance hallway or some sort of escape exit for the building. The ceiling is lower, the walls more narrow than where we'd been moments ago.

We turn right, and head toward the only doorway at the end. It's not until I'm standing at the entrance of the large room that confusion and suspicion weighs heavy on me, and I slowly grab my camera.

The room's lined with lit candles that look like they've been burning for hours. A symbol drawn in a circle on the ground catches my eye. It's not dissimilar to the one I saw in the destroyed encampment.

My eyes don't leave the scene as I bring the viewfinder up to snap a picture, feeling an increasingly odd sense of foreboding with each second.

"This isn't creepy at all." Lennard whispers as he steps up alongside me, and I can't say I disagree.

"Something tells me we aren't supposed to see this." I whisper, stepping inside to snap a handful of photos, raising my camera overhead to take a few distant ones of the symbol.

Lennard walks on the opposite side of the ritualistic looking room as Fredrick's voice murmurs from the radio. Lennard responds with a simple acknowledgement before he crosses the room.

"Did you get what you needed?"

I meet his blue gaze and nod. "Yes. Let's go. I don't want to stay here any longer than I need to."

He follows me out while sweeping the courtyard again for any threats, keeping my slow pace. It's a concious effort not to jostle my abdomen more than intended with each step, and before I know it we've rejoined the others.

My gaze surveys the room, finding Rob's broad grin plastered on his face with a bitter note of anger.

There's nothing more that I want than to smack it off of him.

"Where've you guys been?" He asks, his gaze bouncing between us. "You missed a great view."

I open my mouth to answer with some blasé statement, but Lennard speaks up. "We should have gone with you. The courtyard was uneventful."

I just give a tight smile and a nod of agreement as Fredrick points to the front entrance. "A-team's formed a perimeter, and joined those stationed. We'll need to spend the night here, but if all goes well, we should be back at home base by tomorrow night."

He looks at the four members of B-team around us, including Lennard. "I expect you to support these two for the time being."

The B-team murmurs an agreement, and Fredrick saunters out the front door.

"Well," Rob looks at me, and a pit of dread forms in my stomach. "Should we do some investigating ourselves?"

My eyes gravitate to Lennard as he stands behind Rob stone-faced. "Uh, sure."

Rob turns in a circle. "Anywhere we should look first? Notice anything that could be interesting?"

I shake my head. "Nope. Lead the way."

So he does, guiding us to the front doors and into what I can only assume is danger with the way the B-team has gone full defense. Somehow, whatever we witnessed back in that room has Lennard hovering around me extra cautiously, and each step we take has him inching in front of me, like he expects an attack to hit us at any second.

The contrast between Rob's carefree walk and B-team's barrels taking aim as they walk is stark, and only furthers my suspicion that Rob's changed more than I ever thought.

Lennard suddenly places himself in front of me, as if some sixth sense is warning him of incoming danger. And perhaps it has, because when Rob turns a corner, sudden thunderous pops echo in the air as Lennard shoves me behind him.

I stumble backward, crouching to protect my head as my abdomen screams at me in protest. Shouting fills the air, and we hunch down along a wall as bullets whiz by us. Someone on the roof must have a clear line of sight, because it's less than a minute before the gunfire aimed at us quiets down.

The knowledge that more lives were just snuffed out makes my chest squeeze to the point of pain.

We shouldn't even be here.

Movement in the alley to our left catches my eye, and I hear the gunfire above us first before I see the teenager drop to the ground.

Horror washes over me when none of the others bat an eye, but continue ushering us down the street. When we breach the intersection, Rob glances both ways before motioning for us to follow, and the agony shooting through my core has me wincing with each step.

We shouldn't be here.

We hardly get more than five yards into the road when gunfire erupts from nearly all directions. Lennard shoves me aside into the nearest alleyway, and away from the bullets whizzing past us.

Between Rob leading us to what surely has to be our deaths, and the civilians being shot down, I'm in full escape mode.

So I run.

I run from it all.

I sprint as fast as I can in the direction we came, keeping to the alley as explosions shake the ground behind me. Ignoring the agony in my screaming core, I don't know how far I've gotten as adrenaline pumps through me, just that I need a break to breathe.

My chest heaves with desperate gulps of air as I slow to a stop, bracing my hand on the edge of a nook in the building, bending over as my camera dangles from my neck.

"Maris!" Rob growls behind me, and something dangerously close to disappointment rifles through my veins.

I turn just as he slows to a stop with a wild look on his face. "Where the hell are you going?"

He takes confident steps forward as I straighten, feeling something tear in my core.

"I thought–" I don't get to voice my excuse for why I fled as Rob grabs my shoulders hard, shoving me back into the nook. The throbbing pain in my abdomen has turned into streaks of white-hot electricity shooting all the way down my thighs, but I don't have time to register it as my back hits the concrete with a thud.

"Second thought, good call getting us away from them. This got all my blood pumping and I need to feel you."

I'm still half in shock as he unbuttons my pants, fumbling with them before I realize what's happening, and I shove him off.

"Rob, what the fuck has gotten into you?"

He looks at me with wide eyes, like I'm the problem here. But his surprise only lasts a moment before his expression darkens, replaced with something more sinister. That's when I know the Rob I once knew is gone.

"You know you want it, Maris. Stop playing coy."

I gasp as he grips my jaw and pulls me in for a rough, bruising kiss. My fists slam into his chest only for him to grab them, digging his fingers into my bones as he smashes them into the concrete wall.

He's going to do this knowing I don't want to.

Panic takes over as he leans his body in, snaking his hand roughly into my pants. The buttons snap with his brash, urgent movements, and the sound of my zipper breaking fills the air before his fingers brush the seam of my underwear.

Desperate to make him stop as gunfire sounds out in the distance, I recoil and snap my forehead into his nose. A crunch fills the air on impact, arguably as loud as the surrounding gunfire as he staggers back a step.

"We. Are. Over!" I shout, following his retreat, and bringing my knee into his groin with as much force as I can muster. He keels over and drops to his knees with a groan, dry heaving into the middle of the alley.

I ignore the satisfaction rifling through me at the sight, and run as fast as my legs will carry me. The waist of my jeans rides low, the buttons and zipper completely broken as I hold them up with one hand. I'm only half paying attention as I spot an apartment building towering over neighboring buildings up ahead.

My abdomen's screaming in protest, with each movement lancing echoes of it down my thighs. Adrenaline and nausea twist my stomach into knots, but I can't give it any mind now.

Not when I'm so close to escaping him.

Finally, at the last intersection, I propel myself forward as fast as I can before cutting right at full speed, but just as I turn the corner, I slam into a hard body.

Air rushes from my lungs in a whoosh, just as large hands steady me. Desperate gulps of air have my chest heaving as Rob screams my name angrily in the distance.

My gaze slides up the dark cloak covering the broad chest of the masked man with eyes like the sun. His eyes travel the length of my body before meeting mine, and Rob screams my name once more.

A wave of terror washes over me when he sounds closer than he had moments ago.

Whoever this stranger is, he needs to leave before they get here, and so do I.

I don't know why I care that he leaves. Perhaps because I've seen the horrific acts committed by our soldiers who shouldn't be here, but nonetheless, I reach out and grasp the stranger's solid arms.

His eyes widen, as if this is the last thing he expected, and I hear Rob's voice even closer.

"You need to go. They're coming." Gunfire sounds closer, and I glance around wildly. "Oh, God. We both need to go."

He laughs under his breath, and when Rob's voice sounds like it's mere seconds from us, I fall still. The air suspends in my lungs, and I know it's too late to escape.

Rob's going to turn the corner any second and find me.

His eyes narrow on me, and his rich voice laced with surprise fills the space between us. "You fear him."

When I don't respond, his gaze lingers on the apartment building two blocks away before he mutters a curse under his breath. His large hands find my arms as more gunfire fills the air, pulling my attention in yet another direction.

The masked man tugs me closer, and my heart leaps into my throat.

My only options are to let Rob find me, or see what the masked man has planned, and given my current circumstances, I'm inclined to do the latter.

I don't fight him as his robed arms encircle my shoulders, and he pulls me tight to his broad chest. He backs into a shadowed corner, with his dark robe dangling around us both. Within seconds, he's leaned in to cover my head with his hood, and his arms adjust more comfortably around me.

I'm fully hidden from view, and the masked man's face brushes against my cheek as Rob sprints out from the alley. The dark material is just thin enough to see everything around us, and my pulse picks up.

Still half-limping, Rob pauses in the middle of the road and cups his groin with a wince before he turns in a full circle. As he turns, he looks right at us, and I shrink further into the masked man.

Air suspends in my lungs, and my hands ball into fists at my side, with my nails biting into my palms.

But miraculously, he doesn't see us.

A long moment passes as anger flashes across Rob's features, and he walks down the sidewalk, directly toward where we stand. With each step closer, I think I'm going to be sick.

Memories of his assault and how close I came from a repeat of it flash through my mind. A shudder wracks through me and I turn my face, burying it into the masked man's robed neck.

The logical part of me knows that we're in the open, and there's no way Rob won't see us here, but the logical part of me isn't in control right now.

A light, sweet, floral aroma washes over me, hints of vanilla and cinnamon follow, and I desperately cling to the scent. The distraction only lasts for a moment until Rob's footsteps stop in front of us, and my lungs seize.

A loud bang fills the air in front of us as I jolt. Squeezing my eyes shut, I don't dare to breathe as he shouts in frustration, and the masked man's arms tighten around me.

Rob's footsteps move to our right, fading as he gains distance from where we remain hidden.

I have no idea how he kept us hidden from Rob, but every bone in my body is thankful for it.

Come to think of it, that trick must be how he hid from me in that closet.

It takes a conscious effort to leave the bubble of safety he'd created, but I finally ease myself from the crook of the stranger's neck with a ragged breath.

My entire body trembles with remnants of anxiety, adrenaline, and shock as the pain in my torso worsens. Sharp pangs echo down my shaky legs as my gaze lingers on the sidewalk where Rob disappeared.

"Thank you." I whisper, knowing full well that this masked man just kept me hidden from the one person I should have been able to trust more than anyone.

He straightens to his full, towering height as I take another step back, and I feel uncomfortably exposed.

Taking that as the need to put distance between us, I gingerly pace to the sidewalk, looking in the direction Rob went. A wave of tentative relief crashes over me when I find it empty, even if that means he might reappear at any moment.

The masked man follows me out of the shadows, turning to face me as an odd murmur carries in the air.

His eyes burn bright in the shadows of his mask as he searches my face, and I'm at a loss for words.

Thank you is nowhere near enough.

Yet it's the only possible collection of words that could express even a fraction of my gratitude for the fate he just kept me from.

Movement catches my eye just off to the right behind the stranger, and my eyes widen.

Chapter 7

An orchestra of footsteps fills the air, and I stare down the countless barrels trained on us with a sense of dread.

Soldiers wearing the same gear as those I've been accompanying line the street, the only difference between them is the lack of any identifying badge or insignia. With their faces covered, it's impossible to know which side they belong to.

The masked man tilts his head to the side before he glances over his shoulder. His radiant, sun-like irises survey the soldiers approaching us before they return to focus on me.

His thick, dark lashes flutter slightly. "Are you coming with me?"

I frown at his question, which seems oddly timed when we're staring death in the face. "I beg your pardon?"

Mirth reaches his eyes, and deep laughter rumbles from his chest. "I can't imagine you'd be someone who *begs* for anything, but if you insist."

I gape at him. "We're about to die, and you're cracking jokes."

Like a madman with a death wish, he turns his back to the immediate threat and steps in close—so close that I no longer see a single gun or soldier, and I have to tilt my head to meet his gaze.

"That wasn't a joke, and death is here, but not to claim us." He muses, but I don't get time to process his words.

The earth tremors, light erupts behind him, and shots go off. They whiz past, missing us completely, but I still jolt and flinch at the sound of each one.

"Come with me." He reaffirms, and I hesitate, crouching as a bullet whistles past us to my right.

There's no way I can go back to Rob right now or to base, and there's a chance this guy could be the same magic user Thornton wanted the story on.

The thought whirls around my brain and I don't know if my nerves are more shot from the gunfire or the man in front of me. Engines roar not far away as the thunderous cracks of gunfire die down, and I chance a peek over his shoulder.

My eyes widen at the tall flames that've erupted from the ground, like rotating pillars stretching into the air.

Holy shit.

*It really **is** him.*

Cursing under his breath as a hum vibrates in the air, he moves fast, tugging me into his chest just as deafening explosions go off all around us. His warm scent invades my senses as an explosion rattles the building to our left, and the world suddenly goes dark.

~

My head pounds, and I squint against the invasive light in the room.

"Someone's finally awake."

Searching the room through slits, I bring my hand to my eyes to shield them as they adjust. When my blurred gaze finally finds his shirtless form leaning on the wall near the window, my heart stutters in my chest.

Staring out into the distance with his arms crossed, my vision finally clears, and I finally drink the stranger in in his entirety.

When I don't respond, he turns from the window, and my pulse jumps.

If his eyes alone were captivating before, seeing his entire face without a mask makes me feel as if I might very well be under some kind of spell or witchcraft.

His black hair falls forward over his eyes as he gazes down at where I lie, taking in his high cheekbones, sharp, angular jawline and the dark stubble that lines it. That's not even considering the rest of him in my vision, and I purposefully avoid letting my gaze drop.

I'd almost prefer if he had the mask on because he's inarguably the most attractive person I've seen in my life. I know servilians are conventionally good-looking to most people, but this is an entirely different level of beauty.

I swallow, and his gaze tracks the movement.

"Where are we?" I croak, noticing the angry red and pink scars lining his arms.

"I teleported us somewhere safer."

Teleported? Holy shit.

That only prompts a million more questions in my mind, but I set them aside for now. It doesn't escape me that this stranger is *the* magic-user that I've quite literally travelled thousands of miles to cover a story on, and I know I should be terrified.

He's murdered thousands.

Destroyed countless buildings and various structures.

He's one of the main things keeping the government here from taking control.

I should be frozen in fear.

Somehow, though, I'm not.

Chalking it up to some kind of shock, I move to sit up and wince as a pang jolts my core. "Okay, and where is safe?"

He chuckles, stepping alongside the bed as I swing my legs over the edge, feeling a jagged throb in my abdomen. "Somewhere *safer*. How are you feeling?"

I stretch my arms overhead, and my joints pop loudly. "Stiff, sore. But that's pretty on-brand for this place, it seems." I reluctantly think back to Rob with a bitter note of anger, and he tilts his head.

"Sore? Are you hurt?"

My mouth drops open, but snaps shut as embarrassment washes over me.

"I'm fine."

There's not a chance in hell that I'm admitting to abdominal pain to a stranger, never mind the magic user that I hardly know.

He leans down, his eyes narrowing on me. "If you tell me, I promise to answer any question within reason."

I frown. When I realize how he phrased it, the hairs at the back of my neck stand on end, and I recoil. "Are you trying to use magic on me?"

His bright eyes widen, and even though he seemed taken aback, he recovers quickly. "Surprisingly, it doesn't seem to work. So, no. Well, yes, but also, no."

"You're unbelievable!" I scoff.

He blinks at me. "What's unbelievable is that you say things you don't mean to, and then don't elaborate."

Part of me wants to scream and riot in defense, but I choke the urge down. "I don't even know you."

"I saved your life and kept you away from—who was that guy, anyway?"

My stomach sinks, and I avert my gaze from his, dropping them to my bare, dirt covered toes as I wiggle them uncomfortably. *When did I lose my shoes?*

"My boyfriend—well, ex-boyfriend—Rob"

"Why were you running from him?" He asks, and I keep my attention trained on my feet.

This is the last line of questioning I want. We could talk about anything else—any other painful memory than this. It's too fresh.

Shame coats my veins, and I shake my head, but he just kneels in front of me, bracing a hand on either side of my body. I feel his gaze on me, but I can't bring myself to look at him.

"Did he hurt you?"

Did he? Is it his fault if I let it go on that long? I should have said no sooner. Maybe he got mixed signals.

My eyes slide shut as my head droops, and I feel the lump in my throat grow. Each inhale sends a wave of pain through my abdomen that I can't ignore. The damage from his assault still feels so fresh, and when I realize that I consider it an assault, I know that I'm just making excuses for him.

The stranger's fingers gently tilt my chin up, and my eyes flutter open. My heart squeezes in my chest as anxiety rises in me as I consider everything that's happened.

It's one thing to have gone through it and come out the other side, but to accept that someone you once cared for could **want** to hurt you so willingly and enjoy it... it's a whole new kind of pain to tack onto the physical.

"Did he hurt you?"

Tears well in the corners of my eyes, and I hold his burning gaze as I nod ever so slightly.

The muscles in his jaw tense, and he pushes to his feet. "Alright."

The way he says it is like that's all he needed to know, and when he turns to walk away, my pulse skyrockets.

*I'm alone in some random house, and he's just **leaving** me?!*

"Wait!" He pauses a few feet from the doorway and when turns back to look at me, the red and pink scars that adorned his body minutes ago are nearly gone. "Where are you going?"

His eyes sweep over my body once, as if looking for evidence of Rob's mistreatment before searching my face. "I'm going to go kill him."

My jaw goes slack. "What!?" I glance around wildly before shaking my head. "You can't just go around killing people!"

"I can, I have, and I will." He huffs out and turns to the door as panic rises in my chest.

Surging to my feet, I ignore the agony in my abdomen as I rush to stand between him and the door, blocking the exit as he stares at me with barely restrained humor.

When I don't move his lips tug upward. "You were afraid of him, a mere human, yet you act fearless now—" His twin sun irises search mine for a long moment before understanding flashes across his face, and his eyes harden. "I see."

"You can't just kill him." I don't even know why I'm fighting so hard, but I can only rationalize that it's because I don't want to be the reason for Rob's death.

"Again, I can. And now that I know what he did, I will."

I rear back, and the back of my head hits the door with a quiet thud. "You don't *know* anything."

"He raped you."

My pulse rages in my ears and I grit my teeth. He waits a long moment, watching as two sides of me war with one another.

One side, knowing the pain he caused is not my doing. The other, questioning every moment, and gaslighting myself into believing I could have done more.

I know which is right deep down. Maybe that will be enough to come to terms with it.

"How?" I whisper, and his expression softens for a breath of a moment.

"Educated guess. Now move so I can kill him."

I shake my head. "Please don't."

He tuts, placing his hands on either side of my head and angles himself to be eye-level to me. "Give me one good reason."

The way my heart thrashes and the memory of Rob makes me want to vomit, and when I swallow the bile rising in my throat, his sunlight irises drop to track the movement.

"If you kill him because of what he did, it will be my fault he's dead." He opens his mouth to argue, but I shake my head. "Even if you claim it's your decision, I will still blame myself. So please, do not kill him because of this. I won't be able to live with myself if I'm the reason someone I once cared for dies."

After a long, drawn out moment, he sighs. My tummy flips on itself as he pushes off the door and straightens to his full height. "Fine. He can live, for now, at least."

I blow out a breath, and he steps aside. He gestures for me to move from the doorway and I hesitate. *What if he's lying?*

He must see it written on my face as he releases a low chuckle. "At some point you'll have to move, and I already said I won't kill him yet. I do not break my promises."

I know if he really wanted to kill Rob, he would anyway, and I resign myself to the knowledge that if it happens, at least I tried to stop him.

I slowly make my way to the bed with a huff and wince as I sit down.

At this point, I don't know if the pain is from Rob or how hard I ran to get away from him, but it's a welcomed relief to rest.

Footsteps catch my attention just as he grabs a pitcher and cup from the table before filling the glass. The two items look small and fragile in his grip, like one squeeze and the glass could shatter in his palms.

I swallow at the mental image as he steps in close, handing the cup to me and I down the contents in a few large gulps.

"Thank you." I whisper, and he sets the empty glass on the table. "What's your name?"

"Sitri. And yours is Maris?" He crosses his arms over his chest before something catches his eye out the window.

I nod, feeling like I've completely stepped out of my element by going with him, but at least I'll be able to understand the rebellion's perspective.

My camera sitting on top of the dresser to our left is a relief, though I won't know if it's damaged until I can inspect it.

I *really* hope it's not.

"And you're servilian?"

His brow raises, but he just shakes his head. "No. I'm not from Servilia."

I frown. "But you use magic."

His lips tilt up slightly, and he looks like he can't help but chuckle. "I do."

"You're not human." I know that for sure. He looks more servilian than human.

He inclines his head. "Correct."

I blink at him, feeling my mouth go dry. "If you're not human and not servilian, then what are you?"

Sitri's gaze lingers on me for a long moment before he leans back against the wooden table, and his abdomen flexes as he grips the surface. "I'm a demon."

My mouth opens and snaps shut automatically as I blink at him. "I'm sorry. I think I just had a brain aneurysm because I thought you just said you're a–"

"Demon." He finishes my sentence with a nod of his head.

"Like, as in Hell's legion's kind of demon?" I ask cautiously, equally hoping he just thinks I'm crazy and next he'll say he's a bad guy from Servilia.

He just laughs, and damn if his smile doesn't counteract the wave of horror at the knowledge that the demon that saved me, moments ago, I had no idea existed.

"Sort of. I command sixty of them, so I suppose in some sense that's right."

Did he just say sixty legions?

I am *so* out of my element.

Yet somehow my curiosity is more piqued than it's ever been in my life, and it's all I can do to blame the journalist in me.

I'm still gaping at him, and he just laughs harder. "I'm sorry, so you're like, what, a king of hell or something?!"

For once, he shakes his head, and I don't know if I'm relieved or horrified as he answers. "God, no. I'm a prince of hell, actually. Not quite at Asmodeus' pay grade."

Chapter 8

If I wasn't already sitting, my knees would have given out on me.

"Holy shit." I breathe, and he just chuckles, but my gears are turning with no way of stopping them.

Because if he's a demon, that means that angels are real, which means that there's more than just servilians who can use magic, and we've just grouped them together because we're ignorant of their existence.

That also means that if people blame servilians for his actions, they'll be held accountable for actions they didn't take.

This makes getting the truth out even more important.

My eyes flick to my camera sitting on the table.

I need to go through everything with a fine-tooth comb. There's no way I can put something out that makes servilians look bad.

My heart stutters as I shoot to my feet, gasping when something in my core tears again. Doubling over, I suck in a ragged breath as Sitri moves in to support my arms.

"On the bed."

Obediently, I step backward, and pain tremors through my abdomen again. Tears spring to my eyes, and I'm stuck frozen, unable to move. *Shit.*

He must realize that I can't, and he steps over to my side with his arm around my back. "Lean into me, I've got you."

Urging myself to move, to ease into his grip proves useless—I'm immobilized by the feeling of knives twisting in my core.

I know that if I engage my muscles at all, it will mean pain, but the look in Sitri's eyes is so certain, I have no choice but to let myself fall back, and hope to God he's got me.

Relaxing my muscles, I hold his gaze. I'm only falling for a moment before he catches my body. His large arms securely support my weight as he gently scoops my legs onto the bed.

Kneeling in the middle of the mattress, his arm eases out from behind my back as he hovers over me.

His jaw tenses. "We need to get you checked, Maris. This isn't normal."

The way my abdomen feels like there's a knife being dragged through it makes me inclined to agree, and I nod.

"I'd say to stay put, but..." His words hang in the air, and I huff a pained laugh, wincing when it jolts my core.

The bed shifts with his movement as he pushes to his feet and strides to the doorway. "I'll be right back."

I focus on my breathing, each rise and fall of my chest accompanied by a stabbing sensation that makes me wonder if a stray bullet somehow hit me. It's not long before the door opens, and Sitri reappears with a middle-aged Kharidian woman in tow.

He gestures to me on the bed, and her brown gaze bounces between us for a moment before she leans in to murmur a question to him. I don't miss the pink tinge to his cheeks as he shakes his head and responds to her in a language I don't understand.

Understanding flashes across her features as she pales and hurries to the bed. She drapes the sheet over me before lifting my leg up, and it jolts my abdomen as I gasp as Sitri kneels beside where I lie.

"Anne is going to have to look, Maris." His bright eyes fixate on me as she lifts my other leg, and when I wince, his jaw tenses.

"I understand."

She tugs my still-broken pants down, my pulse spikes as my core flexes reactively, and I squeeze my eyes shut.

It's fine. It's not him. Just relax.

She tugs them to my ankles, and my chest heaves.

"Maris." My eyes snap open to where Sitri leans on the bed beside me, concern etched in his expression with his hand offered between us.

I've just met him. He's a demon–*a prince of hell*–and he's offering for me to hold his hand for comfort.

What the fuck is happening to me?

Sliding my palm into his, Anne murmurs something and the muscle in his jaw feathers.

"What is it?" My voice sounds small, and he brings our joined hands to my chest. He intertwines our fingers as my heart stutters.

"She said you're bleeding." Anne murmurs something else over the sheet, and he just nods. "She's asking when your last period was."

My cheeks burn. "I'm not pregnant."

He holds my gaze for a moment. "How can you be so sure?"

"I have an–" The realization hits me, and I feel my cheeks burn even hotter. "I have an IUD, which is probably–"

He curses under his breath and mutters something to Anne. When she responds, his sun-kissed skin turns a shade more pale. "She said if it's lodged, removal is going to be very painful."

I huff a dry laugh. "Can't be any more painful than when it became lodged to begin with."

My joke doesn't land as his golden irises simmering with rage linger on mine. Anne murmurs something, breaking him from his trance as he nods in response. The hurried way she ushers from the room only makes my heart pound harder, feeling like it could beat out of my throat at any second.

"Are you certain you don't want me to kill him?" His thumb glides along the back of my hand as I choke out a strangled laugh.

"Yes. Let him die of natural causes." *Or at least not one that I'm directly responsible for.*

"Fire is a naturally occurring phenomenon." Sitri grumbles in a matter-of-fact way, and my eyes widen.

Anne comes bustling in with a handful of tools, and blood rages in my ears when I realize what's coming. She says something to him, and he inches closer.

At this point he's hovering over me, and I feel like I'm in a labor and delivery room.

I might as well be.

Anne murmurs something in Kharidian, and I don't need him to translate to know she was warning me, but when the cold tool meets my exposed skin, I jolt.

Anne scolds as I inch away from her. Pain radiates through my core from my movement just as hot tears stream down my cheeks. She goes to smack my leg and Sitri barks something at her in another language, halting her in place.

My gaze remains fixed on the ceiling, and I count the specks of dust that I can see from where I lie, feeling the tool press against me again. She slowly inserts it, and I want to scream, to rage, to crawl backward.

Anything to get away from the feeling that reminds me of him.

Tears continue to stream from my eyes as they squeeze shut, and she cranks the tool open, sending radiating pain through my abdomen.

I gasp in response.

"Maris." Sitri whispers, and my eyes flutter open to his pained expression that might be equally hard to bear.

Because why should *he* feel pain for something Rob caused?

Anne murmurs something over the sheet, and Sitri leans in close, his free hand brushing strands of hair from my face.

"Deep breaths, Maris." He whispers, pressing his forehead to mine as he cups the back of my neck.

That's when I feel it.

It's like she's ripping my organs from my body as my abdomen contracts against the feeling, and I cry out, squeezing Sitri's hand so hard that my fingers go numb. The tugging feeling suddenly stops, and her shrill voice fills the air as she stammers words in a jumbled mess.

My shoulders sag now that the tearing is done, but it's clear that something's off.

It doesn't take a rocket scientist to figure it out.

I was already bleeding.

When you pull the knife from the wound...

Sitri looks at her with wide eyes before his attention turns to me. The resolve in his expression hardens, and he leans in to whisper in my ear. "Think again, Maris. You're not allowed to die before that asshole."

He places his hand on my abdomen, and warmth gives way to heat before the searing starts, and I feel like I'm being branded all over again as I gasp.

I hardly recognize the cry that escapes my throat before the world goes dark.

Chapter 9

The sound of rushing water is the first thing I notice before the dull throb in my abdomen comes front and center.

Recalling the moments that led up to me passing out from pain, I don't know if I should be grateful for Sitri's method of intervention.

I suppose I'm alive, and that's enough.

His quick thinking is probably why I'm not in worse shape... I can't imagine how terrible I'd feel if I'd have lost more blood.

My eyes flutter open, and I glance at the open window, curtains on either side billowing softly with the breeze. Clothes rest in a pile atop the long wooden dresser along the wall opposite of the bed.

I spot the edge of the tub to my left just beyond the open door and make a mental note of where the bathroom is.

The dark, loose-fitting pants hugging my body are most definitely not mine, nor is the soft shirt draped over my shoulders, the sleeves so long that they threaten to hang past my fingertips.

My attention returns to the window as the curtains ripple again, and I watch the stream in the distance with a serene sense of awe. Tall trees line the moving water, guiding it out of view, while giving the area much needed shade.

It's such a stark contrast to the dry destruction I'd been witness to since arriving in Kharidia that part of me wonders if we're still there.

The door to the room swings open, and Anne walks in with long strides. Her momentum comes to a halt when her eyes meet mine, widening for a breath of a moment. She twists on her heel and sprints out the door, leaving me wondering if I grew a second or third head.

I'm only left alone for a handful of seconds before the door opens once more, and Sitri strides in adorned in his black robes once more. The material hugs his body before flowing loosely down his back, swaying with each step closer. Anne follows close behind him, a string of Kharidian words tumbling from her lips.

He gives her a look that I can't quite place before kneeling alongside the bed. He tilts his head, and his dark hair shifts to the side. "How are you feeling?"

His voice is like silk to my ears, and I suck in a breath.

"I'm alright, I think." I whisper, noting the restless ache in my limbs that I can't shake. "How long was I out?"

His jaw tenses, and his golden eyes search mine for a moment. "A week."

My mouth drops open and snaps shut as I blink at him. "Shit." My voice is hardly audible, and a wave of dread washes over me.

Anne's words, even in another language, keep my thoughts from spiraling, and Sitri nods. "She wants to see if you can walk around, even a little."

My stomach twists nervously. "Uh, sure."

Sitri's hands move to my back as if on instinct, and I slowly ease myself upright with his support. The tugging deep in my core is nowhere close to the pain I'd felt when Sitri had gotten us away from the soldiers, and I blow out a breath of relief.

Thankfully, though loose fitting, the pants hugging my hips remain stationary when I turn to hang my legs over the side of the bed. I'm not certain who dressed me, but for whatever reason, I can only assume it was Anne.

Even with my limited knowledge of him, Sitri doesn't seem like he'd be open to doing such a thing when I'm unconscious.

His hands disappear from my back, and he offers them between us as my heart lurches in my chest. His touch is warm and gentle as I slide my palms into his.

It's hard to believe he's a demon, considering the kindness he's shown me since I met him.

The odds of this being an elaborate ruse to gain my trust seems too unlikely, which only leaves the possibility that Thornton and Deliom have both lied.

I hate that that is the more plausible scenario.

Leaning into his strength as my leverage, I slowly push to my feet with a tight grip on him. It takes time, pausing out of an abundance of caution just to breathe before straightening some more. When I'm fully upright, I huff a quick laugh of relief.

Anne glances between us apprehensively, and I just grin at her.

"It's good?" She says in English as my brows shoot up.

"Yes. It's *very* good." I nod, and her shoulders sag as she murmurs something to Sitri. The relief on her face is palpable, like a weight has been lifted from her shoulders, which only serves to tighten the feeling in my chest.

Sitri murmurs in response to her, and she steps alongside him, patting his arm before striding from the room.

"She said to walk around as much as you can, but no lifting anything heavy."

I sigh wistfully. "There goes leg day, I guess."

He ignores my sarcasm with a shake of his head and turns to look out the window. "Are you feeling up for a walk?"

My muscles tremble with exertion already, but I nod. "Anything other than lying down, please."

I know after a week of remaining stationary, I shouldn't overdo it, but the restless feeling in my legs and arms would argue that bed rest could be just as dangerous right now.

Keeping my palm securely in his, he slowly guides me from the room, letting me set the pace. My first steps are more tentative as I test my balance. Teetering once, I grip his hand harder as he shortens the distance between us ever so slightly.

When my leg twitches and spasms, I jerk to a stop and freeze as he remains still at my side.

"Easy, Maris." He murmurs softly, his free hand supporting my arm, to support more weight. It takes another long moment before I'm ready to move again, and he moves fluidly in response, adjusting his position to let me guide us forward.

His presence beside me is calming. In fact, it's so calming that I start to wonder if he was lying about being able to use his magic on me.

Moving at a snail's pace through the kitchen where Anne is, she pauses to watch us with a smile. Whoever this woman is, I will forever be eternally grateful for her, and Sitri, of course.

If Sitri hadn't helped me escape Rob, I don't even want to think of what could have happened. Then, if Anne hadn't removed my IUD, I would still have been in pain, not to mention the fact that there's a very good chance I'd be dead if Sitri hadn't stopped the bleeding.

We continue our slow steps until we're outside, and the sound of running water is a balm to my soul as we slowly make our way toward it.

The conflict in his face when I ran into him in the street comes to my mind, and my gaze slides to his. His attention fixated on the path in front of us, and even though he's clearly looking in the direction we're headed, his mind seems so far away.

"Why are you helping me?"

I don't mean for it to come out rude, but part of me kicks myself for not thinking my question through when I sound more curt than intended.

Thankfully, he doesn't seem too concerned as his expression turns contemplative.

"You helped me before, did you not?"

I give him a sidelong glance. "Our situations were not remotely the same." I say with a huff.

"How so? You had caught me unaware when someone was relying on me for help. You could have easily told the soldiers I was in that closet with her."

I nearly snort a laugh. "You could have just burned us to a crisp. I did nothing to help you."

Finally, near the edge of the stream we come to a stop, and he tilts his head with his golden amber irises trained on me. "Do you think taking lives brings me pleasure?"

My lived experience of servilians wars with the knowledge that many think the worst of them simply because they don't know enough about them.

Who's to say demons aren't much different?

That being said, he did kill those soldiers when I ran into him... and was more than willing to do the same to Rob, though, I feel more inclined to forgive him on that one.

Even though we're not moving, he still gently cradles my hand in his, and my heart pumps hard as I shake my head. "I don't know you well enough to answer that."

His lips twitch, and he exhales a breath as his attention returns to the stream. "If I could live a life without it, I would in a heartbeat. But that's not what Father has in store for me, I suppose."

The ache and longing in his words almost give me pause, but I'm too curious to not ask. "What do you mean?"

His expression pulls into a frown, and the muscle along his jaw-line feathers. "As I'm sure you are aware, those here in Kharidia know me as the one who summons fire to destroy everything around me, including our enemies... But my biggest curse?"

He shakes his head with a wry smile. "I am a demon who can manipulate feelings and curate love where there is none. I'm doomed to lead a life where love is not found but created from nothing."

Something inside of me feels like it might fracture, and I tighten my grip on his hand.

All of a sudden his surprise when his magic didn't work on me makes more sense.

"Why does that make you doomed to never find love?"

His sunlight irises seem to reflect the light peering from the canopy as he takes a deep breath. "Because it isn't true if I've manipulated someone into their desire for me. That would be nothing more than a mirror of obsession."

"That sounds miserable." I mumble, and he huffs a laugh, nodding in agreement.

"And then, there's the war." He adds matter-of-factly. "An eternal conflict, escalated and perpetuated by a group of powerful, corrupt men and women within education, law, politics, government—all to harvest the most valuable resource this world has to offer."

My eyes widen, and I almost don't want to ask—but no matter how horrifying the answer might be, I need to know.

"What resource?" I whisper, the question fading into the sound of the stream and rustling leaves around us.

His gaze finds mine, and I'm nearly certain my heart could stop beating in my chest at his pained expression. His free hand inches closer to my cheek before he tucks a lock of hair behind my ear.

The action is so tender in contrast to my anxious anticipation of his answer, making me wonder if he's doing it soothingly. As if his response is worse than what I could imagine.

Oil and minerals are the main culprits for foreign wars, but Kharidia has none of that, so those possibilities are out the window.

My stomach tumbles over itself as he pauses, as if assessing whether he should tell me. I don't shy away from holding his gaze, memorizing as much of it as I can.

His lips part, and my attention drops, but the single word that comes from him is the last I'd expect.

"Souls."

Chapter 10

A wave of horror washes over me as I stare at him with wide eyes.

"Come again?"

His jaw tenses. "I know this is a lot to take in, Maris."

"Who are '*they*' and why are they harvesting souls?" The words feel foreign in my mouth, and I drop my voice low. "No riddles, Sitri."

He flashes a small grin as he chuckles. "I don't deal in riddles, Maris." Humor drips from his words before his expression turns more serious. "For the *who* of your question, there's no single answer I can provide. It could be your teacher, your doctor, your lawyer, your boss, your local politician, your president, your parent, your neighbor, or your friend. Their roots spread as far as they are deep."

A knot forms in my stomach as I think back to people I grew up with, met in my career and beyond. But it's when my thoughts turn to Rob, Thornton, Deliom and a handful of others that I start to wonder just how close I've gotten to these corrupt individuals.

Sitri gestures down the path that runs along the stream, pulling me from my spiraling thoughts and I couldn't be more thankful. I answer with a nod and take a cautious step toward it, keeping a gentle pace that doesn't push myself too hard.

"Now, as for the 'why' of your question..." His piercing gaze scans the area around us thoughtfully. "Before we fled heaven, corruption had infected some of our most loyal brothers and sisters.

People who loved Samael turned on him for suspecting that something was off. Before we knew what was happening, the hunt for Samael and his supporters had begun, and none of heaven's inner levels were safe."

Everything he says triggers more questions.

Heaven has levels within it? Who lives there? Who became infected? If he and his supporters fled, does this mean the stories we've been told were wrong? What else was rewritten or misinterpreted?

I'm only half paying attention to the path as we move at a snail's pace, with the rest of my focus on the pained expression Sitri wears.

"They tortured Samael's closest friends to uncover his location. When no one gave him up, they winnowed—" He sees the way my brows pull together and clarifies. "—They severed the wings from his followers, and among the insults thrown at them, the most prominent one was 'demon'. It wasn't long before stories of Samael's *rebellion* travelled far and wide, blaming his pride and ego."

I swallow against the lump forming in my throat. "Then what happened?"

A kid shrieks and laughs in the distance, giving Sitri the slightest pause. "Once those of us who escaped had found one another, Samael had a plan to regain control. Unfortunately, so did the forces that had taken over heaven. While Samael worked to counteract their attempts to bolster their ranks, they found ways to manipulate the process of creating future angels. They'd manufacture devastation and trauma here on earth to secure the numbers for their army there."

The thought that the 'good guys' who everyone should trust and run to for help are really the bad guys makes my blood run cold.

"We are at war in every sense of the word, Maris, and humans are caught in the middle. We have been here fighting their influence for centuries while Samael does his part—and for a long time, it was manageable. The impact they have on their charges alters them to be more malleable after death, but we'd counteract their efforts with our own to even the playing field. They'd push a godless man to sin, and we'd be there to whisper in his ear to right his wrongs before it's too late."

My hand grips Sitri's tighter. I know there are no words I can offer that will make anything right or better, but being told such a personal piece of his history—he should know that he's not alone.

"You said it was manageable... is it not anymore?"

He shakes his head, his dark hair shifting with the movement. "Long, long ago, around the time when Rome fell, things took a turn for the worst. They'd created enough influence to drive failures in every facet of the empire, enough so that it created the perfect opportunity for them to install themselves strategically after, to rebuild their own empire in its place—not that the roman gods were happy about that, but they weren't in a place to intervene."

My eyes widen, and when he sees the shock on my face, he just chuckles. "Many think that religion is simply one god or many gods they worship in return for good fortune, leaving no room for others. The truth is, they are all real, but people have twisted the stories over the years to perpetuate corruption and reinforce mistrust. They've gotten more bold over the centuries, and now they harvest souls en masse. They create ritual sites all over Kharidia just before large-scale attacks to manipulate souls, and then harvest them."

I blow out a breath; the revelations keeping my mind far from any discomfort in my abdomen. "So you're telling me you're the good guys, the angels that reside in heaven are not, and we're their targets?"

Sitri nods thoughtfully in the corner of my eye. "I won't say they're all bad, but it does seem like their numbers have exploded in the past few years. It's gotten worse because we are unable to break or bend the rules that are meant to keep us in check... If we do, we risk losing all the progress we've made. So, until someone who isn't bound by our rules can help us, our hands are tied."

His golden eyes pin me in place, burning bright as I absorb his words. "You thought that Kharidians were rebellious radicals when you first arrived, yes?"

Swallowing against the lump in my throat, I struggle to find the right words. "I can't deny I was inclined to believe what news outlets reported... Even if the larger part of me was skeptical."

An odd note of relief seeps into my bones when his expression holds no contempt at my words.

Everything he's said about who the real bad guys are is a tough pill to swallow, but coming here to Kharidia opened my eyes. I can't deny what I've seen, and even though there are two sides to every story, it's clear that Sitri's side is the one that's been missing all this time.

"This rewritten narrative is why people think demons are evil, then?"

A flicker of emotion crosses his features as he nods, giving my hand a slight squeeze.

"Eyes need to be opened to the truth before real, meaningful change can happen. They control the narrative, they always have, and that's where their power lies for now."

He tilts his head to look at me, and my pulse skips under his gaze. "Truth is an ember, Maris. With time and without help, it easily dies out. But for that ember to spread like a wildfire? For that to happen, the winds must help nourish it, and carry it further, to a place where it will grow. That is where we come in. We must be the winds that carry the embers, Maris."

It takes a moment to realize I'd stopped walking to look at him, and I clear my throat. "This is all very..."

"Overwhelming? Life altering?" I meet his gaze, and he just nods in understanding with a quiet laugh. "Yes, it can be, even for me, but now and then, Father throws us a lifeline, and it's up to us to see it for what it is."

We continue further, and the muscles in my legs feel like they've finally loosened to where I'm not worried about falling with each step I take. The dull tension in my abdomen twinges every now and again, but for the most part, I feel better than I expected to, considering the circumstances.

The path loops back to the house, and with each step I feel more relaxed, reassured from the feeling of Sitri's hand in mine.

"So, how will you stop them?"

His thick brows pull together, and he shakes his head. "I don't know if it's possible to stop them now. Their ritual sites are easy to rebuild, and they reinforce them when they get wind of which one is being targeted next."

The room filled with candles comes to mind as I freeze, staring at him with a mixture of disbelief and horror. "The apartment complex, it had—" The gentle breeze blows his robes as he nods, his soft expression telling me everything I need to know. "—That's where you were going when I ran into you."

I don't need him to confirm it as he searches my face. A wave of guilt washes over me when I recall how torn he seemed before he hid me from Rob.

He'd chosen to help me escape, which means they could still use it to harvest more souls...

"You didn't get the chance to destroy it..." I don't miss the way his jaw flexes. "Or did you?"

His lips curve into a relaxed smile, and my shoulders sag. "I took care of it while you were recovering."

The last thing I'd want is to be the reason more people end up in their hands. "So you're just in a constant vicious circle, then?"

He gestures to the house in a silent reminder for us to move, and I take another cautious step. "I have been, and for the foreseeable future, I will be. We need people to see this war for what it is before we can even think of stopping them. Humans need to retake their power from those in control."

"The repetition of destroying ritual sites only for them to rebuild sounds miserable." I grumble, and he just huffs a laugh.

Nearing the front door, Sitri moves to open it for me, a smirk still sprawled across his face. "It's not for the faint of heart."

I can picture him destroying them, clear as day in my mind—returning over and over for the duration of this war. The thought makes my heart hurt.

It's the closest thing to the definition of insanity.

We pass by Anne busily moving about the kitchen on our way to the room, too engrossed in cooking to notice us. It's not until we pass the doorway that I sigh gratefully seeing a fresh set of clothes near the bed.

"Can you thank Anne for me?" I whisper to Sitri before glancing at the doorway. "She's done so much, and she's been so incredibly kind."

His lips twitch. "Sure. Do you think you're feeling well enough to bathe?"

Even if I wasn't, there's no way I'm declining a chance to get clean.

"I'll be okay." *I think.*

He turns away, but when I don't release his hand, he glances back.

"Thank you, for saving me..." I pause, and laugh quietly. "Again."

The air between us feels electric, and goosebumps dance along my arms, making the tiny hairs stand on end.

His lips twitch, and he glances at the bathroom to our right. "Try not to make defying death a habit."

Releasing his hand and suppressing a shiver, I cross my arms over my chest. "Challenge for the highest recorded number in defying death accepted."

Laughing, he just shakes his head and strides through the open door. "Enjoy your bath, Maris. Leave your clothes outside the door for Anne. She'll come get them soon."

Chapter 11

My attention turns to the washroom, and I don't think I've ever been more excited to get clean.

With cautious movements, I gather the small pile of fresh clothes into my arms and pace to the other room. My muscles warmed from the walk, but after a week of not using them, the tension in my body is an obvious reminder that I shouldn't overdo it.

I turn the faucet on and peel off the loose-fitting clothes Anne had changed me into. For a moment, I again consider the possibility that Sitri might have been the one to do it, but when my cheeks burn hot, I shake my head in denial.

Even if he's a demon, he doesn't seem to have adopted the stereotype from what I can tell.

Water continues to rush into the tub, and I stare at the crest-line that slowly rises. My mind wanders to the destruction I'd been witness to since we got here with a bitter note of sadness.

Once upon a time, Kharidia used to be a beautiful homeland to its people—the fact that this place is being used for such horrendous atrocities just urges me even more to spread the truth.

I heard Sitri's unspoken message loud and clear when he said they were bound by rules. What rules they're bound to, I have no idea, but I doubt they apply to me.

The question is, how do I help?

Twisting the faucet, the water stops rushing from the mouth, and I climb into the hot water. Steam rises in wisps, gliding along my skin as I lean back to rest my head.

All I know is reporting, and creating pieces for the news outlets that, once upon a time, wasn't controlled by a few entities with a personal vested interest in keeping people uninformed... or misinformed.

There's a very real, very high chance that everything Sitri said was the truth. I know that there's no actual way to prove or disprove him, but with everything I've seen in my life... it's hard not to believe him.

I'm not usually one to be naïve or believe what people say at face value. The investigator in me would riot if I didn't think I had enough information to make a well-informed decision.

My muscles relax more, and the heat makes the brand on my shoulder throb gently, as if quietly reminding me of whatever ties I have to Sitri.

I reach over to glide my index finger over the slightly raised skin, tracing it mindlessly.

Part of me wonders if the reason he can't use his powers on me is because of his brand on my shoulder, but the logic of it seems too contradictory to be true, so I shove that thought aside.

Whatever the reason, I'm thankful for his inability to coax me so easily. It's made it easier to feel like I can trust him, not to mention the fact that he's been so forthcoming. He could have just as easily told me nothing and let me think he's everything General Deliom claimed him to be.

The video Deliom showed us comes to mind, and though I can only clearly remember some parts, I resign myself to asking him about it.

It's abundantly obvious that I'm partial to him... the reason why might be up for debate, but if it weren't for him, I wouldn't be alive right now, or if I was, I'd be in Rob's *care*.

I shudder at the thought.

My gaze focuses on the bar of soap to my right, and I dip it under the water before rubbing it over my skin. Jasmine and lavender fill my senses as I continue to scrub harder, tears welling in the corners of my eyes.

Water sloshes with my movement, and I move down my arms to my chest and abdomen before working soap down my legs.

Droplets disturb the water and fall to my chest as I choke down a sob.

I scrub relentlessly, making sure soap cleanses every place Rob had touched me, every inch where we'd been in contact over the past few years, and by the time I finish, my eyes are swollen. My vision's still blurred from the tears that have yet to fall, and there's not a single part of my body that hasn't been scrubbed raw.

Besides there.

I lean forward to pull the drain, rinsing the suds from my hair with fresh water before gingerly climbing out of the tub. I've only toweled off my hair when a soft knock at the door catches my attention.

My gaze slides to my dirty clothes on the floor across the room.

Silently chiding myself for not placing the clothes outside the room for Anne beforehand, I wrap the towel around my chest. My hair drapes over my left shoulder, droplets of water still falling to the floor.

I move with added caution, careful not to slip as I reach over to tug the door open without looking.

"Sorry, Anne," I murmur, crossing to the other side of the room to snag my clothes from the floor. When I turn, halfway facing the door, I freeze, seeing Sitri's form filling the doorway.

He averts his gaze, but I don't miss the reddish hue in his cheeks. "Would you like dinner?"

I secure the towel and clothes against my chest and nod. "Sure. I'm starving."

His eyes flick to mine, and I don't miss the way his lips twitch upward. "I'll let Anne know." With an outstretched palm offered between us, his gaze drops to the clothes clutched to my body, and I step closer to place them in his grasp.

"Maris," He whispers, and I see his brows pull together as his gaze flicks to my shoulder. "When did you get that?"

I follow his line of sight to the sigil of raised skin before looking at him once more. "Since we ran into each other that first time..." I trail off, the way his brows furrow sends a wave of anxiety through me. "You mean you didn't do this?"

His golden irises leave my shoulder to lock with mine, and he shakes his head. "Not on purpose—" He says, and he brings his hand up to trace it.

The contact sends a shiver through me. "But you could have?"

"It's possible." He says softly. "I remember feeling like I might lose control of my emotions when I saw him grab you, but I did nothing consciously."

"So, you don't know what this is, then?" I ask, and he tucks the clothes into his body with a shake of his head.

"The sigil is mine. It's used to call on me, but why you might have it, I don't know. Does it hurt?"

I shake my head. "It throbs sometimes, but there's no pain."

His head tilts to the side. "Will you tell me if you feel anything else from it?"

The hesitation in his expression gives me pause and I nod. "Of course." I breathe, and when he goes to move to the doorway, I take a step closer to him. "But does this mean that your magic might work on me, or?"

His lips twitch. "I don't know. It likely means we're tied in some way, and I have half a mind to think Father might be to blame. If I couldn't use my abilities on you to coerce you to give me information, none of my other magic should work on you. If that's not the case, I'd have to think he had some part in it."

He glances to the door as something clatters in the kitchen. "But, we can try to understand it more *after* dinner. If we're late, Anne will behead me."

I chuckle, feeling less doom and gloom as he flashes a grin and slips out of the room.

Chapter 12

Anne sees me striding into the living area, and her face lights up as she gestures to an empty chair at a table with various plates and bowls full of food.

She watches me patiently as I cautiously step closer, feeling exponentially better now that I'm clean and wearing a fresh set of clothes. Even though I'd walked with Sitri and bathed without incident, I'm not trying to overdo it.

The last thing I want is to backtrack any healing I'd done.

I slide into the seat, and my mouth waters at the aroma of cooked vegetables. With the pangs of hunger cramping my stomach every few minutes, I could drool. It takes everything not to as Anne reaches over and places a full plate of food in front of me with a gentle smile.

The deep set lines at the corners of her eyes don't crinkle fully, but something tells me she got them from a healthy share of laughing for years. Given the circumstances, it's hard for me to picture her before the war, when everything was less existential.

I glance at Sitri, whose sunlight irises already watching the two of us curiously. "So, how did you two meet?"

He murmurs something to her, and she blinks, her features softening as she chuckles. His attention returns to me, and I slice a bite sized piece of bell pepper.

"About ten years ago, I'd been looking for survivors from a bomb that was dropped on the eastern region of Kharidia. The civilians only had a two-minute warning to evacuate the hospital and school, but for most, it was not enough time."

Ten years. There's yet another mainstream media lie exposed.

Anne's face grows solemn in my peripherals, and I don't need to ask to know that she understands English well enough to know what story he's telling me.

"When I was searching for people buried under rubble, I'd found Anne pinned between a hospital bed and the concrete wall. I'd brought her here while she healed because this was one of the safest places in the country to hide, and gave her the option to stay."

Their eyes meet, and she murmurs something in Kharidian to him as he laughs. "She said I've been a pain in her ass ever since."

I choke on a piece of carrot and sputter before laughing. When a few seconds pass and I feel no pain, I smile wider before I collect myself. "Why didn't she go to a neighboring country?"

Anne says something to him, and he inclines his head. "The neighboring countries have guarded entry points. Even if people wanted to flee, the blockades and military installments all over make it nearly impossible."

His gaze flicks to her for a moment. "Besides, Anne's stubbornly loyal. She would rather die for those she loves, and she loves her country, and her people."

She looks at me with bright eyes, and I can't help but feel inspired by her courage.

I've learned much since arriving in Kharidia. Enough that any person's head would spin from the conflicting facts warring in their mind. But looking at Anne's proud expression, something in it thrums in sync with the beat of my heart.

If nothing else, I know more than ever what I need to do. I know what my part is in this war.

Anne slices a piece of vegetables as she returns to her meal, and I set my fork down softly. "Would you mind if I took a photo of you, Anne?"

Her brows shoot up, but she nods sheepishly, and I move to stand. But before I can push to my feet, Sitri beats me to it.

"I'll get your camera. Eat. You need your strength." He says, his voice as gentle as it is firm. Within seconds, he's disappeared into the other room, and my eyes slide to Anne.

"Is he always this chivalrous?"

Her mouth curves into a slight grin as she nods, and Sitri strides into the room once more. He offers the camera between us, and I gently take it from his hand—the weight as familiar as it is reassuring.

Inspecting it for damage for a moment, and finding none, I quickly put it to my cheek. Using the viewfinder and steadying myself, I adjust the lens.

Anne's tired grace is captured just as the shutter clicks, committing the moment to history.

I know this image won't mean much to the public now, but it will once they know the truth.

"Thank you." I whisper to Anne, and she smiles softly.

Sitri slides into his chair once more, and I set the camera down beside me, returning to my plate with renewed appreciation.

I might not be a warrior, a soldier, or capable of destruction, but what I do know is that a single story can change the course of history.

Anne murmurs something to Sitri as he chuckles. The sound sends a wave of warmth through me, and my resolve solidifies.

I might not have come here with the desire to get involved in any capacity... But with everything I've seen, I can't help but want an end to come to it.

If only for their sake.

Anne pushes to her feet and starts gathering plates. I notice the exhaustion in her features, so I gather mine to walk to the kitchen.

Her hurried footsteps fill the air before she halts me in place, murmuring what I can only assume is a scolding in Kharidian.

"She doesn't want you worrying about dishes."

I turn my head at the sound of Sitri's voice, seeing him gathering dishes from the table. Anne takes the plate from my hands and my eyes widen as she carries it away.

"I just wanted to help." I whisper, and he just laughs.

"Good luck. It took me six years to help her with anything. She's awfully stubborn."

Anne yells a single word from the other room, and he laughs loudly.

When he sees the question in my face, he chuckles. "She called me an asshole."

I grin as he brushes past me with arms full of dishes, and disappears into the kitchen. When my attention flicks to the front door, I take a deep, centering breath.

If I don't push myself, I won't know my limits.

A few steps toward the door, II'm feeling comfortable enough that one lap won't overexert myself too much. I can always turn around.

Clattering of dishes in the kitchen fills the air, and I step outside, sucking in a deep lungful of fresh air. The wooden door clicks shut behind me, and I amble down the front path to the worn road.

The sun's already disappeared behind the house, casting the sky with hues of orange and pink. I'm a few steps down the road, following the same path that Sitri had led us down earlier when heavy footfalls catch my attention.

I tilt my head to see Sitri jog over, slowing as he approaches. "Miss me that much?" I say with a grin, and the corners of his lips tug upward.

"If I didn't know better, I'd say you're trying your luck at another death defying event." He muses, his golden eyes bright as he offers his arm.

Something in my chest flutters, but I hook my forearm around his. "Great, now you're going to make me responsible for both of us defying death."

He chuckles and shakes his head. "There's not much that can bring me that close. Perks of being immortal, I suppose."

My eyes widen. "So if a bomb dropped on us right now—"

"I'd survive. I mean, it would hurt like hell, but I'd heal."

I grimace at the thought. "I'd rather not imagine that, actually."

He laughs under his breath, and I must have slowed to a snail's pace, because I notice his pace adjust to match mine.

"How many times have you been hurt that badly?" It's hard to picture someone of his size being overpowered, especially with the strength he's displayed.

His bright eyes meet mine for a moment. "Only a handful of times. Certain military units have special bullets that can slow my healing. The first time I'd run into them was a few years ago. I was arrogantly confident in my careless approach to destroy one ritual site. After a few well-aimed shots, I realized I wasn't healing like normal, and I narrowly escaped."

I swallow hard against the lump in my throat. "So, you're not entirely invincible?"

He shakes his head, and after a long moment, his voice carries in the air around us. "Have you given any thought to whether you plan to return?"

My heart stutters, and my gaze drops to the ground. Shadows stretch from the descending sun, and I shake my head. "Not yet. I don't know what I'd tell them, and with everything that happened, I wouldn't be able to face Rob right now." My voice is hardly more than a whisper, and I feel Sitri's free hand rest on top of my arm linked with his.

It's such an insignificant gesture of support, but I hold on to it with everything I have.

"I wasn't asking to pressure you, you know. Stay as long as you need," he murmurs, his thumb gliding along the top of my arm. "Reports came out today saying that you're a prisoner of war, so it's safe to assume they don't know where you are—just that you're missing. They'll maintain that rhetoric as long as they need to, so use it to your advantage."

"I know I'll have to return at some point, but I'd like to stay for a bit longer." While I know I want to stay to make sure I've healed, there's a larger, louder part of me that selfishly doesn't want to deal with Rob, even if I'm determined to expose what's really happening here to the people back home.

I see him nod in my peripherals. "Then stay, recover, and we'll figure the rest out later." He looks over and smiles. "Just don't wander out alone in the dark, preferably." He adds, and I know he's referring to my attempt to do a lap while they cleaned up inside.

"You're really going to blame a girl for wanting to help herself heal?"

He huffs a laugh. "Is that what we're calling that?"

We both chuckle, turning down the path to return to the house.

Something about Sitri is just so easy.

Telling him things, trusting him. It's like breathing.

I don't need to dwell extra on it because it's clear he's already shown me who he is without trying.

The first time I saw him, he was rescuing a child.

The second time, he set aside his original purpose to rescue *me*.

What I don't understand is why he doesn't just end it all. Why play this game and not just destroy everyone he knows is part of the other side?

The question burns on my tongue until finally, I muster the courage to ask. "Why not just kill them all, Sitri?"

His eyes widen, and I know it's because my question is out of the blue, and maybe out of character for how much I dislike death.

When his expression grows more solemn, I inch closer, holding his arm near my chest.

"Remember when I said we're bound by rules?" He asks, his hand still resting comfortably on my arm.

I nod.

"If I were to intervene on a large scale... one that interferes with global affairs or affects humankind in a way that tips the balance, my life is forfeit."

My mouth drops open, but the pained expression he wears has any commentary dying on my lips.

"How?" It's all I can ask, because asking *why* isn't a fair question for him, either.

"Well," he says, leading the last few steps to the house. "The moment I tip the scales, Azrael is duty bound to take my life. Painless, but I'd rather not die and lose the progress I've made, even if meager."

I let that sink in, and he helps guide me past the living room and kitchen. When we cross the doorway to the bedroom, I spot the fresh pair of pajamas on the bed, and my chest tightens.

God. Anne is a saint.

"I know you said there were rules, but the fact that you will literally die, yet they can do whatever they want to corrupt people is unfair."

His gaze drops to the floor, and I decide to quickly change the topic to something slightly relevant. "So... any idea what the sigil on my shoulder is yet?" I ask, withdrawing my arm from his to snag the pajamas.

He steps closer, raising his hands to the collar of my shirt before pausing, a silent question in his eyes. When I nod, he gently lifts the material, setting his palm on top of it.

My body warms with my pulse thrumming in my ears as each second passes. I fall still for a long moment, not daring to breathe before he pulls back and shakes his head.

"I'm sorry Maris. I can't seem to figure out why you have it."

I just shrug. "As long as I won't die from it, I'll just consider it like a new tattoo, just one for you specifically."

He chuckles, moving to the couch along the wall. "I don't know whether I'm impressed or scared."

When he collapses onto the couch, stretching the length of it—his legs are long enough that he has to settle them on top of the armrest in order to fit.

I blink. "Are you... sleeping there?"

He glances between me and the bed. "I can sleep outside if you prefer. There's not much for mattresses here—"

"No." Sitri's mouth snaps shut, and he glances at the door. "Come here."

"Maris, I—" He starts to say, but I point to the bed.

"Sitri, you're not sleeping on a couch you don't fit on. Come here."

I can tell he wants to argue, but he pushes to his feet and walks over to stand in front of me. His tall form dwarfs mine, and I tilt my head to look at him.

"Are you certain you're comfortable with this?"

I nod, gesturing to the bed again.

Truth be told, that he's so hesitant, and that he gave me my space by taking the couch, reaffirms the comfort I feel in letting him lie beside me while I sleep.

He collapses into the bed, scooting to the edge, giving me as much room as possible.

Without another word, I pad to the washroom and change into the sleek pajamas Anne provided. By the time I've returned to the room, Sitri's breathing is even, and I chuckle quietly to myself.

Even immortals need a good night's sleep.

Cautious to not wake him, I crawl into the bed, doing my best to keep it from shifting as the springs creak. I hold my breath after each sound, but to my relief, his breathing remains the same.

Finally lying down, after a long day of pushing my body, I melt further into the mattress.

Sitri's steady breathing is hardly audible beside me, but between that and his body heat, I find myself more at ease than expected. It's a relief to know that that's one thing Rob didn't ruin in his assault—my affinity for physical touch is something I would have mourned.

Listening to each breath feels like a balm to my soul, and my eyes slide shut.

Chapter 13

Anne rushes into the room, her brown eyes wide as she sprints over, rushing out strings of Kharidian.

"Anne, what's going on?"

Her grip is firm as she pulls me off the bed and ushers me to the door. I track the movement as she gestures to the front door and gives me a deadpan stare.

"Sitri," she says more firmly, gesturing to the door again. "Help."

My heart lurches and I close the distance to the door, pushing it open with all my might.

But it doesn't budge.

I turn to Anne, only to find the space empty, and I shudder.

Did I imagine her? Is he in trouble?

Her words echo in my mind, and I push at the door again, only for it to stay closed. If Sitri is on the other side of this door, and needs help... I have to try.

Taking a few steps back, I tense and lunge forward, slamming my shoulder into the door with a loud thud. Pain jolts through my arm, and I gasp, but step back and repeat the action once more.

It creaks on the second attempt, and I take an extra step back to get more momentum, sprinting as fast as I can at the wooden barrier between me and the person I owe so much to.

The moment my shoulder hits the hard surface, it gives way—the wood splinters, falling fast, and I crumble to the floor with it.

I hardly get time to collect my bearings when a familiar voice fills the air.

"Maris, where have you been?"

I groan and roll onto my side to relieve the pressure in my shoulder. Rob's already tall form towering over where I lie prone on the ground.

"Fuck you, Rob."

A grin creeps across his face. "Are you giving me permission?" I hardly get a second to react as he drops to his knees, grabbing my wrists with a bruising grip.

"Rob, get off of me!" I thrash, kicking at him as he struggles to keep hold of me.

"Maris, come back to me, baby." He croons, and tears spill down my cheeks as I shriek in frustration. "It'll be like old times, just you and me at the house. You remember how much you liked it, right?"

He pins me with his knee, and I glare at him. "I won't let you hurt me again."

Rob just laughs, the sound so unlike anything I'd ever heard from him before, but some terrified part of me knows that it's a fitting sound to come from him.

"Come on baby, it'll be fun." He tries to climb on top of me, but I thrash some more, tears scattering in all directions as I shove him away with my hips.

"I won't let you hurt me again!"

I surge upright, my wet eyes searching the empty darkness as I gasp. Twisted blankets wrap around my legs, and my hair sticks to my neck, still slick from sweat.

"Maris—" Sitri's voice is like velvet to my ears as I shudder. "You're alright, it was just a nightmare."

I hear his words, but my adrenaline and heightened emotions refute them, still feeling the echoes of Rob's bruising grip—a phantom touch that no amount of scrubbing will clean away.

I hate him for it.

Sitri's hand strokes circles on my back, and I bury my head in my hands as tears continue to pour from my eyes.

"You're alright." He repeats, his voice hardly above a murmur.

He sits up, adjusting his position so that my hip brushes his thigh, and he gently prods my elbows in a silent request for me to look at him.

My palms and wrists, still damp from my tears, slowly inch away from my face until I find his golden irises, just barely visible even in the shadows of the night. The dark making them look like molten embers searching my face as my breath hitches.

I don't shy away from him as his hand at my back moves to my shoulder, and he pulls me into his chest. The sob that had caught in my throat claws its way out, and my soaked grip finds the material at his chest. Balling my hand into a fist, I grind my teeth as more tears fall.

"Do you want to talk about it?"

His voice is agonizingly gentle, and when Rob's face comes into my mind, I just want to scream.

My body trembles from a mixture of anger and frayed nerves from the adrenaline. "I hate him."

The words I whisper break the stillness of the room, like a confessional that I've desperately needed for longer than I care to admit.

"I hate who I became when we were together. I hate I let him diminish who I am—that I was so fucking scared of what he could do. That my fear kept me from leaving."

Sitri's arms tighten around me more, and my words come out strangled from the emotion clogging my throat. "I hate that I wasn't brave enough. I hate that I feel weak compared to him. I hate that I didn't stop him."

I shake as I squeeze his shirt in my fist as hard as I can, with tears spilling onto Sitri's chest.

His chin rests atop my head, and he takes a deep breath. "Are you *certain* that you don't want me to kill him?"

I choke out a surprised laugh with a shake of my head. "If either of us gets to kill him, it'll be me."

"From your lips to Father's ears, Maris."

Sitri's thumb glides along the length of my arm soothingly, and he leans back in the bed, taking me with him. The action doesn't strike me as overly intimate in any sexual sense, but more-so one of comfort, and I don't make any move to break our embrace.

Maybe it's because even though Sitri looks like a god, and is strong enough that he could pass as one, but he doesn't use that strength for his own benefit.

In fact, I haven't seen him use *anything* to his own benefit or enjoyment. Since the moment we met, Sitri hasn't asked for a single thing from me.

Instead, he's only given me truths I never would have gotten without his help. That knowledge only makes me so much more grateful for his presence, and even knowing he's labeled a demon, I know I trust him.

Arguably more than I should.

I adjust my position to fit better under his arm, his heart thrumming against my ear like a gentle melody to soothe parts of me that his presence alone cannot.

For a long moment, I let my mind wander away from my resentment toward Rob; allowing my curiosity about Sitri's past wash away that toxin like rain to my soul.

Fleeing heaven, fighting in a war that seems to never end... It all sounds like it could be someone's personal hell. I mean, I've been here for mere weeks, and I already want to go home.

I can't even imagine how he feels.

"Do you miss it?" His thumb still glides over my shoulder, not missing a beat as he takes a deeper breath.

"Sometimes. Earth is beautiful, too. To be honest, they are so much alike that sometimes I forget where I am. The only difference is the creatures and surplus of humans everywhere." His chest rumbles with his words, and I squeeze my eyes shut. "It's been so long that I'm not sure I'd feel at home there anymore."

I nearly reassure him he'll see it again, but something holds me back, tying the words to my tongue. False promises can give people a temporary kind of hope, but that can also lead to more heartache.

Of all the pain that exists in this world, I refuse to cause Sitri more than he's already felt.

So I stay quiet.

The silence that falls over us is comfortable, and I'm coaxed to sleep once more with Sitri's steady heartbeat against my cheek.

Chapter 14

Some days later...

"You're not coming with me."

Sitri's tall form leans against the door frame, his dark robes shifting as he crosses his arms over his chest. Birds chirp from the garden near the window, giving the sound of the stream a cheerful ambiance.

It's a stark contrast to the topic at hand.

My eyebrows shoot up. "The hell I'm not." Sitri's golden eyes flash in warning, but I just double down. "I can help. I'm not useless! I can keep an eye out for survivors or something you might miss."

My suggestions are a reach, but he doesn't need to know that.

I just can't sit idly by while he goes to destroy another ritual site by himself.

Turning away from the doorway, I tug my shirt overhead and rest it on the dresser, replacing it with the freshly cleaned t-shirt that I'd been wearing when I ran into Sitri weeks ago.

His tone drops an octave, and I shiver. "The likelihood you'll get hurt is too high. Besides, they already sent out reports that you're a prisoner of war. If they see you accompanying me **willingly**, you'll be deemed a traitor and killed on sight. I'm immortal, Maris, you're not."

"I don't care." I retort, turning to face him.

"Maris—" His pained expression makes my chest ache, but I refuse to let him do this alone.

"No, Sitri. I mean it. Let me help you." I move to stand in front of him in the doorway, and tilt my head to search his face. I know he's going to break.

Somehow, I know he's considering it, even if just a little.

He sighs, running his tongue along the edge of his teeth. "Fine. But you remain hidden, and in a designated location if needed."

I nod, suppressing the victorious surge within me to give him a lazy salute. "Scout's honor."

Something in his expression is unsettling, like he's bracing for the worst-case scenario of this excursion. But when he steps in close, my breath catches in my lungs.

His fingertips slide up my wrists, his palms trailing up the length of my arms before gliding over my shoulders. When he cradles either side of my neck in his palms, I don't dare to move.

But it's not because of any fear or of any desire to be away from him.

My chest tightens, and the realization that I don't want him to release me makes my entire body warm.

His irises, like twin suns, burn bright as he searches my face, and that's when I feel it.

Warmth from his palms travels along my skin, and my line of vision flicks down to the light, scar-like coloration gliding over my bare arms.

Unlike the first sigil that felt and healed like a legitimate brand, this is different. His magic causes me no pain, leaves no lingering wound, and no real scarring where it touches. It dances along my skin, leaving a blazing warm trail before it disappears, and I stare at the symbols now faded into my skin with a tense breath.

It's like the most imperceptible tan line someone can have.

If I hadn't seen it before it faded, I don't think I'd have noticed.

"What was that?" I whisper, tracing the near-invisible lines.

"Protection." Sitri murmurs, retracting his palms from my neck.

I glance over each symbol leading up my arms and frown. "Protection from what?"

He grabs a long cloth from the dresser and steps in close once more. Our chests brush with each breath as he carefully wraps the material around the back of my head. He meticulously covers the lower half of my face with the cloth, securing it as his concern-filled gaze meets mine.

"Me."

I don't get the chance to ask him to explain, because he wraps the dark material of his robe around me. Pulling me into his chest, I inhale a lungful of his warm, delicious scent as his arms encircle my shoulders. My hands ball into fists at my sides, still entirely uncertain what to do with them.

Maybe someday I'll figure it out.

"Closer your eyes." He commands, and they quickly slide shut. His robes cover my body, and my pulse is loud in my ears. Each breath I take only makes me want to relax into him, but it's mere seconds before he lowers his arms.

His robes fall away, and I turn to see an empty alleyway—the sandy road sloping down toward a few larger buildings a short distance away.

Sitri's palm slides into mine, bringing my attention front and center as he turns us in the opposite direction. "This way."

The wind howls eerily over the rooftops as he leads the way up the alley, keeping me securely tucked between him and the wall. It doesn't escape me that he's being extra cautious because I'm here, and I feel the lump in my throat grow.

I don't get to ruminate long before he gestures to a large building no more than twenty feet away. High stacks of solid brick make up the walls; I need to tilt my head to see the roof from here. When I see a cross standing tall atop the highest point, my chest squeezes.

Of course they'd make a fucking church one of their ritual sites.

Typical.

Each step closer feels like an eternity, and Sitri's arm crosses my chest. He halts my steps as he slows his own, using his hand that still encircles mine to position me wordlessly behind him.

If I get hurt, he'll never let me come with him again.

That's assuming he lets anything come near me. With how protective he's acting, it seems unlikely.

My cheeks burn at the thought.

Sitri eases the heavy wooden door open before going inside, and I dutifully follow close. The door creaks before it clicks shut—the sound quiet, but it shatters the stillness around us, only competing with the echo of our footsteps on the old wooden floorboards.

Keeping my hand tightly secured in his, we turn a corner and continue down the hall until we're standing before another wooden doorway. The look is identical to the one we entered to get into the building, but something about this room has a pit of dread forming in my stomach.

Sitri eases the heavy door open an inch, peering through before widening the gap. He leads us inside, and the pit in my core grows exponentially bigger.

The symbols etched into the floor look all too familiar, and the candles lining the room look as if they've been lit recently.

I spin in a circle, feeling better knowing the room is empty.

"Well, let's light this place up." I grin, tossing a candle to the ground with the same gesture that I'd practiced in my youth. With no magic to respond, my moves make me look more like a mime than a magic user.

Sitri chuckles behind me, and I feel his warmth at my back as his palms glide under my arms—the contact suspending the air in my lungs. My pulse rages in my ears as he gently guides my palms to face the ceiling.

Even with the mask that covers his face as he leans in close, I still feel his breath cascade over my ear.

"Close your eyes." He whispers, sending a tremor down my spine as they slide shut. Warmth breaks out in my palms, he leans against my hair, and his lips brush against the shell of my ear through his mask. "Open them, Maris."

They flutter open, and I gasp at the flames dancing against my bare palm. It takes a moment to register that the fire isn't burning me, even as it glides along my skin. My shock turns to wonder as his hands ease away from mine, trailing along my arms before snaking around my waist.

"Well," He muses, securing me in front of him. "You wanted to light this place up."

I turn ever so slightly to see a soft look in his eyes, and when I return my attention to my hands, I swallow hard.

To spend the better part of my childhood wishing I could command some kind of element like servilians, only for Sitri to make that dream a reality without knowing.

The lump in my throat grows impossibly bigger.

When his mask brushes the shell of my ear again, I find myself leaning into him without thinking. "Don't overthink it, Maris. Just feel. My flame is yours to command, as long as you will it."

There's no way that I'm the one controlling it.

As I flex my hands, the flame brightens, and my heart stutters as I look at a nearby bench. Without so much as a thought, as if the flame simply knows my will, it surges into the air before plummeting toward the bench. Within seconds, the flame engulfs the wooden seat as it crackles, and I gasp.

That's impossible.

My gaze bounces between items in the room, and the pillar of fire slams into one before surging toward the next.

As if to prove to myself that I'm controlling it, I look at the desk to our left, but the flame doesn't so much as flicker in its direction.

"You're a natural." He praises quietly against my ear. The flames surrounding us climb higher to the ceiling and dark smoke quickly fills the air.

His hands trail along the back of my arms, and when his palms cover mine, panic takes over. I retract my hands suddenly, thinking that I've burned him, and the flame almost immediately disappears from our palms.

How in the world did he lend me his power?

I grab his hands, bringing his palms closer, squinting through the smoke to see them unharmed and my shoulders sag.

The amount of relief that I feel at the sight of him unharmed is something I don't want to process just yet.

Sitri covers my mouth with a layer of his robe. "Let's get out of here."

Keeping one of my hands firm against my face, with the other held tight in his palm, he leads us out the way we came. The dark smoke in the room billowing into the hallway keeps us lower to the ground as we hurry away from the scene of our crime.

When we finally push past the heavy wooden doors and step into the street, I hear the gunshot before I realize what's happening. The loud bang fills the air, and within seconds, Sitri's thrown himself over me.

A deafening crack like thunder fills the air before the world around us kicks up and my ears ring. Within seconds of his large body covering mine, we're thrust into the brick wall with force.

The breath's torn from my lungs as Sitri absorbs most of the impact—his arm curled protectively around my head. Pain radiates from my limbs, but it's nothing compared to Sitri's torn flesh peeking through tatters of his robe.

My heart nearly stops.

"Sitri." I breathe, and more muffled pops of gunfire fill the air as he tucks me tighter beneath him. I can feel every bullet's impact as he flinches, and even through the panic, tears well in my eyes.

Chapter 15

"Close—"

He hardly gets the word out as my eyes slam shut and heat engulfs us. The warm scent of him mixes with a metallic tang and burnt flesh that makes dread coil in my stomach.

Within seconds, the screams around us die out, and his arms tighten around me. When his robes shift ever so slightly, like fluttering in a breeze, I know he's teleported us somewhere safe.

"You can—" Before he can get the words out, my eyes snap open, and I frantically survey the damage I can see.

The familiar sound of a stream fills the air beside us, and he pushes himself off of me with a pained expression—collapsing onto the ground with a grunt. My hand moves to cover my mouth, and the full extent of the damage he absorbed sends tears spilling down my cheeks.

There's no way he's going to live through this.

Bullet holes decorate his body with chunks of his flesh that were torn from him when the explosion hit us. Blood pours from his wounds, leaking onto the sandy earth as it creeps toward the stream.

There's no sign of it slowing, never mind stopping, and I silently wonder if they'd shot him with any of the weapons that keep him from healing.

Adrenaline pumps through me as I glance around. "Okay, okay." I spot Anne's house only thirty feet away, and relief surges through me. "Let's get you inside."

If I can get him to Anne.

If I can get him to safety.

Maybe we'll be okay.

He has to be okay.

His breathing's labored, and I struggle to haul his massive body over. It takes all my strength to get him into my arms, ignoring the pain radiating through me by sheer force of will. Sitri does what he can to help with the maneuvers, but I know the damage is worse than I thought when I notice him fighting not to lean too hard into me and failing at it.

My legs tremble from both pain and exertion as I haul us both upright, barely supporting our weight as I hobble us to the house one step at a time.

Warm liquid pours over my arm that's supporting his back, and I suck in a deep breath to take another step.

I can't afford to not make it there.

More tears spill over unbidden, pulled deep from the desperation that coats every inch of my being.

He saved me. It's time that I returned the favor.

I owe him that much.

His blood seeps into the cloth around my arms, drenching both of us in crimson, and the overwhelming desperation I'd felt grows almost impossibly greater as we turn into the kitchen.

Hearing us come through the door with a loud thud, Anne turns. Her eyes meet mine first as I sob, but when she looks at Sitri, her face pales.

Her foreign words come out in a rush, and she hurries over to help support his weight. Even with both of us supporting him, he nearly collapses to the ground, and I slam into the wall just to catch him.

When we finally get him into the bedroom where they'd nursed me back to health in mere weeks prior, I feel myself come undone.

Anne and I shuffle him to the bed, letting him collapse onto his stomach. Crimson continues to seep from his wounds as I tear his mask off.

Wincing, he releases a groan as Anne prods something in his back. Within seconds, she's in triage nurse mode, scurrying from one side of the room to the other before placing a thick cloth in my hand.

She places the cloth and my hands over a particularly damaged part of his back, and presses down on it as she speaks a million miles per minute.

Not understanding a word of it, but fully getting the urgency, I just nod, my gaze fixating on Sitri's face as she works.

I survey the damage to his back once more as crimson seeps into the cloth with no sign of stopping.

The moment we left that building, he didn't hesitate to cover me.

Tears well in my eyes again, and my eyes find the gaping wounds in his back, a stark contrast to where torn muscle and ruptured tissue juts out in other places.

The fact that he wouldn't have had to go through this if I just hadn't gone with him.

Hot, wet tears stain my cheeks as they silently spill over, dropping to his skin, and his fingers twitch. Not sparing a second thought, I keep pressure on his wound with one hand and slide my other bloodied palm into his. He adjusts his grip so that his fingers intertwine with mine, and a shudder makes its way through my body.

He'll make it through.

He's not human.

He will be okay. He has to be.

I repeat it to myself over and over as Anne works magic of her own, reassuring myself that he's immortal to placate my frantic mind.

What feels like an eternity passes, and Anne pulls my long-since numb hand from his back and removes the mask from his face. The wound thankfully has stopped bleeding, and when she goes to clean it, he winces against the mattress.

It takes half a thought to remove the material covering my face, and I toss it aside, still focused on his pained expression. The memory of the comfort he offered me when Anne pulled out the IUD comes to the front of my mind, and I shift to lie on my side, facing him.

Unwilling to let go of his hand, my throat feels like it's threatening to shut tight as I scoot in close to press my forehead to his. I don't know if I'm imagining it when his breath hitches, but I bring his hand to my chest.

My eyes squeeze shut, and I just repeat the same thing in my mind over and over again.

He'll be okay.

Please, *please* be okay.

The words replay until it's become a mantra, and I'm so wrapped up in it that I don't notice Anne say anything or leave the room.

In fact, I'm so caught up in begging the universe to let him live that I don't notice how much time has gone by—too focused on feeling his shallow breaths between us, and counting the seconds between them.

~

I'm not sure how much time has passed when the bed shifts slightly. My eyes flutter open at the movement, only to see Sitri's half lidded gaze locked onto me with what I could only describe as relief.

"Are you alright?" He whispers. His twin sun irises search my face, and I huff a dry laugh.

I'm alright in every sense of the word, but I'm no longer the same Maris that arrived in Kharidia.

Something changed in me between meeting Sitri in that building and destroying the ritual site. I know something has changed because I went from not wanting any part in this war to wanting to do anything to end it as soon as possible.

Sure, at first it was because there shouldn't be a war here to begin with.

But now, I'm afraid I hold far too much too close to my heart, and all of it is at risk every minute this drags on.

"I should ask you that." My voice wavers, and he tracks the tear that trails down my nose before falling to the bed.

"They can't kill me so easily." He muses, and damn if that's not music to my ears.

"Thank God for that."

"I guess I should." His lips twitch, and I fight the urge to roll my eyes, but the dopamine hit knowing he's okay has me exhaling a tense breath.

"Did you get hurt?" He winces and raises his head slightly to scan my body.

I just shake my head with a soft laugh of disbelief. "Thanks to you, not really." Guilt rifles through me. "I shouldn't have come with you."

He just frowns. "Why?"

"Because of my insistence, you got hurt." My voice is hardly more than a whisper, but I might as well be yelling with how loud they feel between us.

He shakes his head with a wince. "That's not how this works." My mouth drops open, but he clarifies without me needing to ask. "You can't regret the past simply because of a negative outcome, Maris. Think of the good."

Tightening my grip on his hand, I pull it closer to my chest. "That's not—what if something happened to you?"

Even without my own personal feelings, souls would be harvested without contest, and people like Anne would have no hope. Sure, the rebellion might have some fighters somewhere, but Sitri's the one pushing them back.

His throat bobs, and he sits up onto his elbow, his eyes lingering on where our hands connect against my chest. "We're at war, Maris. The chances of me getting hurt aren't something either of us can afford to worry about."

His thumb glides over the back of my hand, and I squeeze my eyes shut. "Yet I worry all the same." I whisper, emotion forming a lump in my throat.

The admission feels like a weight lifted, but my cheeks burn from saying such a raw and unfiltered statement. When Sitri stays silent, my eyes flutter open, seeing shock etched into his features as he searches my face.

"What is it?" I whisper, feeling that familiar pit of dread coil in my stomach when I consider that I might have said too much.

"Say it again." He whispers as he inches closer.

"Say wh—?"

I hardly get the words out before he interrupts me. "What you just said."

My lips part, and I feel my pulse jump. "That I was worried about you?"

Emotion flickers across his face, and he leans in with his head tilted, his bright golden eyes burning into me from beneath dark lashes. "Tell me why."

His expression is guarded, and I frown. "Am I not allowed to worry about you? Is it so shocking that I wouldn't want you to get hurt—that I *care* about you?"

His guarded expression softens, but I don't get a chance to ask any more as he closes the distance between us. His lips press to mine in a tentative kiss, as if he's testing the waters, or unsure of my boundaries, but my body sings all the same.

Warmth engulfs me from head to toe, and he pauses, pulling back a hairsbreadth to search my eyes.

The look he's giving me is as if he doesn't think I'm real.

Whatever he sees there makes his gaze soften before he leans in, kissing me with more certainty than before.

My heart feels like a bird soaring in the clouds as his hand curls around my neck and into my hair. I never considered what kissing a demon or a prince of hell should be like, but some part of me screams that this is the closest thing to heaven that I ever want to experience.

His lips dance against mine, and even the taste of him is warm; like a summer morning when the light touches everything in view.

My hand moves to grip his forearm for support, and I melt into his touch when his free hand brushes my cheek to move my hair out of the way.

He pulls back slightly, searching my face as my chest rises and falls with each breath. "It's a haunting revelation, but I find myself more and more inclined to abandon this war if it means spending another minute in this bed with you."

My stomach tumbles over itself, and he leans in to place another kiss to my lips. "I can't imagine the others would appreciate that."

His eyes flash, and his fingers tighten, tugging my hair gently. "That's because they have not experienced this." His lips press to mine again, and a growl escapes him. "Nor will they."

The way he kisses me is treasuring but desperate—as if I'm some forbidden yet priceless artifact. Like he's waited his entire life for me, and plans to do this for the rest of his days.

By the time we break apart, I've managed to press myself closer to him in the bed, my lips are swollen, and I'm breathless. Sitri gently tugs my head to lean toward him, and he presses his lips to my forehead in such a reverent way that my chest aches at the feeling.

"The heavens themselves may very well weep to mourn what they will never know." His whispered words make my chest tighten as something clatters outside the room.

A long moment passes as I consider Anne cooking in the kitchen, and civilians being gunned down all while we're laying in bed together.

The feelings I have are so conflicting—it's hard not to wonder if I'm being selfish or insensitive.

Because while I share Sitri's desire to not leave this bed, and abandon everything else to spend more time with him, I know that he won't ever truly be free of the destruction so long as the real demons on this earth exist.

A thick, noxious wave of guilt rifles through me.

Swallowing any fear, and all the anxiety in my body, I meet his gaze. "We will end this war together, Sitri."

Surprise flashes across his face before he becomes more solemn. "I don't want to involve you more than you already are, Maris."

I nearly snort. "I'm already involved. Besides," I run my fingers through his hair, and his eyes flutter at the contact. "I know you won't be able to stop until it is done."

His jaw tenses, the muscle in his jaw feathering. "And if I tell you I don't want to risk you?"

My lips twitch with barely restrained humor. "It's a good thing I make my own decisions then, and I'm choosing to do this."

More clattering sounds out, and rushed words echo from the other room as alarm flashes across his expression. He presses his lips to my forehead again, and I mourn the distance between us when he sits up fully.

He's locked in and listening to Anne's frantic voice before he curses under his breath.

"What is it?" I whisper, almost not wanting to know the answer as he moves to the edge of the bed.

"A civilian town was just bombed." He says quietly, listening to the chatter from the other room. "I need to go, Maris."

The urgency in those five words sends dread through me, unlike anything I've ever felt before.

He just finally healed, only to be needed again.

It really is never ending.

What's worse is that next time, he might not even have time to heal, which only puts him in worse danger.

Because what if they end up hurting him enough to capture him? Or find a way to kill him for good?

The urge to do my part is strong, and it's as if electricity buzzes under my skin with the need to take definitive action.

He pushes to his feet, towering over me as he rolls his shoulders, and I know I'm running out of time.

My mouth drops open, but I hesitate.

Do I even have the right to start requesting such things?

He must notice the conflict in my face, because within seconds, he's reached over to slide his palm into mine—his eyes like twin suns burn bright as he gives me a knowing look.

"Let's go."

Chapter 16

I've never seen so much devastation in my life.

Sitri leads the way through a narrow road between piles of rubble. Dust still thickens the air disturbed by our movement, blocking any chance of seeing further than a few feet in front of us. If it wasn't for Sitri's knowledge of the area, I'd be lost.

The layers of cloth covering my face hardly do much to hamper the smell of death, though it's effective to block the dust particles that's formed a fog all around.

And if it wasn't for my already empty stomach, I would have thrown up at the bodies—or parts of bodies—we pass by every few steps.

Even with death clinging to the air, the sound of distant coughing, shouting and cries fills the air. They grow louder with each step, and it's not long before we spot the first of the survivors.

Some people help move bricks, wooden beams and other items, searching the debris for family, friends or survivors, while others help tend to the wounded.

The sight of blood, limbs torn open, exposing bone and muscle; it all reminds me of how close Sitri had been to what I was certain was death, and I swallow against the emotion clogging my throat.

All of this, just to contribute to some fucking heavenly army.

My camera hangs heavy around my neck, as if the weight of this entire war rests upon it. Feeling like my heart may very well break any moment with how hard it's pounding, I put the viewfinder to my eye and snap a handful of photos as we push further.

It's a minute before we come to a stop near the edge of a half-destroyed building, its walls and roof asunder, exposing the wooden support beams just barely holding it together when Sitri turns to me.

The look on his face is tense. Every hard edge of his jaw seems even more sharp, with muscles feathering as he sweeps his gaze over the survivors.

It doesn't escape me that a demon known for inciting love and everything that comes with it would be passionate—that much he's shown me already, but it's clear that passion is channeled in his own way for the people of Kharidia.

That's when I realize what he intends to do, but I don't have time to say anything as he turns his attention to me.

His golden eyes search mine, and my stomach twists. "Stay here with the survivors."

"I thought we were going to help the civilians?"

"Who said we aren't?" I can hear the grin in his voice as I turn to look at the survivors.

With how many are still searching beneath the rubble, I already know what I'm going to find, but I choke those thoughts away. If I'm going to be of any use, I'll have to focus on who I *can* help.

When I turn my head to look at him once more, his hand cups my cheek in a way that makes my heart turn into a full gallop. "Consider this a challenge—helping one person here can be the equivalent of me killing ten."

My lips twitch. "You're *so* on."

He laughs quietly under his breath, and I hear a cry to my right that catches my attention. A breeze shifts the air surrounding us, clearing the dust ever so slightly, and when I turn to look at Sitri, he's gone.

Damn it.

The cry to my right sounds out again, and I ignore the churning in my stomach as I follow the sound. I'm passing a building that's half destroyed when I hear the cry again, this time right beside me, and I freeze.

My gaze rises to the sundered wall of the building. Sheets and various cloths hang over the edges, twisting into wiring that juts from the rubble. The wall that once erected from the ground, stretching at least thirty feet high, now slopes from the pile of brick near my feet to the meager remnants of the roof.

Another muffled cry reaches my ears, and my gaze lands on the stack of bricks in front of me.

Oh, fuck.

I move on instinct, quickly grabbing fallen bricks one by one and toss them aside. The first few seem easy, and my muscles warm with each successive brick, even with the sharp specks of dust biting into my skin. But, after a minute and a half of squeezing my fingertips against the rough surface, they ache to the point of pain.

Heaving one brick into the air before dropping it a few feet to my right, each one becomes heavier than the last. Each brick gains one pound more than the one that came before it.

The dust and debris that scrapes my palms makes them slick as they ache and throb. Another cry sounds out even closer, and I push forward, not bothering to look at my hands.

Gunfire erupts in the distance, and my heart leaps into my throat as desperation coats my veins, urging me to move faster. The stinging in my palms grows, and I wince as I toss a brick to the ground, seeing a crimson hue coating it.

A little blood is nothing compared to what these people are going through.

With that thought circling my mind, I pull another brick from the pile. From where that brick was, a small hole forms between the impacted bricks just as a loud explosion nearby shakes the ground.

I spot a bare foot in the space before I close the distance to the wall, my aching fingers finding purchase in deep cracks between smaller pieces of smashed bricks.

The ground shudders beneath my feet, freezing me in place to remain upright as crumbles of brick trickle down. My heart is in my throat, as I use the new small opening to grip another. The brick snaps free, dislodging two more that fall to the ground with a loud thud. What remains is an opening just big enough to fit my shoulders through, and I peer through the small opening.

Brown eyes wide with terror gaze back at me, and I gesture for him to come closer as the ground shakes with another explosion. A brick tumbles from the top of the building to our right, and I know I need to hurry.

If this building is already half caved in, I can't imagine the one beside it will endure much more.

Sure, the walls are all intact, but there's a good chance the bricks could give way at any moment.

When distant gunfire rings out, I reach in to wrap my hand around his small arm and tug. He resists for a moment until I'm shouting at him to hurry, and even though I'm certain he doesn't understand what I'm saying, he seems to get the message behind it as he surges forward.

Another rumble shakes the ground, and I nearly drag him as far from the buildings as I can. We've hardly gotten into the center of the street as the building shudders violently from an explosion that's gotten too close for comfort. My legs struggle to keep us both upright as we sprint away, the rumbling growing louder as we put distance between us and the structures.

I hear it collapse before I see any evidence of it, feeling the vibrations in the ground with each step—I don't dare to turn back.

Clutching the boy's arm in my hand, I don't take a full breath until we're near the other survivors, frantically helping one another with an edge of desperation. We just get to the area where a handful of civilians sit bandaging one another when the boy cries out in what I can only assume is a sob of relief.

Heads turn in our direction, but the boy jolts forward into a crowd of people and out of my grip. He weaves around people, stumbling as he shouts something, making a handful more heads turn.

Within seconds, a woman no more than twenty feet away sobs, her tattered clothes whipping back and forth as she dodges the people she passes. Something in my chest twists painfully when she scoops him into her arms, and tears pour down her face.

It feels invasive to capture them at such a moment, but I bring my camera to my face and snap a photo.

Another explosion sounds out, this time even closer than the last, and my heart thrashes.

Are the explosions from him?

Why hasn't he come back yet?

I glance over at the city beyond, my gaze searching each window, every alleyway and street, looking for any sign of his black robes.

But I come up empty.

With my throat constricting, I make my way to a group of survivors slowly working to patch one another, or themselves, up.

Without knowing when Sitri will be back, or if he's even okay, the only thing left to do is help everyone I can.

I might as well try to win this challenge.

~

The orange and red sky filled with smoke has finally dissipated, with the sun's descent behind the buildings that remain. It's been hours since Sitri disappeared, and the gunfire has since quieted down, but I've been on edge all the same.

After clearing through as much rubble as humanly possible, I only stopped when my wrists finally gave out when we were rescuing someone trapped under a collapsed floor—nearly smashing my foot with a cement brick in the process. I joined the survivors who migrated away from the explosions that seemed to get closer over time. We traveled a short distance to the furthest corner of the city, using some long-since abandoned buildings as cover.

The structures here are still mostly intact, though all the windows are clear of glass, with many of them void of any roofs to protect from the rain that Kharidians only see once every couple of weeks.

Being in the heart of summer here, it's likely that they won't see any for some time.

I'm dehydrated. I'm completely spent and every muscle in my body is screaming in pain, but complaining isn't an option for me right now.

I've watched every person in this small crowd of survivors as they band together to help one another, no matter how hurt or tired.

So I pressed on.

A small family that we'd rescued from an apartment building are some of the last to settle in for the evening as I watch the father set a blanket down. The mother, still tightly clutching her toddler to her chest, gives him a weary smile before shakily kneeling on it, and my throat tightens.

Emotions only constrict my throat more when the father sits beside her and presses his forehead to hers. Their eyes slide shut, and I bring my camera up once more, holding the viewfinder to my eye as the shutter clicks.

If they notice or heard, they don't show it as they remain still, finding solace in one another amidst the tragedy around them.

Tearing my eyes from their quiet moment, I blow out a breath. My gaze snags on a man leaning heavily against the corner of the apartment building. His body's clearly shaking, even obscured by the shadows, and from this distance, the tremors in his shoulders springs me into action.

My aching feet throb with each step toward him, but my pain's forgotten when I see him reach for a deep crimson cloth on the ground. Without thinking, I reach into my back pocket for the handful of tattered scraps of cloth I'd gathered in the past few hours.

His hands tremble as I close the distance between us, dropping to my knees at the four inches of exposed flesh in his arm. Thankfully, it doesn't look like it hit any major arteries, even if the wound's still leaking a slow stream of blood.

He murmurs something in Kharidian as I separate one cloth from the others, shoving them in my back pocket. My heavy arms lag in their maneuvers, but it's only a few minutes before I've wrapped the material around his arm and secured it tight.

I keep moving for the first hour, helping as many people as I can as they find a place to rest for the night. I spend as much time as I can helping change dirty bandages for less soiled ones, and as I walk away from a group of injured teenagers, staring at the lone cloth in my hand, I know rest won't find me yet.

Cries and sporadic conversation fill the air around the apartment building as I slip inside one of the side entrances. Dust, dirt, and layers of ash coat nearly every surface. Long hallways with doors blown off their hinges, air flowing in from shattered windows, with garbage and belongings from residents who might very well no longer live scatter everywhere. The rooms are all destroyed; some by bombs, others by the elements that easily got in after the windows were broken.

Ash and dirt cover the few remaining towels and scraps of cloth I find on the first floor, making infection more likely than anything else. I'm about to give up as I open a cupboard in what once was a kitchen, seeing two dusty cans of beans with pull tabs on top.

My heart soars.

Anything is better than nothing.

Tucking them into my body, I push wearily to my feet, returning the way I came from memory.

With no gunfire, the quiet is eerie.

It's like one of those movies where the good guys hunker down for the night, only for the bad guys to show up and the main villain to be at the center of it all.

The thought of Rob and the others showing up here sends a shiver down my spine.

I turn the corner where most of the others have now gathered along the side of the building, and when I reach the first family, six pairs of eyes land on me.

My mouth drops open, but I know nothing I say will matter, so it snaps shut just as quick, and I hand them the two cans. Not bothering to wait as quiet chatter gets louder, I turn and head for the neighboring apartment complex.

It's three stories high, but I only search the first floor, finding a handful of new bandages and fresh, semi-clean cloths. I adjust them in my arms and retrace my steps to the others.

I glance down at the meager bundle of cloths, feeling highly inadequate in my search, but with the way my legs want to give out every time I put my weight on them, I don't know that I could do any more than I am.

Still, what I found is better than nothing, and even with the disappointment circling my mind, I feel quietly triumphant as I find my way back to where everyone rests.

The distance between the exit of this apartment and where the rest of the civilians are is the length of a football stadium. Even the width of the road is the size of a six lane interstate highway, with most of the buildings across the street reduced to rubble.

A distant humming catches my attention, and my mind wanders to Sitri once more as I glance up at the moon that's merely a sliver in the sky.

Even with only a small piece of the moon not engulfed in shadows, it's bright against the blanket of stars that surrounds it. I can't help but wonder if Sitri sees the beauty of it the same way that so many humans do.

I'm hardly more than thirty feet away from where the survivors chose as their resting spot along the wall and hidden in the shadows of the building. When the humming grows louder, people stir from their hiding places, their heads twisting to find the source.

I slow to a stop and frown, tilting my head to the sky and turning in a circle, unable to place where it's coming from.

The constant sound reverberates in the air like it's nearly on top of us when the civilians scatter, most running straight toward me. Shouting erupts as the engine grows impossibly closer—but when I see the chopper appear over the top of the still intact building we were hiding against, I know it's too late for me to run.

I don't even have time to react when the chopper's gun rattles off in short, deafening bursts that crack through the air. Rounds of heavy bullets stitch the ground toward me, and I'm too far from the building to make it in time.

Between that, and the way my muscles feel like lead, I'm a sitting duck.

With seconds before the attack reaches me, my eyes flick to the moon above the chopper and I wonder once more if he's seen it for its beauty.

For a moment, I can't help but consider how pathetically poetic it is that I'd finally find something in this world worth fighting for before being ripped from it.

Chapter 17

My heart's in my throat as the torrent of bullets inch closer—far too fast for comfort. The sky brightens to an orange glow behind the apartment building, and my eyes snap to the chopper just as an enormous ball of flame hurtles through the air.

My eyes widen, and I take a step back as the bullets pelt the ground less than ten feet from me.

It slams into the side of the aircraft as the engines shriek in protest. The chopper careens to the side as the gunfire stops, and black smoke billows into the air before it crashes into the remnants of a building not far away. I cover my ears as the ground shakes with the impact and a burst of flame erupts from the site of the crash. The explosion upon impact has me crushing my hands to my ears as pillar of smoke curl into the air.

I'm certain that explosion would have been heard for miles, and I stare at the smoke with wide eyes before a figure to my right catches my attention.

I don't need to see his face to know it's him, though.

His dark robes billow in the wind as he strides toward me, his eyes like sunlight burn bright against the shadows of his mask. Behind him, uniformed soldiers slip out from the shadows along the alley on either side of the apartment where everyone had once been resting, and my mouth drops open to warn him.

Before I can say anything—before I can warn him—flames erupt from the ground at their feet. Arcs of fire spiral up over their heads before slamming into the ground once more, and within seconds, not a single soldier remains.

They didn't even scream or shout. Not a single sound came from the militia that was just wiped out within mere breaths.

My heart thunders. *I should have helped more people.*

Part of me balks at how quickly and easily he dispatched them, but I know without a doubt there would have been civilian injuries in the crossfire.

And more than likely injury to me, as well.

His stride is confident as he approaches, stopping just before me, to offer his hand between us. The relief in my body—hell, **my soul**—is palpable as my hand slides into his.

"You didn't run." Not a question, but his voice is oddly gentle as his eyes search my face.

I shake my head, glancing over to where the injured hug the wall. The hope in their eyes as they all look at Sitri sends a wave of emotion through me that I'm not sure I'm ready to acknowledge, never mind fully process.

"I guess it's another addition to the list for defying death."

He laughs under his breath. "You did well helping them."

I huff a quiet laugh of denial. "I hardly **did** anything."

He glances down at the cloth in my hands and shakes his head. "Somehow, I don't believe that. And judging by the blood covering your hands, I don't think you are in any place to disagree."

I'm not about to add that the reason I didn't run was because I physically couldn't, so instead I turn to the terrified and hopeful faces peering out from the shadows. "How can we get them somewhere safe?"

Sitri moves to stand beside me, and it takes every ounce of willpower not to lean into him. "We're only about twelve miles from the border. If we can get them there, I'll be able to get them across easily. If we stay here and in the open for the night, though, we'll be in trouble."

He reaches down to slip his hand into mine before leading us to the others. Each step I take is unsteady, and I grip Sitri's hand harder for support. If he notices or minds, he says nothing, only tightens his hold on me whenever I waver.

My gaze slides to what's left of the chopper, with flames and smoke still billowing into the air, forming a thick, dark cloud that extends further and further into the sky.

As the adrenaline fades, I'm left with the knowledge that he just snuffed out over a dozen lives within seconds. But it's an odd feeling to realize that I don't seem to care.

Being a reporter meant seeing some of the hardest things the world can offer, taking the scene with grace and dealing with my emotions when it's appropriate.

I always felt them, though.

When we first arrived in Kharidia, death and destruction would send bile into my throat, leaving an acrid taste on my tongue—but now?

Now, I find these deaths some of the easiest to accept.

Sure, part of me knows they were people with lives; but they were also about to murder innocent families without a second thought.

I can argue all day that I don't feel bad because the responsibility lives with Sitri, but there's a large part of me that knows I would have done the same if I were in his shoes without so much as a second thought.

That might just be the hardest pill to swallow.

Sitri leads us further away from the crash, and I nearly jump out of my skin when a man steps alongside us. His round face is worn with an exhaustion I can relate to all too much, and his brows pull together as he murmurs to Sitri in Kharidian before grasping his arm.

Sitri listens intently until the man's face falls. He sobs when I see Sitri lean in to whisper something back, my heart feels like it's being ripped from my chest.

These people have lost so much.

And for what? Some unholy war?

The man presses his hands to his heart, bowing slightly before he saunters over to where others have grouped together. By the time we've passed them, a line of forms behind us.

Keeping my voice low, I hook my arm with Sitri's and lean closer. "What did he say to you?"

I know I have no right to ask, but something about the devastation in this expression has made it nearly impossible to ignore.

"He said he lost his wife and daughter in the initial attack, and asked me to let him die next time so he may join them." Sitri's voice is agonizingly soft, and I swallow against the lump in my throat.

If my heart wasn't already breaking, it is now.

"I can't say I blame him for asking."

Sitri shakes his head in my peripherals. "No. Nor can I."

A long moment passes, and I look over to see his features more relaxed as he scans the horizon. "So...?"

"So, what?"

"What did you say back?"

His hand tightens around mine ever so slightly. "I told him his business here is not yet finished, and that they would want him to see it through before welcoming him to the afterlife."

I swallow hard, remembering how he sobbed afterward with a bitter note of anger.

"Why not grant his wish?" I ask, feeling Sitri's eyes burning into the side of my face.

"Before meeting you, I would have, but only because it made sense for someone to want to be with the person they love. Now, I find myself torn." I glance over, seeing his brows pulled together. "I understand his desire more than I ever have. But when I put myself into his shoes, I couldn't give him what he wanted."

I squeeze his arm gently. "Why?"

Sitri lets out a long sigh. "Because if I were him, and anything were to happen to you, I'd hunt them all down. I would see this world turn to ash before finding you in the afterlife."

His admission sends a wave of heat coursing through me, and my heart stutters.

Perhaps the most surprising revelation of all of this is that on a fundamental level, I know that if roles were reversed, I would do the same.

Sure, I might not summon fire or have powers, but I would raise hell. I would find a way.

Considering how this war is going, there's a good chance that Sitri might very well end up burning this world to the ground at some point, especially if I have any more moments of defying death.

Truth is, none of us will be finished until this war is done.

Not Kharidians. Not Sitri.

Not even me.

Chapter 18

By the time we're far enough away from the crash to stop, my legs might very well collapse beneath me.

I'm surprised they haven't already.

In the past twenty minutes, I've stumbled twice over nothing. My toes just didn't move properly and caught on the ground, nearly sending me face-first into the dirt. Sitri threatened to carry me if I didn't agree to take a break after that.

I argued, of course. Because why should *I* be the reason for us to take a break when their lives are the ones in danger?

Sitri, however, didn't take that as an adequate excuse.

I lean back heavily against the wall of an intact single-story office building as a handful of civilians move into the two vacant homes across the street, chattering quietly with their families.

Every part of my body aches, and there's a deep-seated exhaustion that even death itself might not be enough to rid me of.

It's been over twenty-four hours since I last slept, and without getting a proper meal, I feel like I might be on the verge of passing out.

My head bobs, and I catch myself as I suck in a breath.

Correction. I *am* on the verge of passing out.

My gaze sweeps over the few people who have settled down to fall asleep outside, and I push off the wall. My movements are rough and unsteady as I stumble away to find something more secluded where I don't need to wear my mask.

When I'm far enough from the others that I can just barely make out the outline of their bodies in the shadows, I turn the next corner and lean back against the side of the building.

At this point, I'm afraid if I sit or lie down, I may very well never get back up. The thought is sobering, and my head tilts to the sky.

"Are you always this stubborn?" Sitri's voice feels like a silken balm to my ears, and I glance over, seeing his robed form slowly approach.

"Some might call it compassionate." I offer, hearing him huff a dry laugh. "I just want them to be somewhere safe."

He focuses his golden amber eyes on me, and it makes me want to squirm. "We will get them to safety, but saving them will mean nothing if you die."

My eyes widen. "It's not like I'm running headfirst into combat. It's just sleep… not *that* important."

Sitri steps closer, and his fingers find the hem of the cloth covering my face as he slowly unravels it. "You say it isn't important, yet you walked here without a second thought to any danger." With the mask still wound around my face, he tugs it toward him, forcing my gaze to meet his. "I could just have easily been an enemy with a gun pointed at you."

The gold in his eyes marbles into flecks of yellow and white, and even though it's dark, I still see the tenderness behind the frustration in them.

He removes the last bit of cloth from my mouth, and the cool night air glides across my skin, sending a shiver down my spine.

"I suppose it's just my luck that I happened to run into a *demon*, of all people." I muse and fight back a yawn.

He huffs a quiet laugh, tucking the cloth into his robe. "Arguably more dangerous."

When he looks at me expectantly, like I'm going to agree with him, I just shake my head. "As dangerous as a marshmallow, maybe."

His eyes flash, and I fail to suppress a laugh of my own before reaching up to remove his mask.

"Clearly I haven't made enough of an impression." He murmurs, the grin clear in his voice.

I shrug, my fingertips gently working to unravel the dark material. "You got style points for the chopper."

His mask comes free from his face, and his tongue clicks in disapproval. The sound makes something in my chest flutter, and I bite back a small smile.

The yawn I'd been fighting finally takes over, and he steps in close as my heart thrashes.

"Come, Maris." He whispers, his hands cupping either side of my neck. "Let's find you somewhere to sleep."

I know my body is tired, but my mind disagrees. All night, with every demand for rest, my mind's been at odds with myself, pushing me forward.

I shake my head. "I can't, Sitri."

He pauses, tilting his head to look at me. "Why?"

"I'm... restless." I whisper. "Sure, I feel tired physically, but I don't know. It's like my mind refuses to turn off. It's like I'm not allowed to rest."

His eyes search mine for a long moment, and even though I'm struggling to understand why I keep pushing myself, his gaze softens as if he already knows.

"Come." He whispers, and leans in close, bringing us chest to chest. My eyes widen as his arm curls around my back, and within seconds of his other arm hooking under my thigh, I'm being hauled further into his chest.

I choke down the shrill sound of surprise, but it just comes out strangled instead. He just chuckles, and my arms and legs instinctively wrap around him for support.

"What are you doing?!" I hiss, feeling his forearms support my ass while his hands splay over my lower back.

"I'm bringing you somewhere you can **rest**."

He strides a few paces before kicking a door open; the sound echoing into the empty space. My arms that had snaked around his neck to stay upright tighten around him, though some part of me knows it has nothing to do with any fear.

I look around at the abandoned remnants of an office, rows of rooms with doors wide open, filled with computers and filing cabinets. Papers of all kinds scatter across the floor, pencils, and other various items mix with the dust and debris that's blown in from the windows that line the outside walls.

If he thinks a change of scenery is all it will take to clear my mind, he's wrong.

He walks with purpose to a room with windows on either side of us and a small hole in the ceiling. Stars paint the sky through the opening, with the moon peering in the window to our right.

A breeze glides over my skin as Sitri steps to the wall, leaning his back against it before sliding down to the floor.

Straddling his hips, my heart's frantic, and my pulse spikes as I lean back to look at him.

"You think *this* is resting?"

His lips twitch, and he glides his palm along my jawline to cup the back of my neck. "It's better than standing against a wall, half asleep and alone, in the middle of an alley."

"Clearly I wasn't alone." I whisper as he leans in, his bright gaze reflecting the low light of the moon.

He's so close that his breath skates over my lips, and my stomach trips over itself. His scent invades my senses from this distance, and I'm certain that if you asked me for my name, I wouldn't be able to answer.

If he hadn't already told me that his magic doesn't work on me, I'd be accusing him of it.

His gaze drops to my mouth, and my core tightens. "You'll never be alone again, Maris."

I don't have time to process his words as he closes the distance between us. His lips, his stubble grazing my skin, the way his sharp teeth tug my lower lip, the low growl in his chest when I gasp, it's hardly been more than a minute, and I've never needed someone this badly in my life.

My still tender hands find purchase in the robes along his collar, and I lose myself in him.

The way Sitri kisses is like a game, because for every sound he coaxes from me with a bite of pain, he rewards me with more of him. For every response I offer to his touch, he answers twice over.

Leaning further back into the wall, and taking me with him as he throbs between us, I feel inebriated. My arms tighten around his shoulders, but even though I'm melding to him, desperate for *more*, his hands don't leave my neck.

I pause, pulling back ever so slightly.

He's intense, commanding, and attentive.

Yet he's holding back.

"What is it?" His silken voice is gruff, and I search his heated gaze for a moment with desire pulsing in my core.

Part of me doesn't know how to answer, because speaking what I want aloud wouldn't do it justice.

Tugging the hem of my shirt overhead, I toss it aside, and when my gaze finds his, I feel a hint of vulnerability wash over me.

I know what I want.

But his refusal to go further contradicts the way he's looking at me with a hunger that makes his restraint seem like it teeters on a knife's edge.

"Do you not want to do more than just kiss?" I ask, feeling more unshielded than ever.

He gets a slight up tilt to his lips before he smirks in earnest. "I would burn down heaven *and* hell to have you, Maris—but I will not take more than I should. Not until you're ready."

My chest squeezes, and even though I feel like I'm about to jump from a plane without knowing if my parachute works, everything inside me screams to throw myself into a free fall.

There's no doubt in my mind that I want Sitri in ways words can't describe, and even with everything we've been through, I have had no negative inclination toward him.

No. If anything, since the first day, he's been my safety net.

The prince of hell who destroys entire military units, encampments, ritual sites, and drives a silent revolution is the only source of peace to my world.

"I'm ready." I whisper, feeling like I'm toeing at that edge of the plane, ten thousand feet in the air.

His burning gaze meets mine as it darkens, and he releases my neck just to drag my hips to his. I gasp as the length of him throbs against me and his lips crash to mine.

Desire in my body responds in full, and I shift my weight in his lap, desperate for more friction, more of **him**.

The way he dominates our kiss makes my head spin, and I'm hardly aware of the brisk night air licking my bare skin. The heat radiating from my body keeps the cool air at bay as his fingers bite into my hips.

Even with the clothes between us, he throbs hard against my clit and swallows my gasp as I grind into him, desperate to ease the ache as his chest rumbles.

Within seconds, his arm around my waist secures me to him, and he slides forward, not breaking our kiss as he lays me on my back. The position gives him control as his hips squeeze mine into the ground. He straightens, leaning back for a breath of a moment before reaching down to shrug off his robes.

Moonlight cascades in through the windows, giving me just enough light to see each inch of skin, and the flex of muscle as he tosses the material aside.

I swallow.

Sure, I've seen him shirtless before, and damn did I appreciate his body then, but never has it been more clear how perfectly inhuman Sitri is.

A handful of scars decorate his skin, reminders of the creative ways people have found to ensure his injury, the corded muscles around his abdomen would be enough to make most women salivate, but it's the deep lines along his hip that have me swallowing.

All of a sudden, the pretty words he's said since we met have me in a state of disbelief.

Because how could a demon like him feel this deeply for a human?

My heart leaps into my throat as he crawls over me, and I see his shadowed gaze search mine. "Why do you look sad?"

I hadn't realized my internal turmoil was so visible, but I've already placed my entire life in his hands.

Asking the question couldn't hurt, right?

"You're a demon, and surely much older than me." His lips twitch. "I guess I just don't understand why you feel this way about me. I'm not special. Just a human—average, at best."

His concern melts into understanding as he leans down to place tender kisses along my neck. Trailing them to my collar, he murmurs against my skin.

"You are not *just* human, Maris. You're so much more than that." He continues lower down my breasts and stomach until he's hovering above my hips, his gaze not leaving mine. "You are not average. You're spectacular. You give freely. There's something in you—something untouched by this world's corruption. Your heart is one that's proven to me that there's still hope for humans to overcome the trials and tribulations—the atrocities—that have befallen them."

His hands glide under my body, and I feel his fingers hook under the waistband of my pants. "I might summon fires of retribution, but for years, Maris, I'd lost faith. I'd let my flames burn low because I couldn't see an end to the fighting. Yet somehow, from the moment you walked into that building, you stirred them—like pouring fuel into dying embers. They've burned for you ever since. And there's no human, servilian, angel or demon who could stop them from bending to your will."

He tilts his head to the side as he gently eases the material down, and the cool night air sends goosebumps along my spine. "There isn't one simple answer to your question, Maris. You could call this love, but that word is too shallow, too small for what binds me to you."

He slides the material down my ankles before tossing it aside. "I have waited my entire life to feel this way, and spent just as long certain I never would." He leans in to trail kisses down my stomach, pausing between my thighs. "So if words fail me, I hope you understand—there are no languages on this earth or any other that could do us justice."

I stare down at his mess of dark hair between my legs, and before I can process what he's said, his mouth is on me. He sucks and laves lazily, teasing my clit as his fingers bite into my skin.

It's a contradiction, the way he devours me like we have all the time in the world, while his grasp on my hips says otherwise, like he's keeping himself back more than holding me still.

The thought makes my mind whirl.

Each flick of his tongue makes my hips move on instinct, and he pushes me closer and closer to the edge of oblivion.

My orgasm crests—and he must feel it—because he pauses, tugging down his pants as he crawls up the length of my body. He towers over me, all hard muscle, honed to withstand anything, yet here he is, leaning onto his forearms to make the world around us disappear.

Selfishly, I preen at the thought of feeling him everywhere.

Since the moment I met Sitri, his actions have spoken what words never could, and there's nothing more that I want than this.

I'm set ablaze at his touch. His words make my soul ache. His presence is my safest haven.

That's how I know my trust is not misplaced.

By the time his searing kisses reach my jaw, his length grazes my entrance and I shudder. My legs wrap around his, squeezing him closer as he releases a dark laugh under his breath.

The sound sends me into a haze, and I wrap my arms around his neck as his lips press hungrily to mine. The taste of myself mixed with his warmth makes desire coil in my core.

In the most apocalyptic way, I need him.

Wasting no time, he notches himself against me and pushes in. His pace is agonizingly slow, but I'm silently grateful as I struggle to accommodate his size.

Even as soaked as I am, it's still a tight fit. But he gives me more, inch my inch, his length massaging my walls. He gets halfway before I know I need a moment to breathe, and my nails dig into his shoulders to keep quiet.

Not for fear of retaliation or punishment, but because I don't care about the pain.

I would walk through fire, run myself through with a blade, or dive headfirst into turbulent waters if it meant being close to him.

He must feel it too, because he pulls back just a little, then pushes in deeper. I gasp into his mouth as he reaches between us to tease my clit, and the moan that follows makes him throb inside of me.

There's no brutality in the stretch, not with the way he keeps coaxing pleasure from my body. By the time my legs twitch and my toes curl, he's fully seated in me, and I've never felt needier in my life.

Chapter 19

Sitri

A small whine escapes Maris as I withdraw my hand from her clit, but she doesn't have to wait long before I start to move.

My forearm braces the length of her back, curling around her shoulder to keep her in place as I pull out to the tip. My body protests the distance, echoing her desperation in the way she digs her heels into me before I thrust in deep.

Meeting her felt like fate. Kissing her was the purest desire I'd ever felt in my life, but being inside of her?

There are no words for this.

Rarely do I find myself speechless, but more and more, it seems like Maris is a long list of firsts for me.

I continue my long, languid movements, rocking her into my grip, and her breathing picks up. It was selfish of me to bring her to the edge earlier without giving her what her body begged for, but I'll be damned twice over if I don't feel her come undone around me.

My muscles tighten at the thought, and my thrusts become more erratic as I lose myself in her.

Her soft skin. Her scent. Her sounds.

I have to remind myself not to go too hard, but fuck if all I want is to bury myself in her for the rest of my God damned life. With everything she went through, the physical damage was bad enough to give me pause. Even if she's fully healed, I won't subject her to more unwanted pain.

She deserves more than that. All of it only makes me want to kill that asshole even more.

I didn't lie to her when I said I find no pleasure in killing humans—but his, I would enjoy more than anything else.

My hips snap against hers with a bit more force, and her nails dig into my back, dragging a groan from my throat.

Well, I wouldn't enjoy it more than this.

My heart stutters as she breaks our kiss, and I'm silently cursing myself for letting my anger get the best of me as her forehead presses to mine.

"Harder, Sitri." She gasps, grinding into my hips. I groan at the pleasure shooting from my dick all the way up my spine. "Please–"

Fuck. I'd tried to save her from pain, but who am I to deny her what she wants?

She clenches around me as I thrust with more force, and each one nearly makes me spill over into her. I drive in harder, rocking her into my grip in my desperate need to keep her close. When she shudders beneath me, I don't dare stop.

Her body's a fucking vice grip, clinging to me through her orgasm. My balls tighten, and my abdomen goes taut before I pull her closer. Buried as deep as I can possibly get, her lips brush mine and I come undone.

My hips press harder into hers, like my come might reach depths I can't. She meets my slow thrusts until I'm spent, but I'm not finished. Not a chance in hell.

I've waited all my life for her—and I intend to spend the rest of it very, very wisely.

Reaching down, I take her hardened nipple between my fingers and squeeze lightly as she arcs into me. My dick throbs, and a shiver runs down my spine as she moans into my mouth.

She's fucking perfect. Perfect, and all mine.

Chapter 20

Maris

My body was exhausted before, but as Sitri throbs inside me, I'm a puddle in his arms.

I'm covered in sweat. My hair sticks to my neck and shoulders, and muscles deep in my thighs won't stop twitching as I come back down to reality.

But as Sitri starts to move again, I don't stay there long.

His grip becomes more demanding as he cups the back of my neck, drawing out in long strokes that sends little bolts of pleasure through my core.

Every thrust, mixed with the way he devours my mouth feels more and more possessive, and I know with every fiber of my being that I'll never be the same after this.

As much as there's a possessive edge to his touch, I can't help but feel it too.

Because, God, if he's claimed me—and the way he's fucking me says he has—then I'll be damned if I don't reciprocate.

Meeting Sitri was our worlds colliding, and since then I've lost track of where I begin, or he ends. I feel irrevocably and unequivocally changed. I feel more strongly than ever before that this is where I'm meant to be, and my heart squeezes to the point of pain.

I might be Sitri's person, but he's *my* prince of hell.

I break apart from our kiss, breathing hard as his twin sun irises search my face. "Tell me again."

He seems to understand as he reaches up to curl his forearm around the back of my neck. His palm rests on my shoulder as his other cups my cheek, and he presses his lips to mine, long and slow.

His thrusts echo his kiss, and we move in sync with the hard, unforgiving floor biting against my back.

Emotion clogs my throat at his tender touch, and how he slides into me like he never wants to be anywhere else.

I can't say that I disagree.

He says more with his actions than he ever could with words. Each languid thrust hitting a spot that makes my toes curl. The hard planes of his body flex against my skin. My hands trace old scars at his back, and between my mumbled pleas for him not to stop, I find myself silently cursing his enemies.

As his thrusts become more urgent, I clench around him—my orgasm crests with the way he hits the same spot over and over, jolting pleasure up my spine.

Clinging to him like my life depends on it, he fucks me into another wave of euphoria. The moment it tremors through me, he's buried himself deep, and he stiffens as he spills into me.

My limbs go slack, and he rolls us until I'm straddled on top of him, curled into his chest.

"I can't feel my legs." I murmur, melting into him as he chuckles.

I feel it reverberate in his chest, and he encircles my body with his arms. Keeping himself buried as deep as possible, he sits up a bit, shifting back further until we're against the wall.

"You should rest." He whispers, pressing his lips to my forehead.

My mouth goes dry, and I lick my swollen lips as he throbs inside of me again, contradicting his suggestion.

"I should."

My head tilts up to capture his lips, and he throbs once, twice, three times as I moan.

At this rate, I'm never going to sleep, and he's going to have to carry me to the border.

Honestly, not a bad idea.

Chapter 21

We get to the border five hours after sunrise, and as I look over at the soldiers standing at the only exit on the main road. Tall metal fences run along the border as far as we can see in either direction, with the only road in or out manned by a handful of soldiers.

My attention drops to the automatic rifles strapped across their bodies and the handguns holstered at their hips. I don't know how we're going to make it through them unharmed.

We lost two people to their injuries overnight, which left us with two dozen civilians to rescue; most of which haven't eaten a proper meal in days, maybe weeks, never mind their injuries.

It's a miracle we only lost two.

Sitri's imposing form steps in close, his face obscured by his mask. "Stay here."

I just nod, not trusting my voice as he leans in to press a kiss to the top of my head. He murmurs something to the others in Kharidian before disappearing around the corner. With each second he leaves us behind, my heart could beat out of my throat.

Anxiety swirls in my head, mixing with every admission he'd made last night, and I can't stand his absence.

Crouching down, I peer around the corner, watching Sitri stride confidently to the entrance of the blockade. The first soldier that notices him tenses, his hand gripping his automatic rifle firmly.

When I see the other soldiers mirror the first man's tension, I might vomit.

If they fucking hurt him... I swear to God.

He steps up to the soldiers, and though I can't see his face, I can definitely see theirs. The way their brows go slack before they nod and gesture behind them tells me that somehow, he's convinced them to let the refugees through.

My eyes widen. *He used his powers on them.*

Sitri turns, jerking his head toward the blockade as one soldier radios to the others.

That must be the sign for them to go.

I turn, waving for the others to go to Sitri, and they start to make their way over. My camera feels heavy in my hands, and I snap a couple of photos as Sitri helps them through.

Explosions sound in the distance, and the civilians pick up their pace. The panic on their faces is clear as they pass by the soldiers who don't even try to stop them.

Sitri turns toward the sound, and a pit of dread forms in my stomach.

Even after all this, there are still so many more civilians that need help.

So many more people are losing their lives.

The explosions get closer, and gunfire erupts in the distance as the last of the civilians get past the blockade. When the soldiers form a line along the road, with no civilians left in sight, I finally exhale a sigh of relief.

Sitri strides over as more gunfire fills the air, mixed with a familiar hum of a chopper, and I don't need him to tell me it's not safe here anymore.

Part of me already knows that we can't get into any kind of fight here without bringing attention to the civilians that just got through the blockade, so I already expect it as he pulls me into his arms.

He backs me into the wall, and I revel in the feeling of his body against me again. "Close your eyes, Maris."

They snap shut, and I feel his robes brush against my back as the wind picks up.

Distant chatter fills the air, and I'm surrounded by Sitri's warm scent that's come to feel like home as I hold him close. The hard muscles in his back flex under my grip, and his arms slide down my shoulders.

"You can open them now."

The first thing I notice is the solid wooden walls of the cramped space. Sitri's size only serves to make the room feel smaller as I turn in a circle. Spotting the single bed along the far wall with the small dresser beside it, I turn to look at him again.

"Where are we?" I whisper, hearing more relaxed chatter outside—it's an odd contrast to the explosions and gunfire we just teleported away from.

"Northwest side of the country. When the war began, most people who could escape the major cities came to the northwest because it was designated a safe zone; it remains largely untouched. There's only been one strike that hit this town, and that was a little over a year and a half ago."

My chest tightens. A year and a half.

The way he says it is as if that was yesterday, but most reports from major outlets have all had the same timeline.

Two years ago, the conflict began as rebels caused terror attacks on their own government.

With everything I know now, it's clear that everything they've said has been lies to further an agenda the general population shouldn't know about—a way for them to get support from civilians.

"How long has this been going on?"

He leans down and presses his lips to my forehead. Even though his mask creates distance from the contact, my chest tightens all the same.

"Far too long. You can rest if you'd like." He adds, tilting his head toward the bed.

My mind wanders to last night, and how we'd chosen to spend our time instead of sleeping. At least, until Sitri noticed my sheer exhaustion, and held me in his arms until I'd fallen asleep.

Still, it was hardly enough to combat the ache that reaches the marrow of my bones.

Even though I've hardly slept, part of me wants to explore the safe haven these people have, and take photos for my story—the real story... so I shake my head.

"Can we walk around?"

Sitri inclines his head, his hand tucking my hair behind my ear before threading through the length at the back of my neck. "In a moment." His fist closes, and I sigh as he pulls me into his chest. "Just give me a moment." He whispers and presses his lips to mine.

The quiet plea in his words, the yearning and pain mixed with the tenderness in his kiss, the desperation in his touch; all of it makes me want to rage against those who have kept him in this hell away from home.

Because wouldn't anyone wish desperately to experience anything than death, if only for a moment?

My arms wrap around his neck, and he walks me backward. The back of my thigh hits the bed as his hand roams the length of my body, supporting my weight as he lays me back.

His free hand glides over my breast, teasing my nipple through my shirt and I moan into him, the sound catching in my throat.

"Tell me you're real," he whispers against my lips. "Because if I lose you, or wake from this dream, I don't think I'll come back from it."

He kisses down my jaw to my throat, and my legs wrap around his body.

"There's only this, Sitri." I whisper, my back arching into him when his hand that was teasing my nipple slides between my thighs. "There's only us."

He circles my clit through my pants and my eyes roll back. My nails bite into his shoulder as he works my body, my thighs twitching against his hips.

After last night, some part of me knew that being a demon that incites love, he'd know a thing or two, but damn if I wasn't still surprised at how well he'd known my body.

Sure, he's attentive, but it's like the moment I felt something, needed something, desired anything, he knew.

And fuck if he didn't give it to me.

Sitri sits up, tearing his robes from his body and tossing them aside. The springs in the mattress creak with his movement and within seconds he's hovered over me once more.

His words linger in my mind, circling like vultures to my anxious thoughts, knowing what waits for us outside these walls.

I'm mortal, which means I'm his biggest weakness.

While I don't expect anything to happen to me, we're at war...

His lips find mine in a hungry, lingering dance—like every moment he spends not kissing me could be his last. When his fingers slide under the waistband of my pants, I echo his urgency, helping him slide them off and toss them aside.

"Promise me," I murmur, dragging my shirt overhead, and it falls to the ground beside us. "Promise that no matter what happens, you'll find a way through."

His reverent touch glides over my bare skin, followed by his lips leaving a burning trail as he kisses his way up my collar to my jaw. When his breath skates over my lips, and our noses brush, I ache to close the distance.

"I promise," he whispers against my lips, his forehead pressed to mine. "If this is the only time we ever get, I will be eternally grateful. But mark my words, Maris Sylvara, I will hunt down every angel and demon here and in heaven to find you and bring you back to me." Pressing his lips to mine, tears slide between them as he shudders.

The promise in his words spring tears to my eyes, and he leans his delicious weight onto me. His arms wrap around my body, and I know without a doubt that he would bring me home.

Not to any place or time.

But to him.

He throbs against me, and my hips move of their own accord. I'm desperate to feel him, given the unspoken grief in his words, and the anxiety in worrying that this war will tear us apart.

Sitri must feel it too, because he adjusts his hips as he throbs again—positioning the tip of his dick against my soaked entrance, and he eagerly pushes in deep.

My heels dig into him as his teeth nip at my lower lip, and he keeps easing in deeper until he's buried inside of me. He crashes his lips to mine once more, throbbing as I squeeze him into me.

I understand now why he said to forgive him if words fail him.

He pulls out halfway before driving in harder, and I roll my hips to meet his.

If Sitri's taste is warmth, his touch is eternity given form. It's infinite in the way that I never wish to stop feeling him. Intoxication doesn't begin to describe how I feel as he languidly rolls his hips into mine.

The bed creaks loudly, and without breaking apart, he rolls us until he's on his back. His hand moves to cup my neck, thrusting up into me as my hips roll.

The sound that escapes him goes straight to my core, and he breaks our kiss. His golden eyes search my face, and something in me fractures at the vulnerability in his unguarded expression.

"I need you, Maris," he chokes out, his voice cracking. "Not like I've needed anyone. I need you like my lungs need air—I need you, or I won't survive."

I search his face for a moment, realizing that this might be the first time that Sitri has ever allowed himself to want. He's given, and given, more than anyone should ever be expected to. But for me, he's finally allowed himself to be undone.

My hands glide from his chest to cup his cheeks, and his eyelashes flutter, but his twin sun irises don't leave me.

"You already hold my heart in your hands, Sitri," I whisper, pressing a kiss to his lips. "And my soul. I've been branded in more ways than one."

Chapter 22

My hips roll, and as much as pleasure coils in my body, I focus my attention on him. The way his lips part, the heat in his eyes as he thrusts up into me.

He's given me more than I'd ever asked for, but has anyone done the same for him?

I hold his gaze as I ride him, paying attention to every action that makes his breath hitch, or his eyes threaten to roll back. Every movement I make is with the sole purpose of giving to Sitri each ounce of pleasure, tenderness and love that he's shown me since we met.

His breathing picks up, and I mirror it with my movements, rolling my hips until his fingers dig painfully into my skin. My orgasm simmers beneath the surface, but I ward off the pleasure, determined to focus on him.

Sitri suddenly leans forward and grabs a fistful of my hair. I gasp as he captures my lips, thrusting into me hard as I cry out into his mouth.

He buries himself deep, tugging my hair to the point of pain as his cock hits a spot that tips me over the edge.

I moan as my pussy clenches around him. My hips gyrate on their own, riding out each aftershock of pleasure, with Sitri's hard length throbbing as he comes.

I'm panting as we break apart for a moment, searching Sitri's face before he leans in to press a tender kiss to my forehead.

He leans back onto the bed, not bothering to pull out as he drags me with him. Fingertips brush my hair from my face as I listen to his heart rate slow.

"I need to tell you something, Maris."

My heart slips into my stomach. "Sitri..."

He chuckles, and the sound eases my mind, if only a little. "Do you know what a daevari is?"

I frown and shake my head lightly. "Never heard of it."

His fingers run through my hair, gently placing it away from my face. "Daevari are rare. Only a handful have appeared in recorded history. For the most part, angels are only meant to help guide humans, so reproducing with them... it does not happen often. Falling in love with a human is an even more rare occurrence, especially now."

I file away the existence of yet another species that exists beyond servilians, angels and demons, and nod along.

"Though they are rare, they do not have abilities like angels do. They do, however, tend to live a very long life. Longer than any true mortal once they reach a certain age."

His heart rate picks up, and I frown, wondering what might have caused it.

"Maris, I'm telling you all of this because you should know," he whispers, like it's too much for him to say it normally. "You are a daevari."

I freeze. My pulse rages in my ears and I push up onto my elbow. My eyes meet his, and my question for him to repeat himself dies on my lips when I see the uncertainty in his gaze.

My chest rises and falls heavier, and it's like the oxygen in the room's thinned. "You're certain?"

That's the only question I can muster, but I already know the answer. Sitri wouldn't have told me if he wasn't sure.

He nods, his bright eyes still fixated on me, as if he's worried that I might suddenly change my mind about everything.

"What—" I begin, but my words cut off when I change my line of questioning. "How? I know my parents. They are both human, and they're old, Sitri. There's no way one of them was human unless they—"

My eyes widen when emotion flickers across his face, and my mouth snaps shut.

I was adopted.

This can't be real.

"I—" My breaths quicken, and Sitri quickly sits up, cupping my cheeks.

"Maris, breathe. It's okay. This changes nothing. Do you hear me?"

Tears well in my eyes as he presses his forehead to mine. Even though it feels like my entire world was just shaken, flipped on its head and given a new axis.

I exhale a ragged breath. "Why are you telling me this?" I whisper, and his arms encircle my shoulders.

"Because the daevari might not have abilities, but they're strong, Maris. Strong-willed, and resistant to corruption. There's only been one daevari that they converted into their army, but that was long, long ago. He died in the last war between heaven and hell."

His lips press against the top of my head. "I only tell you this because I know every time you take photos you plan to go back to them at some point, and as much as they want to stop me, I know they will also try to get to you. They can't learn what you are, Maris."

My heart stutters, and my eyes slide shut, because I know he's not wrong. There's a million questions I could ask him—I should ask him—but I can't deny, none of the answers truly matter.

Denying his words, asking him to explain how he knows or what daevari are... none if it changes our reality.

And that reality is that at some point, we were going to have to split up for me to do what I need to.

I've just been delaying the inevitable.

"I won't deny your plans, or try to change your mind, Maris. I trust you to make your own decisions, but—" his arms tighten around me, and he shudders. "—please for the love of God, promise me you will go into whatever plans you have with a fresh set of eyes."

I nod against his chest. "I promise."

"They're cunning, Maris. If they find out what you are, they'll poison you, they'll trick you, they'll lure you into their trap."

He pulls me into his lap, and while his actions are charged with intimacy, there's no sexual tension in them. Just a need to be close.

He cups my face, and warmth explodes over my skin as I suck in a breath.

Lines of heat swirl down my neck to my shoulders as his gaze burns into mine, and even though I trust him with everything I am, part of me is viciously curious about what he's doing.

The searing lines aren't painful at all as they travel down my chest and stomach before swirling down my right leg. The pinkish lines settle at the top of my right thigh where a circular sigil has formed on my skin.

My heart thunders, and when my eyes find his once more, his expression softens into what I can only describe as relief.

"What's this for?" I whisper, my chest tightening because of the way he's looking at me.

Dear God, I love this demon.

"I gave you one to protect you from me," he whispers, leaning in to press a tender kiss to the top of my head. "This one is insurance." His fingers trace just around the outer circle, and a shiver wracks through me. "Save it for a rainy day; when the hour is darkest, and you ever need me. Should that day ever come, break the sigil."

His actions make sense, in how he knows they would want to hunt me down if they knew what I was, but the context behind why I'd need it makes the pit in my stomach grow.

I swallow. "Break as in—"

"Slice, cut, or tear." He offers, pulling me into his chest and back onto the bed as I release a long sigh.

Even though I understand his reasoning, suspicion coats my veins. "Is there something I should know?"

His thumb glides along the back of my arm soothingly. "If we're going to go head-to-head with them to disrupt their plans, Maris, they'll be backed into a corner. That's when they'll be most desperate, and dangerous. It's more of a Hail Mary than anything else. I hope we never need to use it."

I glance up at him, searching his face for a long moment before exhaling a tense breath. My head settles against his chest, hearing the steady thrum of his heartbeat.

The last thing I want to think about is anything happening to either of us.

... Because if I lose you, or wake from this dream, I don't think I'll come back from it...

My chest squeezes.

No. Nothing will happen to us. I won't let it.

Chapter 23

The safe zone is busier than I ever could have imagined.

Following Sitri down a narrow road filled with Kharidians, it's not hard to see that this has been one of the longest standing safe zones in the country.

I suppose it only makes sense, being the one safe zone in the entire region that hasn't had an attack in over a year—people understandably would flock here.

Looking at how crowded it is, it also makes sense why people decided not to come.

People have set up a handful of tents along the sides, offering handmade clothes, essentials, and various other items. Two lanes divide the walking space for opposite foot traffic.

There's hardly room to exist with how many people crowd the streets, and more pouring from the houses erected from debris and remnants of the downed buildings nearby.

Even though it's been years, the wreckage from the bombings Sitri mentioned still remains—like a haunting visage of what used to be. It looks as though most people have just learned to live around the damage, or make the most of it.

It's beautiful, in its own horrific way.

After walking for twenty minutes, I've snapped a handful of photos that I know would garner attention from mass audiences overseas, giving us a better chance of getting the story out—and getting Sitri out of this damned groundhog's day from hell.

One photo I'd taken was of a group of kids sitting in front of a woman. She looked to be teaching them something as she sat in front. They all listened attentively as she looked at each of them.

Though I couldn't understand a word she was saying, I could feel the weight of her words.

The next photo was of a young child, no older than twelve, helping a younger one with peeling potatoes. An older woman sat a few feet away slicing some various vegetables, and I knew I needed to capture it.

In fact, most of the images I'd taken were of children or elderly, but I don't need to ask Sitri why there seems to be such a wide age gap dwelling here.

Only maybe ten percent of the population living in this town is older than twenty, and the rest seem to be well into their sixties.

Just another thing this war has ripped from the Kharidians.

Sitri and I come to a stop in front of a communal garden, where a handful of people are tending to various plants.

"There's no way that garden can sustain this many people." I whisper, and Sitri nods.

"There are some trucks that deliver extra rations and other important items—medication, medical equipment, and fresh water. With the attacks ramping up recently, it's been nearly impossible for towns like this to get what they need, though."

I swallow hard against the emotion clogging my throat. "It's not enough."

In the corner of my eye, Sitri's head shakes. "It never is."

Chapter 24

It's been two days since we arrived, and my heart has broken multiple times only for Sitri to put it back together again.

Seeing damaged buildings I can handle, seeing injured people is hard, but I can usually manage. Seeing children arrive, scared, alone and crying for their parents, only to be welcomed in by complete strangers?

I can and can't handle that.

A bell rings in the distance as countless Kharidians wander in from the south entrance. Judging by the way the children hold hands in groups of five, with only ten adults among them, it's safe to say that most of them have lost their families in the conflict.

This group makes up the third wave of refugees to arrive today.

Three.

In one day.

Somehow it seems the fighting has gotten worse, and which has only made Sitri more on edge, more determined to take any kind of definitive action.

I wave over a group of three children and one older woman, gesturing for them to head toward a small tent. The family who lives there rearranged their beds to accommodate as many as possible, and surprisingly, this family headed in will fit perfectly.

The woman inclines her head and murmurs something in Kharidian as she continues past me to the tent. The lines of heads passing by us in the street have me blowing out a breath, feeling a weariness settling into my bones.

If I thought this town was busy when we arrived, we're now crammed in like a can of sardines.

We spent the entire day finding places for the newcomers, even with many families having parents sleep on the floor in already tight quarters, just for those arriving to have a place to recover.

I glance over at the last sliver of sun descending behind the buildings in the distance with a deep yawn.

"Come on, Maris." Sitri slides his hand into mine, and I give him a weary smile that doesn't quite reach my eyes.

"Leaving so soon?" I whisper, but he just searches my face with his brow quirked up.

"They will manage without us for the evening." He tugs me along behind him as he leads us with foot traffic. Putting one foot in front of the other, it feels like an eternity before we finally get back to the room where Sitri and I have been staying.

After mentioning it to Sitri, we'd offered the room to share with people, but everyone had refused.

In fact, everyone seemed more inclined to rearrange their living areas than impose on Sitri's place of rest.

Pros and cons to being the literal key to everyone's survival, I guess. We were more than willing to, but they were insistent on giving him space.

These people can't keep this up forever though, even if Sitri is powerful and on their side. He's bound by the rules; limited in his actions.

But now, as I stand in the middle of the cramped room, looking at his guarded expression from where he sits on the edge of the bed, it's clear that we need to make our move sooner than later.

"Can't we bring them all to the border?" I offer, but my heart sinks when he shakes his head.

"The two dozen we brought across would have already caught their attention. If we try it again, especially with hundreds, we could get caught in the open outside of the safe zone." I turn to look out the small window. "Even without catching their attention, there's a good chance that my actions could have tipped the scales enough to summon Azrael to keep the balance. While I feel emboldened because he didn't show up, I don't think it's wise to tempt fate more than once."

Chewing the inside of my lip, I know he's right, but damn if I didn't wish there was a better option.

"Maris."

The creak of the bedsprings fills the air, and when I turn, I'm face-to-chest with Sitri. His bare skin and defined muscle makes me swallow.

My head tilts to look at him, and when he tucks a lock of hair behind my ear, I melt into his touch.

"There's nothing we can do about it right now. It's late, and you spent the entire day helping people get settled. You. Need. Rest." He murmurs, his index finger gently prodding my collar with his words.

I release a deep sigh as he circles to my back, directing me to the bed.

"Why do you always have to be right?" I groan, crawling into the bed. The single mattress is hardly big enough for the two of us, but Sitri hasn't seemed to mind.

Just like last time, he climbs in alongside me and pulls me into his chest, draping half my body on top of his.

If I didn't know better, I'd be certain that he's using me as his own personal blanket.

The warm scent of him invades my senses, and I burrow my head into his collar, breathing him in deep.

Regardless of what anyone says, Sitri is the furthest thing from a demon. Sure, he might be a prince of hell, but there's not an evil bone in that man's body.

Or is he an angel?

Something in my chest flutters at the thought.

His arms tighten around me, and I melt further into him, eyeing my camera on the desk beside us.

I know I'm going to have to return to the military base sooner than later, and when I do, I'll have to pretend that everything is normal just to get this story out.

That's assuming Thornton will even publish it.

Sitri places a kiss on the top of my head, and my heart stutters.

If he doesn't, I'll just find another way.

Chapter 25

It's hardly sunrise when loud bangs erupt in the distance, and I awake with a start. My heart ricochets against my rib cage, and I sit upright, squinting at the window that's just barely lightened with dawn rising.

"It's alright." Sitri murmurs, pushing himself onto his elbows just as an explosion in the distance overtakes the gunfire.

Anxiety rises in my chest as I scoot to the edge of the bed. "We should help people pack, just in case."

"No."

My head whips toward him so fast that it cracks. "No?" I whisper, the soft question a stark contrast to the urgency I feel in my limbs.

Even in the low light from the window, I can see his contemplative expression, and a pit of dread settles in my gut.

"You're going to go after them."

Twin sun irises flick to mine, and his features soften. "I can draw their attention away, Maris. They'll want to come after me more than civilians."

My stomach churns uncomfortably, and I move to the center of the room, pacing back and forth.

I don't like this.

What if they hurt him?

I don't want to split up.

Another explosion sounds out, and cries from children nearby fill the air as my chest squeezes to the point of pain.

We don't have a choice.

Sitri rises to his feet, and steps in close as the pit of dread in my stomach grows impossibly bigger. "I'll be back before you know it." He whispers, his fingers leaving a blazing trail of electricity along my arms. His palms cup my cheeks, and he presses his lips to mine. "Not even God himself could keep me away from you now, Maris."

Fighting the tears that have welled in the corners of my eyes, I just watch silently as he pulls a shirt over his broad chest, draping his robes over his body before covering himself with his mask.

A thunderous crash rumbles the ground closer than before, and he steps in close. His hands tenderly return to my cheeks as he presses his forehead to mine, and I'm thrown back to that moment in the bed of Anne's house.

So much has changed.

Including me.

I squeeze my eyes shut as his hand falls from my face, and when the wind blows my hair, I open my eyes, knowing that he's gone.

The tears that formed in the corners of my eyes slip down my cheeks and I choke down the ache in my being from his absence, as if boxing it away could work.

The humming of engines fills the distant air, and I tug my shirt over my head. Without Sitri here, it takes extra time to wrap a mask around my face with trembling hands, but I manage.

A rumble like thunder fills the air in the distance, and my mind jumps to Sitri as gunfire follows it.

My limbs are jittery with the need to move, to do something, and even though Sitri said he could draw them away, I need to prepare.

Some part of me screams that something is wrong, and as much as I want to chalk it up to them drawing Sitri out, I can't shake the feeling.

We need to get ready to go.

Just in case.

Snagging my camera and securing the strap around my neck, I walk out the door and onto the main walkway. Even with the small shelter being so enclosed, the gunfire sounds exponentially louder, and my pace to the road quickens.

When I turn the corner, I nearly trip over a man's feet as he kneels, praying with his eyes squeezed shut. Someone bumps my shoulder and I stagger forward, only to lock eyes with a panicked elderly woman. She murmurs something before hurrying away, but between it being Kharidian and the rumbling in the distance, I can't make heads or tails of it.

I dodge out of the way of a kid sprinting from the chaos, and my gaze sweeps over the people running to take what little cover they can and others helping comfort their neighbors or friends.

The familiar humming of a chopper gets louder, and by the time it's overhead, people scream as they run for cover.

They wouldn't attack here, would they? Not with so many civilians in one place.

When the candlelit ritual rooms come to mind, I swallow.

The aircraft passes over without firing a single shot, and I almost think we've made it out without incident until a piece of paper flutters to the ground in front of me.

Another swooshes to the ground before another, and I reach down to pick one up.

The flyer is double-sided, one in English, the other in Kharidian. But it's the large, bold words plastered to the top of the English side that make me wish I'd listened to the pit in my stomach earlier.

I stare at it for a long moment, silently praying that my eyes are playing tricks on me.

SAFE ZONE EVACUATION IMMINENT

The rest of the flyer outlines for refugees to travel to a nearby city, but without intimate knowledge of the area, I'll have to rely on everyone else to know where they're going.

Movement catches my eye as a younger boy picks up a flyer. He glances it over before yelling something to the others.

That's when all hell breaks loose.

People frantically collect what little belongings they have, gathering their loved ones. Most people, already torn from their homes and displaced, grab what is closest to them and walk down the street.

Watching people up and leave everything behind, only bothering to grab essentials before hurrying down the road; it all feels like I'm frozen watching a movie scene play out.

I'm only frozen for a moment when a little girl trips in front of me. She tumbles forward onto her knees, wailing as I hurry over to help her up. The crowd continues to grow around us, and everything inside of me is screaming in urgency.

Trusting my gut, I wrap my fingers around her tiny arms and pull her to her feet, wasting no time as we follow the crowd. She sniffles, but says nothing, taking three or four quick steps to match mine.

I'm murmuring words of reassurance that I'm certain she doesn't understand, but she stays quiet. Her hand firmly clasped in mine squeezes lightly every time more thunderous cracks erupt behind us.

The image of Sitri fighting and leading them away comes to mind, and my heart stutters.

He'll be okay.

This isn't his first rodeo.

Keeping the girl's hand firmly in mine, I use my right hand to grab my camera as a little boy in front of us lifts the flyer. The camera's weight feels like it's doubled as I bring the viewfinder to my eye and capture the moment with the click of the shutter.

With everything I've seen, taking stills of the horrific tragedies here will never truly capture what these monsters are doing.

Releasing my camera to let it hang against my chest, I exhale a ragged breath.

Until people band together and do something, what hope do we have?

Sitri can't fight this war on his own, even though it feels like he is. There has to be more I can do.

We walk for what feels like an eternity as the sun rises behind us; the little girl sniffling every now and again. The sound makes the tight feeling in my chest worsen, because I know there's nothing I can say or do to change our situation.

Cracks of gunfire fill the air, echoing in the direction we'd come from before a rumble follows it, and I can't help but wonder if it was Sitri or a bomb.

The journey is exhaustive even though I'd nearly gotten a full night's rest. But I know I'm not the only one feeling the effects. Every now and again, someone staggers unsteadily or trips over their own feet, and I can't help but wonder how long it will take for us to get to safety.

We slowly make our way between buildings that grow increasingly tall, and I scan what likely was once the downtown of a small city.

The stream of refugees turns down a street that looks oddly familiar, and my eyes narrow on the buildings, trying to pinpoint where I recognize them from.

It takes a few minutes before I recognize the area, but it's because we're approaching from a different direction from when I last saw it. When the tall apartment where I'd escaped Rob—and ran into Sitri—comes into view on our left, my blood runs cold.

I vividly remember the soldiers that lined one side of the road behind Sitri, but by the time my head turns, it's too late.

We're literal fish in a barrel.

A deafening crack has us all ducking as a man to our right drops like a stone. The little girl screams as more shots fill the air, and she rips her hand from mine as she sprints in the opposite direction.

The shout that escapes me as I call after her to get her attention is hardly audible over the gunfire, and I twist to chase after her as more shots ring out.

Bodies drop in my peripheral, and I rush toward her with as much speed as I can muster.

She'll never make it.

With my next step, something hits my leg, and I cry out, my thigh buckling as I put weight on it. Careening forward, my knee slams into the ground before something heavy collapses on top of my back, shoving me further onto the paved road.

Covering my head with my arms, I watch in horror as the little girl only makes it another fifteen feet. She suddenly flinches, and her small form falls limp to the ground.

They're killing everyone.

I don't dare look away as they fall, committing each soul to memory. One by one, I watch the civilians gunned down in cold blood, and my head spins with the wave of nausea washing over me.

The evacuation was a distraction. They led us into a trap, effectively luring Sitri away from us.

It was a fucking trap.

The ritual site I'd seen that day with Lennard comes to mind, and my mind's a jumbled, chaotic mess between unspoken vows of violence.

The body on top of me is crushing weight, and I don't need to look to know that they're likely dead.

With how lightheaded I am, there's a chance I might not be long for this earth much longer either.

At least if I go, that means Sitri will take them all out with me.

Darkness creeps in at the corners of my vision, and the world around me spins before it goes dark.

Chapter 26

Rhythmic beeping that keeps in time with my heartbeat is the first thing I notice.

That tells me I'm alive and in a hospital.

I don't know whether I'm relieved or disappointed.

Not that I'd want to lose my life, but at this point, it feels like it will take some kind of divine intervention for us to even the stakes.

Peeling my crusted eyes open, I squint against the light as they water, burning at the invasion. The sound of footsteps grows closer to my left, and I turn my head toward it.

"Maris? Maris, can you hear me? Thank God you're okay."

My heart sinks into my stomach at the sound of Rob's voice, and I freeze.

For a heartbeat, I nearly wonder if I'd imagined everything. But then my gaze lands on the bandage covering my thigh, and all my memories come flooding back.

Rob stands beside the bed, grasping my hand in his, and I stare at him with wide eyes.

Does he not remember that I *ran* from him? That I broke up with him before he tried to assault me again? That I kneed him in the groin before disappearing?

He must assume my reaction is for some other reason, and he pats the back of my hand. "You must have been so scared, stuck with those infidels for so long. It's a wonder you weren't more injured."

It takes a conscious effort not to scowl at him.

He leans forward to pet my hair, and I inch away, seeing the way his face grows more serious. The emotion melts away from his expression, turning his features more cold than I've ever seen.

"You're in shock, that's all," he murmurs, pushing to his feet. "You just need some time to... get acclimated again."

Sitri's warning rings through my mind, and I find my voice as Rob strides to the door.

"Rob," he turns to look at me with a guarded expression. "I meant what I said that day. We're over."

His jaw feathers, but he says nothing as he disappears out the doorway, and I listen to his footsteps recede before exhaling a ragged breath.

At least I won't have to pretend.

It takes everything I have not to walk through the moments before I'd passed out. Every time I feel myself creeping closer to those images, I suck in a deep breath and focus on Sitri.

The last thing I need is to break down in a hospital far behind enemy lines. My gaze falls on the camera to my right; the bullet hole in the opposite side from where the memory is stored makes me swallow.

To think I might have been that close to dying.

My eyes slide shut, and I let myself picture Sitri, burning soldiers to a crisp somewhere with a weary note of satisfaction.

The beeping drones on, and I'm in and out of consciousness as my thoughts wander to Sitri.

I'm not sure how long has passed when a nurse comes in with General Deliom in tow. The hard lines in his face seem like they've only grown since I'd last seen him, and with everything I know now, I seriously want to throw up.

"Ah, Ms. Sylvara. Good to see you finally awake." He says gruffly, and the nurse walks over to stand beside my injured leg.

I say nothing as she slowly unravels my bandages, and Deliom clasps his hands in his lap. "I'll expect a full written report on what you observed during your imprisonment with the rebels, but given our current circumstances, I'd like a verbal report now."

Shit.

My blood pressure skyrockets, and the monitor beeps faster.

"What are our current circumstances, sir?" My voice sounds so much smaller than I'm used to, and even though I hate it, I can't deny that it's working to my advantage since they think I was kept as a prisoner of war.

Deliom scoffs, crossing his bulky arms over his chest. "The rebellion invaded the safe zone in the northwest region twenty-four hours ago. We sent a few units to investigate, but they never reported back. It looks like the magic wielder killed everyone in the city to clear the way before taking out our units. The city has been leveled."

No fucking chance they're trying to blame this on him.

Still, at the thought of Sitri, my heart squeezes in my chest.

I know he's capable of destroying an entire city, but he wouldn't have killed civilians. Not like they would.

It takes everything in me not to let my thoughts wander to him as I nod. "That's horrible."

Deliom must feel like he's getting somewhere with me, because his features relax as he nods curtly. "So, you can understand why a full detailed report on what you saw might be helpful, but for now, I'll take the short version."

My heart thunders, and the traitorous monitor mirrors the spike. "Um, I... I don't really know." His eyes narrow, and I know I need to feed him something. "I saw the magic wielder once, but he wore these black robes, and there was fire around him... Other than that, they kept me in confinement, and it's all a blur."

He doesn't look convinced. "So you don't have any knowledge or insight?"

My monitor beeps faster and I swallow hard. "I don't know, I—"

"It might be best to give her some time to process what happened, General. I'm sure it was quite a traumatic experience."

My eyes flick to the nurse changing my bandage, but she remains focused on my thigh as Deliom grumbles under his breath.

Surprisingly, he drops it altogether, and pushes to his feet. "How long until she's discharged?"

The nurse glances at me before her eyes settle on Deliom. "Sometime this afternoon."

He nods, albeit reluctantly, and heads for the door. "Fine. I'll expect your written report tomorrow morning, Sylvara. No later, or I'll come retrieve it myself."

I don't bother responding as he turns the corner, disappearing from view as his footsteps grow more faint.

"Thank you." I whisper, and the nurse straightens, turning her head toward me with a grin. Her fingers gently tap my thigh, and my eyes gravitate to the area before a wave of horror washes over me.

The sigil. She saw it.

"With this," she taps it again. "A thank you is never needed."

I blink at her, confused by how her words contradict my crippling fear of being found out. "I'm sorry, I'm afraid I don't follow."

She chews her lip, glancing at the door. "You think *he* works alone?"

The way she says it has a double meaning in her tone. On one hand, the way she says it implies that she's curious if I think he does, but her eyes locked onto me as her fingers hover above the sigil tells me she might be my only ally in this godforsaken base.

My eyebrows twitch upward. "You—"

"Ah, would you look at that, Ms. Sylvara. You're right as rain now. Here I thought you'd need longer." She muses, tossing me a wink as she unhooks the wires from me one by one. I watch as she breezes over to the head of the bed, her hand clasping my arm with her voice low. "Be careful now, Ms. Sylvara. I'm sure *many* people are relying on you to stay safe."

My heart pounds in my chest, and she gestures to the door. "You're free to return to your quarters."

"Right. Uh, it was nice to meet you—"

"Kira." She offers with a smirk, and turns to clean up the worn bandages.

Not wanting to put my newfound ally at risk, I swing my legs off the bed and pull on my clothes left on the table. I hear her behind me bustling about, but I say nothing as I snag my camera from the table and head out the door.

The sooner I can get everything in order, the better.

Even with the injury I'd sustained, there's no pain as I navigate the long hallways that look more foreign than ever.

Who knew that coming to Kharidia would change my entire world this much?

I hold my breath each time I pass a soldier, choking down every anxiety of what could happen if they discover the truth.

When they discover the truth.

Turning the last corner to my quarters, I can't help but release a dry laugh as I key my pin into the pad.

How ironic it is that the soldiers and military brought me here to uncover Sitri's atrocities, yet theirs are the only ones I've found to expose.

The door slides shut, the lock clicking in place as I glance at the clock. It's late, and even though I know I should rest, I pull my chair up to the desk, flip open my laptop and get to work.

If I have any chance to end this war, it'll be with the footage I took, convincing the greater population of humans that demons are real, living beings walking this earth, wearing human skin.

They're real, and they're murdering thousands for their own gain.

God, I hope it's enough.

Chapter 27

It's been hours, and after uploading all the photos to my laptop, I lean back in my chair and rub my palms into my eyes.

I can't help how much I feel like I'm in the belly of the beast.

Surrounded by militants, including Rob, with Sitri nowhere close by... Every move I make is a calculated risk from this point on.

Outside of Kira, I'll have to assume that everyone is involved with what the military is trying to achieve here.

My mind wanders to Lennard, and my stomach flips. Even if he was nice to me, and acted surprised when we saw the ritual room... it could have been just that. An act.

I spend the next few hours drafting out a story line before writing out an embellished yet vague report on what occurred when I was gone for Deliom.

After weeks of 'imprisonment,' I know they'd want more than just a single page of detail... so I wrote a page and a half. My account mostly describes how I was held in a room, fed, and allowed to bathe, until a plane flew overhead, at which point they evacuated me and the others.

My report focuses more on the small room where they confined me, with a single bed and desk than anything else, and I know that alone will drive Deliom up the wall.

Keeping my story as minimal as possible makes it so that I can recount it later if needed. Keeping it aligned to how I ended up back in their hands without me having to worry about losing track of the lie.

Forwarding the report to Deliom's email, I heave a sigh of relief and stand with a wince. The dull pain in my thigh has slowly gotten worse as the painkillers wore off, but I refuse to take more.

I need to stay as alert and lucid as possible, and who knows what the fuck they put in the drugs here.

A shudder runs through me as I gingerly walk to the bed and throw myself into it. The bullet missed major arteries and ligaments, so really it's more superficial than anything.

Still, Kira said to take it easy for the night, and who am I to disagree? It's not like I'm going to adventure through the base on my own any time soon.

Blowing out a breath, my eyes trace the lines on the ceiling, and my mind wanders to the one person I miss more than life itself.

My eyes squeeze shut, and I'm deluded to the point where I'm almost convinced that if I willed it hard enough, I might somehow make him materialize from thin air.

His absence feels like more of a physical wound than the one in my leg.

Does he even know where I am? Or what happened to the people in the evacuation zone? Will he think I was killed?

My heart squeezes painfully at the thought.

As much as I'd like to see Sitri take out everyone on this godforsaken planet in this rampage, I don't want the guilt of taking that many lives on his conscience.

He deserves better.

But if he thinks they killed me, he's going to end up leveling towns all the same. I need to find a way to show him I'm still alive, without *completely* outing myself for being a mole.

My thigh throbs some more, and I chew the inside of my cheek before my eyes slide shut. I'll figure it out tomorrow.

One day at a time.

Chapter 28

A loud knock at the door jolts me awake, and I surge upright, searching the dim room with wide eyes.

For a moment, I no longer recognize the barren, minimalistic walls, the lone work desk across the room, or the small dresser with my carry-on tucked in beside it.

It's like I expected to see a dimly lit window with him standing cross-armed in front of it—his broad chest and corded arms silhouette against the dark of the room.

Disappointment crashes over me when my mind reconciles fantasy with reality, and the loud knock echoes into the room again.

"Sylvara, it's Rob."

My heart sinks into my gut. *Shit.*

Throwing the bedsheet off of me, I hobble to the door, thankfully feeling more stable than I did last night. Glancing at the t-shirt and shorts I'm wearing, I don't have time to change into something that'll cover me more.

At least his sigil is covered between the bandage Kira wrapped around my leg and my clothes.

I exhale a steadying breath and pull the door open. "What is it?"

Rob looks like he just got out of the shower minutes ago, and he glances down the hallway. "Deliom said you never responded to his email this morning. He wanted me to come get you." His eyes trail my body, and I want more than anything to shrink away behind the door. "Can you be ready in five?"

My eyes widen. "Oh, uh, yeah, sure. Just give me a few."

Shutting the door on Rob's face, I gingerly pad to the dresser to pull on a pair of stretchy dress pants and a comfortable blouse. I feel odd in my old clothes, and I can't help feeling more than ever that the Maris who arrived in this country has changed forever.

The material, my old style, the vibrant colors, all feel so foreign to me now.

By the time I open the door to the hallway, Rob's impatience is clear as day on his face. His jaw feathers, the muscle rippling from his teeth grinding together, yet he says nothing as we walk the winding halls to Deliom's office.

It's an odd feeling to have once cared so deeply for someone, only to see who they really are at their core. It's even more odd to walk side-by-side with the man who nearly killed you while defiling your body.

War changed Rob, in more ways than I expected.

I suppose, in a way, it changed me too.

Still, maybe because of my relationship with Sitri, or what I've learned about who–or rather *what*–I am, walking beside him in silence is more of an annoyance than it is anxiety inducing.

Or perhaps I've gotten a false sense of security from being in a military base filled with people making me walk taller than usual.

We turn down the final hallway, and the thought of being in front of Deliom wipes out my excessive confidence.

One minute at a time, Maris. Fake it until you make it, one minute at a time.

"Mr. Paulson, Ms. Sylvara." Deliom grunts as we walk through his door and make our way to the seats in front of his desk. "I'll cut to the chase. I read through your report, Ms. Sylvara."

Blood rages in my ears, and it takes everything in me to keep my breathing even.

"It's clear that you have been through quite a lot. More than we'd ever want any correspondent to suffer, and after much consideration, we wanted to offer you the chance to return home."

I'm sorry, what?

They want to... send me *home*?

After all of this?

I want to scream that my home is here, fighting against their forces every day to help the people of Kharidia survive. But I don't.

My heart rattles in my chest, and I nod slightly. "Oh..."

I know I can't seem too averse to leaving, because who wouldn't want to after seeing such traumatic events? I mean... Horrors *were* witnessed, but not by the people they want me to blame.

There's a good chance they think my report could be used to further their agenda, and explain why they've leveled entire cities and towns.

But I won't buy into it.

I swallow hard, meeting Deliom's gaze. "I appreciate your offer and consideration... However, I would be remiss if I didn't see this through, especially considering everything I've witnessed."

It's the truth, but not for the reasons he'll think.

Deliom considers me for a moment and I have to fight the urge to sag my shoulders when he nods. "Very well. I will have to warn you, though, tensions are on the rise. The rebel's attacks on our bases have increased in both voracity and frequency over the past two days. We assume it's because of our retaliation against the rebellion leaders' control of the safe zone."

I nod along in agreement, silently filing away the information with a light feeling in my chest.

Does this mean Sitri's looking for me? Maybe he's searching for where they might be keeping me?

How can I give him a clue?

Deliom braces his forearms on the desk, clasping his hands in front of his face as his hard eyes flick between us. "Since neither of you have an issue with it, Fredrick's team leaves in half an hour. I want you both to accompany him. The footage we get from this mission could be critical in getting support for our efforts back home."

Rob and I both murmur an agreement before leaving the office, and it's a quiet, awkward silence until we pass Rob's quarters. Thankfully, he says nothing as he breaks apart from me to key the pin into the pad. When I hear the door click shut behind me, I exhale a sigh of relief.

I don't know what is in store for us, but I need to figure out how I can use it to my advantage.

My mind wanders to Sitri as I open the door to my room, taking a moment as I slide the lock in place. My back presses to the door, and my eyes slide shut as I recall every moment between us, every touch.

To remember how he felt. The way he cared for me in a way no one else has. To feel the ghost of his touch in the palm of my hand or against my cheek.

Footsteps pass by on the other side of the door, and my eyes snap open, landing on my carry-on where I keep my spare camera.

Soon. I'll get to him soon.

Chapter 29

"Good to see you back, Sylvara."

Fredrick stands near the armored vehicles with his hands clasped behind his back and nods when our eyes meet. He's decked out in full gear, but he looks like he's aged since I saw him last.

I guess war will do that to a person.

"You as well, Fredrick." I pace past him to the open door of the armored truck and hoist myself in. The pain in my leg surprisingly dulled to where I hardly notice it at all. Feeling the weight of my camera swinging loosely against my chest, I settle into the vacant spot in the corner. "Where to today?"

His eyes meet mine for a second before he steps aside, and Rob climbs in, dousing a wave of ice over me as he takes a seat. Still, he says nothing, and Fredrick's head peers in the doorway again.

"We're headed to a southern encampment to help establish their new location. Intel says we may run into trouble, but if we timed it right, we should be okay."

He shuts the door with a loud crack, and my gaze sweeps from one side of the truck to the other, searching for any familiarity. When I don't see a pair of bright blue eyes amongst the soldiers with us, a pit forms in my stomach. Fredrick walks around to the front and climbs into the driver's seat.

I'm sure Lennard's fine. He's probably in the other vehicle.

Not like I care, anyway.

Everyone here is the enemy.

The vehicle rocks back and forth as we exit the camp, and I survey the vacant buildings we pass by. When we arrived, I'd assumed that the conflict here had cleared them out of these areas, leaving a central location for our military to set up a base. But now, I know better, and every second I spend back here, it feels my blinders are off.

Here I thought we were coming to find out what the rebellion was doing, but everyone back home was just as oblivious to the truth as I was. Whether willfully or unknowingly, but I have to believe that if the masses knew what the military was doing here, they'd act.

Because what if this was their *family* being slaughtered?

Their **kids** being injured or orphaned?

Would they rise up, knowing that these are somebody's daughters and sons? Would the knowledge that these are somebody's loves... their soulmates... would that be enough?

My gut wrenches, and the car lurches as we wind down a main road with weather-worn buildings on either side of us. They appear abandoned, with shattered windows, tattered drapes hanging from them, but outside of that, they appear mostly undamaged outside of the scattered bullet holes.

Something tells me it will take years to rebuild the areas where most of the damage lies. Even then, it hurts my soul to think of how many people won't have lived long enough to see it restored to even a fraction of its former glory.

Sure, cities here weren't the most progressive in terms of tech or construction, but they were quaint. Now, tragedy and suffering conceal the character and love those cities once held.

Much like the blood that coats the hands of those responsible, I'm not sure if they'll ever be free of it.

I don't think the real demons deserve to.

My thoughts wander for the rest of the short drive—my own way of keeping my attention away from being this close to Rob, and it's not long before we lurch to a stop in front of a series of connected buildings.

"A-team out first. B-team will cover the correspondents." Fredrick says loudly before he climbs out of the vehicle. The others follow his lead, swinging the door open and filing out into the area with their weapons drawn.

I wait patiently for Rob to climb out, and I ease across the seat, placing my hands on the sides of the door. I'm about to hop to the ground when I see a familiar set of sky-blue eyes peering back at me.

As expected, Lennard's geared up with his rifle in his arms at the ready, and even though I know he's just as much to blame as everyone else here, an odd sense of relief washes over me at the sight of him.

He nods his head in acknowledgement before scanning the area, and I climb out of the truck.

Lennard moves behind me as two members of the B-team lead the rest of us into what looks like an abandoned mall. The barrels of their guns aim in all directions as we gain more distance from the truck.

To say my pulse is racing would be an understatement, not because I fear any attack directed at us, but instead, it's the opposite. Every second we spend here, I listen for how many lives they'll take for their unholy army with each bullet.

My heart rate doesn't calm down until we're inside, and B-team clears the room. Muffled shouts echo from all corners, and relief washes over me like a warm blanket when each unit member lowers their weapons to the ground.

I slowly pace to the center of the room, my gaze sweeping across the debris scattered around us. Whatever used to be stored in here is long gone, with only desks and chairs remaining amongst the dust and garbage.

In my peripheral, Rob murmurs to one soldier, and he nods once before moving to the others.

Could he be planning something?

Suspicion coats my veins like hot oil, and my muscles tense as he walks over. I feel myself lean to my left on instinct, away from Rob and toward where Lennard approaches my other side.

"They're going to check upstairs and the rest of the building—"

"Ah, me and Lennard are going to check out the north side of the building." I offer before he can finish.

Rob looks at Lennard, and one doesn't need to be a mind reader to know the thoughts circling his brain as his jaw feathers. It doesn't help when Lennard just nods like it was our set plan all along.

Thank God.

Some small piece of me hopes he's not part of this, even though he's wrapped up in the middle of this mess of a war.

"Right. Well. Be safe, I guess," Rob grumbles before he whirls around, and the rest of B-team escorts him in the opposite direction.

Watching them disappear down the hall, I exhale the breath that had caught in my lungs.

"Your ex-boyfriend gives me the creeps."

My eyes widen as my gaze slides to Lennard, only to see his crinkling at the edges. He huffs a laugh as if he can't help himself, and I just shake my head, unable to bite back a dry laugh.

"You and me, both."

"Come on," Lennard whispers, and steps toward the north exit. "We should leave before they change their minds."

I nod, following close behind Lennard as he clears room after room. His steps are methodical and practiced, stiff but ready, and I can't help but wonder how many innocent civilians he's taken the lives of.

The naïve Maris that showed up in Kharidian would have thought none, but now?

Now I'm afraid I don't want to know the answer.

Minutes go by, and we've followed one vacant hallway into another, and when we cut left into a smaller passageway, the smell of candles burning invades my senses.

I freeze.

Could it really be? Here, of all places?

Lennard must have noticed me, because he pauses and turns toward where I stand, waiting for me to catch up. When my legs move once more, each pace is slow and cautious, as if one wrong step could expose us both.

Our eyes meet as I grow closer to him, but neither of us utters a word as he nods, leading the way at an even slower pace than before.

By the time we find the doorway of the ritual room, the smell of burning incense and candles is so strong, it could give someone with the highest tolerance a headache.

Wooden benches line the room, with a symbol drawn into the ground, and candles scatter in a pattern around it. Hay or straw covers the floor, piling in a handful of areas around the room and under long curtains draped from the ceiling.

"What the fuck." Lennard whispers harshly. "Another one of these fucking places?"

An idea forms, and my gaze bounces from the candles to the rest of our surroundings as butterflies ricochet in my abdomen.

Two birds, one stone.

Hurrying into the middle of the room, Lennard curses behind me under his breath. "We need to get out of here, Sylvara."

Ignoring his recommendations, I bend down to grab the nearest candle and turn to look at him with a broad grin on my face. I'm nearly certain that, given the situation, he probably thinks I've lost my mind.

Judging by the way he's glancing wide-eyed between me and the candle in my hand, I'd say I'm right in that assessment.

"Give me one minute, and we can blow this joint." I whisper, whirling around as wax splatters onto my hand. I hardly feel it amidst the excitement that has gone from brimming to raging in record time.

Finding another candle on top of a bench, I scoop it up before walking to the wooden table in the center of the room. Lennard says nothing as I gather hay nearby and shove a candle underneath.

It takes only a minute for the hay to catch, and soon the flames spread to the dry wooden chair legs before stretching higher.

I repeat the action until the fire bleeds over each surface, and when it catches on the curtains that line the walls, I know it's time to go.

Scraping my boots through the etched symbol on the ground, I follow Lennard out, and we hurry back the way we came.

He doesn't question my actions, or accuse me of anything as he leads us out, his surgical precision hurried as he guides us back. I'm elated as we near the room where we'd split from the others, and my heart could burst from my chest. Voices fill the air nearby, and before I can catch my breath, Rob and the others appear in the doorway.

Their eyes are wide as they glance between Lennard and me before sliding to the doorway behind us.

Dread sinks into my stomach like a boulder.

They'll know it was us.

There's no way they won't think it was us.

"What happened?" Fredrick steps forward, his eyes trained on Lennard. When their eyes remain glued to the doorway, I turn slightly to follow their gaze, only to see dark smoke pooling at the top and into the room.

"Fire. There's smoke coming from the hallway. We need to go."

"Fuck." One man behind Rob says, and another murmurs inaudibly in response.

Fredrick mutters something into his radio before turning to us. "It might be the magic user. You two, get outside and hide near the car. Lennard, stand guard. The rest of you, with me."

Lennard ushers us out of the building and around the corner before pacing from one end to the other to clear our surroundings. When a gunshot rings out nearby, he glances between us hesitantly, and another goes off in the same direction.

Lennard walks closer, his hand against my stomach as he walks me closer to the wall. When my heels hit the concrete, he stops and surveys the area one last time.

"Stay hidden here." He says in a low tone before stepping off to the side to clear the area.

Another gunshot goes off, and Rob steps closer. He keeps his attention fixed on my right as I squeeze myself closer into the building.

Being in such an exposed location like this, all it would take is one or two well-aimed shots to finish us. If I were demons harvesting souls, it wouldn't take much to manufacture a gun-fight to cover for two reporters deaths.

Something crashes inside the building, making it shudder in response and Rob looks at me with wild eyes. My last memory of him comes rushing back as he surges toward me, backing me further into the wall.

His hands grip my biceps to the point of bruising. "What the fuck is wrong with you, Maris?"

I don't have time to respond as a gloved hand encircles his arm, ripping him away from me. Lennard's blue eyes burn bright as he shoves Rob back against the wall, crowding Rob's space as he presses the barrel of his automatic rifle under his chin.

"Give me one reason I shouldn't pull this trigger right now, and end your miserable, useless, vermin life."

Rob looks like he might shit himself as he stretches onto his tip-toes to put space between him and the barrel. Lennard just raises the tip further, waiting somewhat patiently for his answer.

"I was just stressed. I didn't do anything, I swear."

Footsteps grow closer just as Lennard pulls his weapon back. "Go to the truck, correspondent."

Rob glances between us before he sulks away, disappearing around the corner. I could sob in relief as I rub the tender spot where he'd held me. When I go to follow Lennard's instruction, he stops me in place by sliding his hand across my stomach.

"Not *you*, correspondent." He says with a more gentle tone.

My eyes find his, and there's a knowing look in them as I fight the tears pooling in the corner of mine. "Where do I go then?" I whisper, swallowing against the lump in my throat.

He listens for a long moment before his low voice fills the air between us. "Go to B-team's truck. Wait there for me."

With that he heads in the direction that Rob went, and I put one foot in front of the other until I'm at the opposite truck to the one we arrived in. The armored door is so heavy that it takes all my strength to swing open the door and climb in before a shudder wracks through me.

That was too close. If Lennard hadn't been there...

I don't even want to think about it.

My gaze flicks up to the windshield, and my eyes widen as flames rise into the sky from the top of the building. Black smoke billows from the columns of fire, and I watch for a long moment before the A-Team appears from all corners. They keep their barrels aimed as they move in sync toward Fredrick and the rest of B-Team.

They talk as a group for a moment before splitting, and B-team heads straight for the vehicle I'm sitting in.

I snap a photo of the burning building before sliding back into my seat. The door pulls open, and Lennard is the first to climb in, taking the only seat next to me before the others join.

The truck is silent as everyone loads in, and within the minute, the engine rumbles to life, and we head back the way we came.

Before everything happened, before Kharidia, the silence would have been tense, but now I welcome it like an old friend.

Between not talking to anyone and not having to worry about Rob for the entire ride, I'm able to think through what my next steps need to be with a little more peace of mind.

By the time we're pulling through the gates of the base, I know what I need to do.

I need to finish writing up the story.

I have all the documentation.

Now I just need to convince Thornton to publish it.

Chapter 30

I'm on high alert as I stride down the hallway to my quarters, keeping a close eye out for Rob at each turn.

He'd hurried out from A-team's truck when we pulled up, so something tells me he wasn't exactly interested in sticking around.

Something about it was unsettling, though.

He's not usually the type to forego pleasantries with people he respects, and even if he's a fucking psycho now, he still respects Fredrick. Yet he disappeared into the front doors of the base without so much as a word.

When we'd filed out of the truck, Lennard pretended like he knew nothing, which, as much as it sucked feeling alone, I understood the distance he put between us.

He's a soldier, after all, and he was out of line by threatening Rob.

Part of me can't help but wonder if he'll end up getting some kind of punishment for his actions, or if Rob will keep his mouth shut about it.

Something tells me it's not the latter.

By the time I'm sliding the lock in place on my room door, I exhale a ragged breath of relief. Today was hard, but knowing the fire I set would be visible for miles, along with keeping the military's attention away from where Sitri might be, it was well worth it.

My feet carry me to my desk, and I open my laptop with a deep yawn.

Even with how tired I am, there's still so much I have to do to prepare if I'm going to make this work.

I slide into the chair, spending the next three hours on my report, feeling the weight of my exhaustion heavy on my shoulders. But I push through, knowing it has to be perfect.

Things don't get any easier, because compounded by the exhaustion weighing me down, is the memory of each photo I'd taken, from the moment I'd landed, to when I met Sitri, until we'd been separated. My heart aches as I gaze into faces that might no longer be alive, all while fury and a hard note of resolve keep me focused.

Because their deaths won't be for nothing.

I won't allow it.

By the time I'm done, sliding my laptop closed, I yawn deeply, struggling to keep my eyes open as I push to my feet.

That's as good as my story is going to get.

All the elements are there. Emotional ties, empathetic response, shocking factors that will make them question everything just in time to feed them all mere pieces of the real truth I collected.

There's no way they'll run the story if I bare it all for the world to see, so a fraction of the truth will have to do.

Flopping into bed, with my eyes fluttering shut, I melt into the hard mattress.

The rest of this will be tomorrow's problem.

~

A loud knock jolts me from my sleep, and I surge upright with my heart in my throat as it echoes through my small room.

What the—?

The knock comes again, but this time it sounds more urgent, and terrifyingly more angry.

My limbs tremor as I slide off the bed and approach the door. Easing the bolt out of its locked position feels like I'm walking the plank of my own volition, and a lump forms in my throat.

Did they finally realize I'm not the same person who was captured?

Did they finally find out what I am? Or maybe Deliom saw through my report, and they're coming to arrest me now. Or maybe Lennard told them everything.

That thought makes my heart slink into my stomach.

Oh, God. What *if* Lennard told them everything? Or Kira told them about the sigil on my thigh?

I pause before fully withdrawing the lock, and when another loud knock reverberates into my hand on the knob, I swallow my fear.

Whatever they have planned for me, I'll have to face it head on.

It's not like I can hide in this room forever.

The lock clicks out of place and I pull the door open to see Deliom, Fredrick and Rob standing before me. The realization that my worst fears might end up being reality settles into the pit in my stomach as I glance between them.

Fredrick's face is unreadable, but the look in Rob's eyes—the malice in his expression—sends a shiver down my spine. I'm reluctant to admit he almost looks excited, and Deliom clears his throat, pulling my attention to him.

"Ms. Sylvara, we're going to need you to come with us."

A statement, not a request.

Shit.

Okay, just play dumb. It's fine. It's cool. Play it cool.

"Uh, sure." I murmur, gesturing to my pajamas. "Can I change first?"

Fredrick and Rob glance at Deliom as he shakes his head. "No need. We won't be going far."

"Oh, okay. Lead the way then."

Blood rages in my ears as alarm bells go off in my mind, but I have no choice other than to follow Deliom and Rob with Fredrick at my back.

They lead the way through the barracks, but instead of turning left to go toward the Deliom's office, we cut right and into a wing I've never been in before. I'm entirely out of place beside them as we pass other military operatives in full gear, most glancing at me for a moment before their eyes drop to my pajamas.

The flash of confusion each person gets, or the quirk of an eyebrow I catch, tells me that this is entirely out of the ordinary, and the lump in my throat grows.

At least they haven't put me in handcuffs, right?

That has to mean something.

.... Right?

We come to a stop at the end of a hallway, and Deliom scans his badge over a small screen on the wall. It beeps twice, and we file into a small room filled with floor to ceiling windows. In the middle of one of the windows, another badge-scan type door looked to be the only entrance or exit from another, larger room.

Deliom leads us to the second door, scans us through and my feet move of their own accord, bringing me closer to the single chair in the center.

The pit of dread in my stomach grows bigger as Deliom pauses his movements to turn to me. When he gestures to it, I want to throw up.

"Sit please, Ms. Sylvara."

The way he says it isn't a request even if his word choice disagrees, and my anxiety riddled mind sends my heart plummeting into my stomach. I turn hesitantly, nervously glancing between the three men before easing to the seat.

The metal against my bare skin feels like ice, and the cold seeps through my thin pajamas as I settle into it.

"What's the meaning of this, General Deliom?" I ask, keeping my focus on Deliom as Fredrick shifts to my left.

He crosses his arms over his chest as the sound of metal fills the air, and before I can fully turn to look at Fredrick, a metal clasp encircles my wrist.

I jerk my hand away two seconds too late, and I stare at the handcuff with wide eyes as Rob tightens one around my other wrist.

Lennard or Kira. It had to be them.

"I didn't do anything!" My voice is shrill, and my wide-eyed gaze bounces between the three men.

"We are fully aware of your innocence, Ms. Sylvara." I freeze, and my heart feels like it could break free from my chest with how hard it's beating. "However, given the instances where you've been present, and the magic user has appeared, we've determined that the best way to draw him out, is with you."

My jaw goes slack. This has to be the worst-case scenario.

They're going to bait him into a trap?

"You can't be serious—" When none of them say anything, I shake my head in disbelief. "There's no way that will work. I'm nothing to him. Besides, how would he even know where I am?"

Deliom grins broadly. "Oh, he'll come. We distributed flyers across every corner of the region announcing Maris Sylvara's imprisonment for crimes against her country."

I'd say if only they knew, but a part of me worries that they actually just might, and this is them killing two birds with one stone.

"There's no way this will work." I mumble, and my gaze drops to the cement floor.

"The flyers stated you had two hours before you'd be executed for your crimes, and that was an hour ago, so we shouldn't have to wait long." Deliom says gruffly, and a muffled voice comes through Fredrick's radio.

He lifts it and murmurs something back before turning his attention to the General. "All units are in place, sir."

My eyes widen. "You're not going to kill him, are you?" The question pours from me before I can stop it, and Deliom's eyes narrow. "He seems strong. It might be useful to study him." I add, hoping to god that he ignores my first question.

"You have your orders. Everyone out." Deliom barks, and I watch the three men file out of the room. They form a line on the other side of the windows, their faces mostly darkened with shadows as they peer in at me.

Seconds turn into minutes, but each one feels like an eternity.

Three pairs of eyes remain glued to me, and my fingers encircle the arm of the chair, if only to stay still.

Part of me considers how funny it would be if another hour goes by and Sitri *doesn't* show up—the look on Deliom's face might be one for the books.

The other, louder, and more rational part of me knows that even if Sitri knows this is a trap, which he probably does, he'd run in headfirst, anyway.

That's what I'm afraid of.

After what happened when we destroyed that ritual site together, and I'd almost had to carry him to Anne, the last thing I want is for him to be in harm's way again.

What's worse is that, as more time goes on, and the more I consider everything that could happen, the more I'm convinced that either Sitri or I will die in the process of escaping.

A dull sense of resignation settles on my shoulders as I count the seconds that pass, praying silently with each one that he doesn't take the bait.

If they have all units ready at the main base, and even *some* of them have the bullets that block Sitri's healing, we are so beyond fucked.

Chapter 31

Thirty minutes is as long as it took for Sitri to show up.

The only reason I know this is because the gunfire outside is almost constant, and I squeeze my eyes shut.

Each distant pop sends my heart into my throat, and I can only pray that they miss their mark.

The thunderous gunfire gets closer before an explosion sounds out, shaking the walls all around me. The faint smell of smoke carries in the air, and an odd thrill shoots down my spine as my gaze bounces between Deliom, Fredrick and Rob. Because they might be the ones who set this trap for Sitri, but unless they take him down with those bullets, they're the ones ill-equipped and unprepared.

Another explosion sounds out closer than before, just as more shots erupt on the other side of the wall behind me.

The thought that Sitri saw the flyer and walked headfirst into a trap just to save me from execution makes my chest tighten, and I have to fight the urge to smile.

Another explosion rumbles behind me, and dust falls from the ceiling as a long web of cracks lines the wall. Deliom barks something at the others, and they turn away, disappearing into the shadows and out of my sight.

Within seconds another blast goes off, rattling the chair beneath me. My fingers tighten around the arm of the chair until they're numb, and when pieces of the ceiling start to crumble to the ground, I twitch away from them. The rumble of gunfire around the room gets louder, and when another explosion goes off, sending pieces of wall flying out from behind me, I flinch.

Dust fills the air and I squint against it as I cautiously raise my head, still hearing pieces of debris fall around me. Footsteps grow closer to my right, and my heart's in my chest as Sitri's tall form comes into view. The familiar sight of his robes draped over him sends a wave of relief over me, and that relief is doubled when he doesn't seem to have any concerning injuries.

With his face still covered, my heart stutters as his burning gaze falls to my wrists. Even with most of his face covered, the rage in his eyes is clear.

"Did they hurt you?"

His silken voice is a balm to my soul, and tears brim in the corner of my eyes as I shake my head, but my tears aren't because of any fear or terror I'd felt.

No. The tears forming in the corners of my eyes are because he came for me. He fought through an entire military base and risked everything to keep me from being executed.

He kneels in front of me, finding the cuffs holding me hostage as he curls his fingers between my skin and the metal. It takes mere seconds for it to melt away. The remnants of it drip to the floor as his hands rest on my legs, and he tilts his face to meet my gaze.

He freezes as the mechanical whirring of the door behind him fills the air, and my eyes widen as a unit of soldiers spread out along the wall with their weapons aimed. But they're not trained on Sitri.

They're directed at me.

My heart thunders, and he glances on either side of him, his sunlight gaze flicking from each of the barrels before settling on.

I see the decision in his eyes as he makes it.

"Don't." I whisper, and his hands cup the back of my thighs. "They will kill you."

I don't care if they hear me now. Not when I'm on the verge of losing the one person I trust. The one person who knows me. The prince of hell who saved me, but showed me the real light in this world.

The man who became the light to me, when everything was cast in shadows.

They say to be loved is to be seen, and damn if Sitri didn't show me every moment of every day how he's seen me.

I know I'll spend the rest of my life hoping I can do the same for him.

But he needs to *live* for that to happen.

"Time is up, magic user. Give yourself up or she dies."

"Leave." I mouth to him, but I see that it's no use. Not with the way his fingers flex against the back of my knees, and before I can even understand what's happening, he jerks me into him.

My body slides off the chair faster than I can comprehend, and within a fraction of a breath, I'm completely covered by his body. Two shots ring out before heat engulfs the area, just as a deafening explosion goes off.

The ground beneath us erupts just as Sitri's body's ripped from mine, and we're hurled in the opposite directions. I'm only airborne for a moment, twisting in the air as my vision becomes a blur.

I slam into something solid and my head collides with a hard surface before everything goes dark.

Chapter 32

A radiating throb pounds through my skull, and I peel my eyes open.

A rhythmic beeping in tune to my heart rate picks up, and I survey the familiar hospital room with a dull sense of panic. My monitor beeps even faster as I recount the moments before I passed out.

If I'm here, that means that Deliom is probably still alive...

But then what happened to Sitri?

Footsteps in the hallway grow closer, and Kira's the first to walk in at a brisk pace. Surprise flashes across her face before she schools her features, and my mouth drops open to ask her where Sitri is, but the words die on my lips as Deliom breezes through the doorway behind her.

The heart rate monitor beeps faster, and it takes a conscious effort to slow my breathing.

"Ms. Sylvara. Glad to see you're recovering well."

I meet his gaze and nod, not trusting my voice as he strides closer to the bed. His gaze travels over the bandages on my legs and arms, and I fight the urge to squirm.

Did they see the sigil before they'd brought me here?

Or are they going to use me to lure Sitri back?

Whatever the hell he wants, it's clear that Sitri didn't kill them, so I stay quiet, waiting for him to break the news that Sitri got away.

That'll teach them to lure him into a trap.

"I know our methods were unconventional, but I hope you can understand, Maris. What we did was for the good of everyone. There was no other way." The Kira keeps herself busy beside me as his calloused palm roughly pats the back of my hand. "Your invaluable assistance in helping us capture the feared magic user will have us all forever in your debt."

My blood runs cold, and the beep from the monitor mimics the way my heart stutters.

Did he just say capture?

No. That can't be right.

Sitri, *captured*?

A full bag of fluids plops onto the bed near my knee. "I'm sorry, General. I believe she's still shaken from the traumatic event." Kira murmurs, and Deliom just nods.

"Ah, yes, yes. Well, I'll take my leave. But Sylvara, when you're rested, you and Robert will accompany Fredrick as we make one final push against the rebellion to help local authorities crush what remains of the resistance."

He takes a few long strides before he disappears around the corner, and my gaze slides to Kira's as she unravels the bandages over my limbs.

When there are no injuries beneath them, I frown, keeping my voice only a whisper. "What's with the bandages?"

Her gaze flicks to the door as she continues to unravel, but she taps the sigil on my thigh gently. "Who else do you know heals *this* quickly?"

Come to think of it, my bullet wound had healed fast, too.

The lump in my throat grows that he'd given me a portion of his power that would keep me alive, knowing that if they knew who I was, they'd try to kill me.

My brows shoot up, and she nods almost imperceptibly. "I think you'll be ready to go into the field, Ms. Sylvara. Just keep your back to the wall and your eyes open."

I swallow hard as she methodically unravels the rest of my bindings, her eyes flicking between her hands to the doorway.

Guilt twists my gut when I remember that I'd assumed she'd told them about my sigil.

Kira sets the used bandages aside before shifting her attention to the myriad of cords attached to my chest. When she hovers over me to peel the last and furthest one from my skin, her voice is hardly audible.

"There's a top level security facility ten miles south. They will keep him there until he breaks, or they kill him."

Sitri would never break, which means...

My eyes are wide, and adrenaline pumps into my veins in earnest as footsteps pass by the door to our room and she straightens.

"Thank you, Kira." I murmur, swinging my legs from the bed and sliding my feet into the slippers waiting for me.

She walks over and hands me a fresh set of clothes, but she says nothing—her attention split between me and the door, as if worried that someone could walk through it any minute.

"I'll give you some privacy to change." She murmurs, not waiting for my response as she exits the room, closing the door behind her with a click.

I don't stop to think, I just move. Within seconds, the hospital gown drops to the floor, and I tug the jeans and shirt on quickly. My feet carry me toward the door, and Kira's gaze meets mine.

She just gives me a nod, and I'm on autopilot as I navigate the corridors to my quarters, mulling over my next course of action.

If I go straight to this facility for Sitri, I'll be out-manned and out-smarted. There's no way I can get into a facility like that with nothing but my bare hands.

Still...

Sitri's freedom needs to come before they make the final push against the rebellion though... Otherwise, all of this will have been for nothing.

And I refuse to let that happen.

The sigil on my thigh is almost burning as I key the pin into the pad of the door to my quarters and slip inside. The door clicks shut, and I slide the lock into place.

No, this has to go perfectly... starting with my story.

Opening the laptop, I get to work, adjusting what I'd written to tell even more of the truth than I'd originally intended.

What's the worst Thornton can do? Say no? Have Deliom arrest me?

I'd like to see him try.

It takes me an hour to finalize everything, but by the time I'm done, I search up the email address for Casey Warner from Channel Five News—Thornton's biggest competitor, and my heart thrums steadily in my throat as I hit send.

I draft the same email and send it to Thornton, and a handful of other outlets I know would be interested.

Casey will run with the story, I know that much, but if I can get it into the mainstream circuit? That's the lottery.

My eyes widen at the idea that forms, and I type in the address to a well known streaming site.

The chances of this working are low.... but not zero.

And I need to do everything I can.

It takes me another twenty minutes to set up the stream to loop the content, and I leave my computer open as my watch's alarm goes off.

Shit.

Changing into a dark pair of jeans and one of my t-shirts, I hurry out the door. My footsteps feel louder than ever as I navigate the barren hallway. Part of me is grateful for the lack of foot traffic, but the more rational side of me has to wonder if it's because Sitri killed so many or because Deliom called them elsewhere.

By the time I get to the front entrance where Fredrick stands with both his teams and Rob waiting, my nerves are frayed.

Fredrick nods his head once as our eyes meet. "Let's go, Sylvara. War waits for no one."

Rob files into the first truck with the rest of A-Team, and even though habit pushes me to follow, I pivot to the left. Falling into line behind Lennard, I don't waste a second as I pile into the truck with the rest of B-team.

Lennard slides into his seat, his gaze focusing on me as his eyes widen, and I hurry into the seat next to him. He says nothing as he adjusts the muzzle of his rifle between his knees, aimed to the ground.

I wish I could see Rob's face when he realizes I'm veering off course from what he would consider normal, but I'm more eager to get this over with.

Because the sooner I can get into wherever they're holding Sitri, the better we'll all be off. And if they don't bring me to him willingly, I'll just find some other way.

The vehicle lurches into motion, swaying back and forth over the uneven road as we leave the gates of the base behind. We aren't on the road for long before we pull past another enormous set of gates, guarded by not two, not four, but *six* soldiers armed to the teeth.

For whatever reason, this base is more guarded, but the buildings within are a mere portion of the size of the main barracks. The main building we pull up to is dome-shaped, with plenty of cameras aimed at, and away from the entrance.

The truck lurches to a stop, and I watch through the windshield as Fredrick takes long strides into the building. No one else moves to get out, and my heart thrums steadily.

My thigh where the sigil's burned into my skin gets more warm, and I gently glide my thumb along it.

With how close we are to the main barracks? Could this be where they're holding him?

For a moment, I allow myself to imagine it. Waltzing into the building and demanding entry, only to be denied and subsequently try to force my way in.

The sigil burns so much that it's become itchy, and I rub it with more force to ease the sensation.

I'm lost in my imagination when Lennard's leg bumps into mine, and I freeze as I snap back to the present. Pressure in my fingertips drags my vision down, and I stare at where my nails have dug into my thigh overtop the sigil.

I swallow hard.

My gaze slides to Lennard's bright blue irises, and I ignore the note of concern in them. Inclining my head, my attention focuses on the building beyond the windshield once more.

One thing at a time, Maris.

The truck in front of ours rolls forward as ours follows, and something deep inside of me wants to rage against leaving. It's like my blood is rioting with every inch of distance we gain, and with every passing minute, I get more and more antsy.

By the time we come to a stop again, I'm vibrating with the need to get out of the vehicle and spread my legs... And maybe sprint all the way back to that building.

Fuck.

He has to be there.

Everything in me knows it.

I don't know how or why I know it—maybe because of these sigils, but I do.

B-team starts to unload from the vehicle, and I follow in close with Lennard at my back. It's an odd comfort having him around, one that I don't give myself a second to think too much about.

Because if he's part of this, then he's just as bad as the rest.

Still, it doesn't mean I can't appreciate his presence. He's been an ally this long... let's hope he doesn't stop now.

B-team heads toward the nearest building that stands tall beside the other vacant offices that surround it. Soldiers stand ready on either side of us, and I feel Rob's burning gaze on me as we pass by A-team, but I can't focus on him right now.

Not when I'm fighting the urge to become Kharidia's greatest track star.

Fredrick leads the way inside, and that's when the stark difference between our other excursions and this one suddenly hits me. All the other encampments we'd accompanied them to didn't have anyone stationed there already. They were empty as far as we'd known.

So then why does this one not only have a full company but also now us supporting it?

Unease washes over me, and we file into the large main room as Fredrick steps aside to talk with who I assume to be the one in charge.

My watch vibrates, and I bring my wrist up to look at the screen. Seeing Thornton's name, my heart rate spikes, and I read through the first two sentences before my teeth grind together.

Thornton: Your story is a fantasy, Sylvara. One which doesn't align with our vision...

I don't bother to read any further and turn my gaze to the television in the corner of the room as a local news station runs their own stories. Without audio, and how far away it is, I can only make out the man on the screen's general appearance as he talks into the camera.

My leg bounces quickly as my mind runs through the various ways I could get back to that gated facility when Rob suddenly fills my line of vision.

"We need to talk." He murmurs, and I roll my eyes.

"We have nothing to talk about, Rob."

Rob just glowers, glancing around us. "Maris, I'm serious."

The way he's keeping his voice low sends a hint of curiosity through me, and he gestures to the door behind us.

"Can we talk?" He searches my face. "Please."

Even with all the horrible things he's done, there was a part of Rob that I'd once trusted. One that I'd spent months on end with, working and living together.

This is one of those moments where I have trouble reconciling that the Rob I knew would so easily have done what he had to me.

Holding his gaze, I just nod, and he quickly brushes past me, with the B-team falling in line alongside us.

I don't know why he's suddenly interested in discussing things, but as long as Lennard and the others are with me, I'm not overly concerned.

More so Lennard than the others, actually.

He might be the only person here that I have a modicum of trust in.

That's a dangerous thought.

The six of us turn left down a hallway, and Rob continues to lead us down a long corridor before cutting right into a side room. Once we're all inside, Rob pulls out his phone for a moment, touching his screen twice before tucking it into his pocket.

His hard gaze scans the room before landing on Lennard, lingering on him for a moment before settling on me. "Who was he?"

I frown. "Who?"

His jaw clenches. "The magic user."

My heart stutters in my chest. Clearly he doesn't know, but deep inside, the terrifying notion that Sitri's survival hinges upon my ability to break him out makes me wonder what the risk is if he figures it out.

"I don't know what you're talking about, Rob."

"Don't lie to me, Maris." He barks and catches himself with his palms out. "Just tell me the truth. You owe me that much."

A radio sounds out in the room, and my gaze slides over Rob's shoulder to see Lennard's eyes widen. The other soldiers murmur to one another, and file out of the room.

Remembering the text Rob sent when we got in here, my heart stutters wildly. Was this a fucking trap?

Rob sighs and turns to face the wall to my right as Lennard looks like he's going to go against direct orders just to not leave me alone with this asshole.

His blue eyes bounce between me and Rob, but I shake my head before jutting it toward the door. He seems to reluctantly get the hint, and I turn toward Rob.

Hearing Lennard's footsteps disappear into the hallway, Rob sighs as he turns around. "Why was he so obsessed with finding you, Maris? Why did the trap work?"

I frown again, blood raging in my ears as the door behind me clicks shut. "I have no idea."

In typical Rob fashion, his entire demeanor changes now that we're alone. He stalks up close, searching my eyes as if he's looking for the root of my deceit. The unhinged way his wide gaze searches mine makes me nervous, and I take a tentative step back.

"They will torture him, Maris. They'll do things to make him wish he were dead." Unable to stop myself, my eyes widen, and I take another step back. "And if I were them, I would start with *you*. I'd torture you in front of him and make him watch as they break you and put you back together. Because if he cares enough to run into an enemy military base, seeing you die over and over again would be the worst torture of all."

His hand snaps forward faster than I can register, and his fingers bite into my throat as he walks me back three steps.

I lose my footing on the third and trip on nothing. My weight shuffles backward, bringing him back with me as if he'd rather fall than let me go.

My back slams into the unforgiving flooring, knocking the air from my lungs and within seconds, his weight's heavy on my chest. I thrash to push him off, but he's locked both hands around my throat.

"I won't let them, Maris—I won't let them hurt you."

His words are a stark contrast to his actions, and the pressure in my head is so great that it could explode as his fingers tighten around the column of my throat.

Stars fill my vision, and the sigil on my thigh burns to the point of pain as I dig at it with my nails through my jeans. They tear at my skin through the thick fabric as my vision dims.

Sitri's face is the only thing I see as I force my nails impossibly deeper, ignoring the pain as I dig at it, scratching my thigh until I'm near certain my nails are bleeding.

I was a fool to come here. My false sense of security was just that. Not even Lennard can save me.

Heat engulfs my leg first, and my eyes squeeze shut as it spreads over the rest of my body.

Warmth like the sun, a feeling that I welcome like my lover's embrace covers every inch of my body.

Rob's screams are the first thing I notice before his grip disappears from my neck entirely, and my eyes snap open to him hurling himself from my chest.

His mouth drops open in a silent scream, and he rolls on the floor, writhing in pain as the flames devour every inch of his body. The worst shock comes as his eyes burn in their sockets first, sinking in as his skin literally cooks in front of me.

I don't look away as his body becomes unrecognizable; the skin sloughing off before bubbling on the ground, with his muscle and bone quickly charring.

It only takes mere seconds before he's a heap of black and white dust on the ground, but those seconds lasted an eternity to me. The worst part is that I don't know if I'm more horrified by what happened, or my reaction.

I shouldn't be relieved.

I shouldn't be happy.

Yet some sick and twisted part of me is both.

Movement to my right catches my eye, and my face snaps to the doorway, only to find Lennard standing there with wide eyes.

Shit.

His gaze drops from me to my thigh, and I glance down, seeing the blood that's seeped through my jeans over Sitri's sigil.

Blood from the wound that's already healing.

"It's not–"

"Save your words, Maris." He pulls down his mask and flashes a broad grin. "If you hadn't killed him, I would have."

I blink at him. "Are you not concerned about—"

"You controlling flames? No. I'm relieved, actually."

My brows shoot up. He can't be serious right now.

"Why *relieved*?"

Lennard's smile just grows impossibly wider. "Because you're going to light this place up."

Chapter 33

There's no way he just watched me burn my ex-boyfriend alive and has no issue with it.

"You can't be serious, Lennard." I whisper, glancing between him and the door.

"It's our only shot, Maris. If they think they have the wrong guy, we can use that to our advantage."

Our? He's talking as if he's...

"You're a demon." I whisper, and he lets out a dark chuckle with a playful tilt of his head.

"You didn't think we'd just lay back and let these guys run rampant, did you? We might have rules that stop us from taking over, but joining the ranks and being shit soldiers doesn't break any rules."

I gape at him, which only makes him laugh harder.

"I have to admit, though; it's pretty satisfying that you turned your ex into dust using Sitri's power. Kind of poetic, actually." He sighs wistfully, and I push to my feet.

Pacing toward him with a wince, each movement jostles the cut to my thigh. For whatever reason, that cut seems to take longer than usual to heal, and I can only imagine it has to do with the sigil.

Once I'm standing next to Lennard, I turn around to look at the room. "You're sure about this?"

He just laughs under his breath. "As sure as I'll ever be. Light 'em up, Maris, so we can go stir up some shit."

It takes everything in me not to smile at the sudden change in Lennard's behavior, but I suppose if he was playing the perfectly imperfect soldier when I'd met him, it only makes sense.

My gaze sweeps over the room, landing on the large pile of ash on the ground in the center.

The problem is, I don't know how the hell I managed to do that, nor do I know how to do it again on purpose.

If only Sitri were here to show me.

"How do I—?" Before I can finish my sentence, flame erupts from the floor in a circle, with lines in the center forming in an intricate pattern. The lines and curves of white flame meet before separating, and within seconds I'm staring at a fiery pattern that matches the sigil on my shoulder.

"Holy shit." Lennard breathes before the flames rise higher. The wood and tile is the first to char as the fire spreads to all corners of the room. It consumes everything in its path, moving across cement and brick before rising along the walls.

Sitri's magic travels along the ceiling, turning everything it touches bright red and yellow before it turns to coal. The wooden beams overhead groan, and my eyes widen as they warp and buckle.

I'm still staring at it all with a sense of wonder when Lennard's hand wraps around my bicep and tugs me toward the door. "While I trust you to call them off when you need to, we need to go before we get caught out."

He wraps my arm around his shoulder and reaches down to grip the back of my legs. Hauling me into his chest with ease, he takes long strides from the room and down the hall as the crackling of burning wood grows louder behind us.

Dark smoke has already lined the top of the hallway, and I swallow hard at the fact that I wasn't going to leave the room, even with everything burning down.

I think part of me was relieved to have a piece of Sitri so close... but if I'm going to free him, I'm going to have to be more careful not to get wrapped up.

We're nearly to the main room where everyone else waits, and his pace quickens. "Follow my lead."

My eyes squeeze shut, and I lean into his chest as he bursts through the door to the main room. My heart's in my throat and everyone's faces turn to us, their weapons in their hands jerking at the sudden movement.

A handful of eyes widen at the sight of blood on my leg, and the soldiers shift to the walls to make room for us, while others raise their weapons and hurry to the hallway.

"The magic user is here." Lennard bellows, and that's when chaos ensues. Bodies rush past us toward the hallway as they hurry to inspect the scene of the crime.

My crime.

"What's the meaning of this?!" Fredrick's voice cuts through the madness that's taken over everyone around us. "The magic user was captured."

Lennard places me on the floor and rips part of his shirt off to press it to my thigh that has since stopped bleeding. I could almost laugh at how well he's selling it, so I wince at the pressure and inhale sharply. My acting must be too good, because Lennard's pressure on my thigh relaxes ever so slightly, as if he thought I might actually be in pain.

He levels Fredrick with his stare. "Then there must be more than one, or we got the wrong guy. I just walked in the room as the other correspondent was being burned to a crisp and a hostile fleeing the premises."

"And you didn't take a shot?" Fredrick's eyes burn as he glares at Lennard, and my heart pounds.

"It's my fault!" Lennard's grip tightens on me in what I'm certain is a warning. "I was screaming for help. I distracted him, I'm so sorry."

His grip loosens, and Fredrick murmurs something into his radio before turning his full focus on Lennard. "Secure the correspondent. This operation is on hold until we get eyes on the magic user. A-Team, with me."

I silently wonder if this alone will be enough to convince them that the magic user is here, and at that same moment, an explosion shakes the house.

The sudden quake that rattles the walls has everyone ducking, eyeing the ceiling warily.

I don't have time to speculate if that was my doing or some kind of curated response from Lennard as he wraps a long strip of cloth around my leg, and I wince as his arms jerk to tighten it.

A-Team's a rush of bodies following Fredrick's barked commands as they disappear down the hallway we'd come out of. Not that they'll find anything.

Lennard's arms hook under my body, and he hauls me into his chest with practiced ease. His strides to the door are long, purposeful, and my jaw drops when I see the armored truck we arrived in burnt black. White flames still engulf the body of it, and some part of me balks that I don't even remember thinking about wanting to do that.

Lennard angles me away from the searing heat as if it could hurt me, and rushes to the remaining truck with the other soldiers of B-team following close behind. He throws open the door, and hauls us both inside with so much ease that I start to wonder if carrying me is even challenging at all for him.

Is it a normal demon trait to be this strong?

By the time we're settled into the back of the armored truck, the others from both units have climbed in with us. Those who don't have seats sit on the ground while the others stand over them.

Fredrick shouts for his second in command to drive, and the engine rumbles to life before we lurch forward, tires spinning as we make a series of left turns.

My heart is in my throat as we head back the way we came at break-neck speeds. Each turn lurches the truck to one side, and everyone leans to counteract the weight. Through it all, Lennard remains steadfast at my side, his large hand covering the wound on my thigh to—at the very least—keep up our story.

It's a relief that Fredrick demanded to get eyes on the magic user, but the question is, how the fuck do *we* get inside?

We need to make sure they bring us, not just leave us in the car.

I chew the inside of my cheek, and my eyes slide from Lennard's hand on my thigh to his face. He focuses his bright blue irises on the windshield, and the truck sways as we hit a bump in the road.

What if the magic user were following us? That might put more pressure on them.

It takes us half the time to get to the smaller base, and when we pull up to the gates, my eyes slide shut. My limbs hum with the need to find Sitri, which has only gotten worse with every second we've spent driving toward the barracks.

God, I hope this works.

Within seconds, shouting breaks out and Fredrick's second-in-command bellows over the rest.

"The hostile's still in the vicinity, Captain." My eyes snap open to see Lennard's fascinated blue gaze already fixated on me.

He says nothing, but I can see the mischievous glint to them, and I already know he'd be praising my use of Sitri's power.

The thought is as reassuring as the look in his eye, and I drop my gaze to my thigh.

The vehicle lurches forward again as the driver slams his brakes, and we all slide toward the front of the truck before it comes to a full stop.

Soldiers file out in a hurry as Lennard hauls me into his arms, and I stay quiet as we follow Fredrick inside. A handful of soldiers stop to stand guard at the main doors, leaving just Fredrick, me, and Lennard with the rest. The panicked admin behind the front desk looks at us wide-eyed as Fredrick barks orders, not bothering to stop to talk to the concerned admin.

Fredrick leads us through winding hallways before coming to a stop in front of an elevator and scans his badge. He quickly punches in a code, and my heart hammers so hard against my rib cage that I'm almost certain it could beat out of my chest.

The elevator doors slide open, and we file into the tight space that's grown even more cramped with so many of us trying to fit. My hand covers my thigh as I grow more antsy, fighting the urge to squirm as the doors shut once more.

As if he can sense my nervousness, Lennard's hands tighten on my body, and I lean into him, inhaling a centering breath.

We're almost there.

I can feel it.

It's as if this sigil on my thigh can sense Sitri like radar, and with every second we grow closer, my body is nearly vibrating. If Lennard wasn't clutching me to his chest, I'm almost certain that my knees wouldn't be able to support my weight.

The elevator drops lower and with each breath, each heartbeat, it feels like I might implode.

Our descent slows to a stop, and a long moment passes before the doors slide open at an agonizing pace that has me wanting to scream. Each inch the doors widen exposes the room beyond, filled with people closely monitoring computers with touch screens, flashing and beeping lights.

It reminds me of some alien movie, like they've got some organic being that isn't of this world that they're keeping confined and away from the rest of the human race.

I suppose, in some sense, they might be.

We step out of the elevator, and Deliom's voice booms as I flinch. "What the fuck is the meaning of this, Fredrick?!"

"Sir, I know this breaks protocol—" Watching the two at odds with one another is odd, since Fredrick isn't a small man by any means. Deliom's presence is just intimidating enough that he seems larger than life as his face reddens.

"Breaks protocol? You're lucky I don't execute you all on the spot. You have five seconds to explain yourself before I take action."

Fredrick nods, and his throat bobs. "There's a hostile magic user on our trail, sir. This is the safest place for us to be."

"What the *hell* are you talking about, Fredrick? There's only one magic user in this damned country, and he's on the other side of this wall, wrapped in rhodium cuffs and fed a palladium diet."

My jaw clenches as Deliom paints the picture of what they've done to Sitri, and I lock eyes with Lennard. The barely contained fury in his expression tells me everything I need to know about what rhodium and palladium will do to Sitri.

"How do you know for sure that you have the magic user?" I ask, shifting in Lennard's arms as he moves to set me on my feet.

Fredrick twists as if he suddenly remembered he had an audience, and Deliom's face turns an impossible hue of reddish purple, with the vein in his forehead looking like it might burst.

"Are you implying we don't know who we captured?!"

I fight to school my features, but can't help the way my brow rises. "Judging by your defensiveness, I don't know that you do. Did he even use magic when you captured him? Did you get proof of his abilities?"

The vein in his forehead pulsates, looking like it might finally rupture from his skin as his chest heaves. "There's no way for us to know without him using it in front of our equipment, and it would be impossible for him to use his magic now."

I preen at the opening he's given me, but keep my features schooled. "So you captured some random man without proof of his abilities? When were you going to seek me out? Considering I'm the only person who has seen his actual face."

Deliom's face turns a shade pale, but instead of screaming or yelling at me, he turns his attention to the workers sitting near a thick, reinforced door.

"Open the doors." When the attendants hesitate, he slams his fist against the table nearest to him, and I jolt. "I said open the fucking doors!"

The attendants face forward, typing onto their keyboards before pressing a few buttons on the touchscreen, and my heart thrashes in my chest.

Deliom stalks over to the door with Fredrick and a handful of others, and it slowly slides open.

This is it.

We're coming, Sitri.

Chapter 34

The door inches open, I haven't thought through what I'm going to do once I get to him, and this bridge I knew I'd have to cross at some point is fast approaching.

I'd pictured finding him with no one around, and helping a fully lucid and powerful Sitri to escape. It was stupid to think they'd have let him keep his powers while captured.

My heart thrums steadily as I count the heads that wait in a line, prepared to witness me confirming Sitri's identity. There's a chance I could lie and say he isn't the magic user, they'd probably try to kill him, though and his immortality would prove me wrong, anyway.

Knowing who we have in this room, and the opportunity it presents... Could the risk be worth the reward?

My gaze finds Lennard's, and even though his face remains mostly unreadable, the rage behind his bright blue eyes mirrors my own, and that's when I know exactly what I plan to do with this bridge I'm crossing.

"Lennard, guard the elevator." I whisper, and he inclines his head, swinging his rifle over in front of his chest. He takes a step back to stand in front of the doors and squares his shoulders.

Deliom, Fredrick and a handful of others step into the oval room, and I slowly follow in after them as my resolve settles deep into my bones. They line either side of the room, but my eyes remain glued on Sitri's prone form, face down on the concrete floor.

Two solid metal chains embedded into the cement are taut to his wrists, with a third visible beneath him which I can only assume tethers his neck to the floor.

Seeing the strongest man I've ever met, chained and unconscious, solidifies every decision I've yet to make, calcifying it into the marrow of my being.

Everything I'm about to do is nowhere near what they deserve.

My next steps feel more steady–*more sure*-than they ever have, and I turn to look at Lennard by the elevator once more. His eyes are bright, and he taps the side of his rifle twice in acknowledgement before I turn back around to face Sitri.

Deliom gestures to his limp form impatiently. "Well? What are you waiting for, Sylvara? Hurry up and tell us if this is the fucking magic user!"

My gaze slides from one of them to the other, looking directly into the eyes of the bridge I'm about to burn. When they settle on Sitri once more, I feel the sigil on my thigh sear even hotter than ever before.

It's a comfortable heat, and I welcome the burn as it turns scorching. My gaze lingers on Sitri as an incessant beeping resounds behind me.

"He must be waking up." Someone says, their words rushing from them as they step back toward the wall.

"Sir—!" Someone shrieks and their words cut off abruptly before they can continue. I don't need to turn around to know that the machines are picking up my use of Sitri's power.

"Sylvara! Do it!" Deliom shouts, and Fredrick suddenly throws his weapon to the ground with wide eyes. The handle of his rifle has turned red from the heat, and he upturns his scorched palms.

His chest heaves as his eyes turn to me. "You. It's you—you're the magic user."

Obviously not, but I won't tell them that. Wouldn't do any good since they're about to die, anyway.

Time to burn this fucking bridge down.

My hair whips around as heat engulfs the area and flames erupt along the edge of the room, blocking the way out with a wall of fire. They flick higher as Deliom and the others turn in a circle, looking for a way out.

But they won't find one.

Flames encircle Sitri's body, curving over him protectively as I step close. The flames on the outskirts of the room mimic my movement, spreading wider, and with each consecutive step I take, the men surrounding me scream out frantic pleas.

But I don't stop.

Three steps in, the first of them catch fire. His piercing wails should have given me pause, but I can't bring myself to stop as I remember the little girl I'd held hands with being gunned down. The flames latch onto his body as he flails, as if hungry to devour him and he runs toward the others.

"Sylvara, stop this!"

I watch them dodge out of his way, and he collapses against the wall before I take another step. The flames leap at another one of Deliom's officers, barreling into his chest and quickly swallowing his face with white-hot flames.

"Maris!" Deliom bellows.

When the skin sloughs off his cheeks, I turn to face Sitri again.

The moment my foot leaves the ground once more, I see the fire launch toward Fredrick, and he stumbles back, falling into the flames that surround him.

Another step has white flames curling into the air like a cage around Deliom before surging forward from all angles. The sound of his screams is such a desperate contrast to his barked threats, and it takes everything I have not to smile.

One by one, the flames devour each soldier, and by the time I've taken the last step toward the dome that covers Sitri, none of them remain. The beeping from the other room has become a constant alarm, and the dome of white fire extinguishes as I kneel before Sitri.

How still he is, even with the fire surrounding him, makes emotion clog my throat, and I choke it down.

My palms cover the metal at his wrists, and without a second thought, the flames around us grow higher as the metal heats. The silvery white metal sweats, beads of metal running down the sides as I melt through the cuffs. Even though it takes time, there's a poetic justice in the way I feel it melt away from his wrists —the same way he must have felt when he destroyed the cuffs they'd put on me.

Screams from the other room die down, and I roll Sitri onto his side to get access to the metal around his neck. His handsome features are slack, and when I see the red and purple welts in his skin, spanning from his cheeks to his neck, something in my gut twists.

If I hadn't already killed them all, I would have now. Just more painfully, and much, much slower.

When the chains around his neck don't melt like the cuffs did, I frown and urge more scalding heat into it. Slowly, the metal warps, beading down and dripping to the floor at an agonizing pace. By the time the metal's disappeared from his neck, Sitri hasn't moved an inch, and my heart's lodged in my throat.

My fingers brush his cold skin first, and my palms flatten against his shoulder as I prod him gently. "Sitri." When he doesn't move, I repeat the action with more urgency. "Sitri, please."

Maybe if I can just get him out of here and somewhere safe, whatever they gave him can run its course. There's no way I can carry him out of here, though.

Glancing over my shoulder as the flames in the doorway dissipate, I lock eyes with Lennard, and he takes long strides into the room without a word. The still burning flames disperse as he walks, clearing a path to where I kneel alongside Sitri.

"Help me get him out of here." I whisper, and Lennard kneels beside me.

I know whatever this palladium diet is has weakened him, but I already nearly lost him once. I never want to get that close to losing him again.

When Lennard leans forward, he pauses, and my gaze slides to his. "You'll have to clear the way to the truck, Maris."

He searches my face and I nod, knowing that he's really saying I'll have to kill more people than I already have.

It wasn't so hard when I knew they were directly responsible for Sitri's imprisonment because I'd seen firsthand the grievances of their involvement.

"What about others—like you?"

He flashes a devilish grin. "They've cleared out of the barracks. Most of them are at safe houses that Sitri's created over the years, and others went to help civilians to steer clear of the military encampments. Knowing how many powerful people are involved in this conflict, I wouldn't be surprised if something drastic happened in retaliation."

Filing away the information, I push to my feet. "Then we find somewhere safe for Sitri to recover."

I don't mention the hint of a plan that's formed as Lennard hauls Sitri's large body over his shoulder. That he picked me up with ease seems to pale in comparison to him lifting Sitri with minimal effort.

"You really aren't human, are you?" I whisper, and Lennard chuckles quietly with a shake of his head.

"Human-passing maybe." He muses, and I huff a dry laugh as I lead the way to the elevator. Dismembered bodies lie scattered on the floor around us, with splattered blood coating almost every surface.

Between the damage to the bodies and me not remembering a single gunshot being fired, tells me there's a lot to Lennard that I don't know yet.

When we get to the elevator, I press the button, and it dings before the doors slide open. For a moment I debate asking Lennard about how he killed them to satisfy my curiosity, but the other part of me would rather not know.

If they have any surveillance to hear his answer, he'll be on the run for the rest of his life, or until they kill him, too.

Even though we've freed Sitri, there's no telling how much information they have on him now or how many people in high places are aware of this operation in Kharidia. Never mind the connections they might have.

The doors slide shut, and I stare at Sitri's unconscious form with a bitter note of frustration.

If the humans and servilians in the world knew the truth, would they rise up? If they knew that a secret war between demons and angels was curating tensions to farm souls for an endless war, would they do something to stop the violence?

Would they be inclined to rage against the system that oppresses them from the shadows for its own gain?

Or would they simply choose to remain silent because they fear for their livelihoods?

Part of me knows the latter will happen regardless, but if enough people mobilized, they wouldn't be able to be stopped. City by city, country by country, we could change *everything*.

But it starts with us—the wind that blows the embers of truth toward them.

It's what the rest of the world does with the truth that will determine the future.

The elevator slows to a stop, and the doors slide open as we come face to face with an armed soldier. He glances between Lennard and me before his eyes settle on Sitri, and I see the moment he realizes what's happening.

He jerks to bring his weapon up, and my heart thrashes wildly. "Stop!" I whisper loudly, and the man freezes. His eyes glaze over as they fixate on me. "Escort us out, and if anyone asks, we are transporting the prisoner to a secured location per General Deliom's orders."

The armed man blinks twice slowly, and robotically turns away from us as I swallow hard. We follow in close as we keep a brisk pace down the hallway. Footsteps not in time with ours grow closer, and when an officer turns a corner toward us, my heart stutters.

The officer eyes the four of us before landing on the soldier escorting us with a narrowed gaze.

"We don't have transport orders—what's going on here?"

Our movement halts, and I glance between the soldier and officer as anxiety builds in my chest. I'm about to speak up when the soldier's voice fills the air, and the words die on my lips.

"Orders came down from General Deliom—immediate evac authorization. We're cleared to move without delay" The officer stiffens, before giving us a tentative nod.

"I'll be confirming that with Command." He jerks his head in the direction he came, but doesn't push further before he continues walking.

His footsteps disappear behind us, and I know we need to hurry before we're caught.

"Let's go. We don't have much time." I whisper, and Lennard whistles quietly.

"I half expected to have to kill him." He muses. "Good work, Maris."

We have to stop once more when questioned, but the moment General Deliom is brought up, we're ushered on our way. The soldiers who had remained guarding the doors are gone as we hurry out of the entrance, and I spot the second armored truck parked just behind the one we'd come in.

I only know it's the one we'd come in because of the charcoal that coats parts of it, like it had driven through a forest fire. With adrenaline pumping through me, we reach the truck and I notice the soldier straighten. He gives me a stiff salute, pausing, and I realize he's waiting to be dismissed.

"Return to the elevator and complete what you were planning to do prior to assisting us."

He drops his hand with a nod and turns on his heel to head inside once more. The soldier heads back the way we came, and I watch Lennard secure Sitri in the passenger seat. I lean in to press a tender kiss to Sitri's drooped forehead, and my chest tightens when he's entirely unresponsive.

We both walk around the front to the driver's side, and as Lennard climbs in, my gaze lands on the man I've seen at death's door two too many times.

Ever since the day I met Sitri, my life hasn't been the same.

He's brought color to a black and white canvas plagued with grey.

The moment we met was a one in a million chance, a needle in a haystack, and yet, just meeting him was enough to alter the course of my life.

Lennard turns the key as the engine rumbles to life, and I slide my gaze to the truck behind us, feeling tears pool in the corners of my eyes.

Sitri deserves to live a life free of their influence, free of war, free of fighting and cruelty. He deserves happiness, and he has the rest of eternity to find it.

What is my measly life compared to the good he can achieve in twice that long?

"Maris..." Lennard's voice is half warning, and I feel a rogue tear fall. "Don't do what I think you're about to do."

My eyes find Lennard's and my resolve settles in. "Bring him to Anne so he can recover. Tell him—" the lump in my throat grows, and I shudder. "When he wakes up, tell him I loved him." I whisper, and the taste of something sweet makes my mouth water.

Lennard's ocean blue eyes brim with red, and he just shakes his head, but he puts the truck into drive. "Tell him yourself, you stubborn woman."

"Go, Lennard. Now." Bouncing back on my heel, I slam the door shut and head for the driver's side of the second vehicle at full speed.

Thankfully, the keys are still in the ignition, and as I feel the reverberation of the engine beneath my feet, it takes everything to swallow my own nerves.

This is crazy.

This entire plan is crazy.

But maybe crazy is exactly what we need.

Chapter 35

The gates of the main barracks come into view as the truck barrels down the road, and I already want to throw up.

I never thought about what my last day on this earth would be like, but if you had asked me to picture it, I would have probably described something boring.

Trivial.

Uneventful.

Natural.

Never in a million years would 'drive into an enemy stronghold to sabotage their master plans and sacrifice myself' be anywhere near the top of the list.

Yet here we are.

Every inch closer to the main base feels like an eternity, and I wipe the sweat from my palms on my shirt. Pulling up to the gates, I roll down the window and peer down at the soldier before me. "Let me in on Deliom's orders."

The first time I'd used Sitri's magic like this, I hadn't noticed a thing, but when I'd used it on Lennard to send him away, I tasted it on my tongue.

Like a hint of sweetness gracing my taste buds, and I click my teeth as the soldier guarding the gate gestures to the others to open them.

That was way too easy.

The base seems more busy than usual, with soldiers and their units travelling in groups from one building to the next. There's a very real possibility that what I'm about to do will result in many of them dying, and I swallow hard.

A thick layer of guilt washes over me as I remember Sitri saying taking lives was not enjoyable.

Sure, it might not be *enjoyable* to take lives, but to see their operations halted or paused? That is satisfying.

Killing them is more of a necessity than anything close to pleasurable.

I park the truck near the main entrance with the memory of meeting Fredrick and the others for the first time still fresh in my mind.

It's an odd feeling to remember the calmer moments before everything changed.

Turning the ignition off, silence falls around me, and I suck in a deep breath.

Deliom is gone, but I probably only have another few minutes before word spreads of his death, along with who caused it.

I keep a quick pace, hurrying through the front doors, before scanning my badge at the front. But, instead of heading straight for the conference room, I cut left toward the media office.

The walk is short, but busy as people walk past, giving me a nod that I quickly return. I would have thought, given my reason for being here, I'd be more nervous, but when I walked through the front doors, a sense of calm washed over me. It's like since I'd made my decision, every step I've taken has been one of confidence.

Because truth be told, part of me is eager to get this over with.

Whether because of my desire to free Sitri or to end this war for once and for all, I don't know.

Probably both.

Scanning my badge at the door to the media office, it beeps and a red light flashes.

Denied.

Interesting.

I knock three times, hearing a chair roll on the other side before footsteps grow closer. The door opens a few inches and Martin, one of the producers, peers out from the other side.

His eyes widen when he sees me, and I know I need to act fast.

"Let me in and help convince the others that Deliom gave us orders to publish this story." Sweetness bursts on my tongue, and his pupils dilate before he nods.

"Yeah, sure. Guys—" He opens the door wide and turns around. "New orders direct from the General. We've got a breaking news story to pivot to."

Desks covered with papers, coffee cups and computer equipment fill the room, and I look at a handful of curious faces. Heads turn in my direction, and a middle-aged woman near the back perks up.

"Do we have Thornton's approval to run it? Has it run through edits?"

My mouth drops open, and before I can tell her the entire segment is ready to publish, Martin nods his head. "We have everything we need. Just get your shit together and be ready to run it, Linda."

God, Sitri's power is cool.

Martin turns to me and offers his hand between us. "Assuming you have it stored on a drive?"

I nod, reaching into my bra for the small flash drive. Placing the tiny device in his palm, he turns and breezes away, plugging it into the computer.

"Is this media to be syndicated to our other networks?" Linda asks, typing away at her computer.

"Yes." I whisper, knowing I only manipulated one person in this room, but all of them have quickly fallen in line. This is the second time using Sitri's power this way has had a domino effect, where I only coerce one, but the impact trickles down.

I file that information away for later.

"Which networks?" Linda looks over at her monitor, waiting for my answer.

My gaze flicks at Martin, and my heart thrums steadily in my chest. "All of them."

~

After leaving the media office confident that within the hour, the whole truth will be broadcast to as many networks as possible, I'm still riding the high of my success as I approach the conference room.

I still don't entirely know what the hell I'm going to do once I'm inside, but apparently I'm good at improvisation.

The long corridor from the media office branches out, with the conference room being at the far end on the right. I'm five minutes late, and it'll take some convincing to get security to let me inside.

That much I know.

It's what I'm going to say once I'm able to tell my story. That's the part I'm most concerned about.

Turning the corner, two tall security guards stand on either side of the double doors, and I walk up to them with more confidence than I have any right to feel.

The first security guard puts his palm up. "No more reporters are allowed in."

Glancing between them, my pulse hikes. "Let me in, so I can address our entire nation, per Deliom's orders. I am not to be interrupted."

I have no idea if I need to use him as a crutch for validity as something like sugar coats my mouth, but I figure it can't hurt. The guards both nod and step aside, with one stretching his arm out to tug the door open.

"Right this way, ma'am."

The doors open and a handful of heads turn to look at me as Phillip, the foreign affairs minister, stands at the podium. Cameras aimed at him are rolling, but I can hardly hear the drivel he spews from the teleprompter.

I pick up a "peace" here and a "negotiation" there, but none of it means anything to me. Not when I know without a shadow of a doubt that everything he's saying is lies.

There's a clear path to my left behind the cameras, and I follow it, taking long strides toward the front where security stands near the steps. When I go to walk past, his hand in front of me, and I repeat my statement from the others.

By the time I'm walking up the steps, it's only taken me a minute to get to the lectern, and Phillip stares at me with wide eyes. "What are you—?"

"Step aside, Phillip, I have orders."

The taste of sugar fills my mouth, and his eyes glaze over as he nods, stepping over near security to make room for me as I take my place behind the microphone.

Cameras pan to me, some flashes go off, and I exhale a breath. *Here we go.*

"Hello everyone. I'm here to address our nation about the atrocities that have been occurring here for months—years even." More photos snap with flashes of light, nearly blinding me as I look into the lens directed at me. "We are being lied to, but I am here to tell everyone the truth."

Phillip gasps and stutters toward the stage, but the security guard I'd coerced stops him as I bite back a smile. "Our military has been killing innocent civilians in Kharidia—displacing families, bombing without discretion, and gunning women and children down in the streets. By now, all news outlets should be running a story—the true story—that I sent to them. I know the atrocities are all true because I witnessed it firsthand."

Not a single reporter raises their hand as I continue. "There was a rumor of a magic user causing horrific acts, but after thorough investigation, I uncovered that this magic user was not causing any of the tragedies occurring here, nor was he servilian, but he is yet another species of beings that lives among us."

That should cover servilians from being targeted. "Your news media has been purchased, bought out by the highest bidder, and all they want is to keep you negligent. They don't want you to not see Kharidian's truth because it will show you the terrible things that ***our military*** is doing in the name of God. Resistance is here, but we need your help."

God, please let this work. "Everyone watching this today at home must wake up and help others see Maris Sylvara's story about how our government is killing people en masse. Wake up and join the resistance fighting for the good of humanity. It is not enough to be aware of the crimes they're committing, but we must act, and we must act ***now***. Even through their efforts to break him, the magic user that protected so many Kharidians is alive, and yet ***we, the people***, are the ones who hold the power to create change."

The sugar on my tongue is a relief that floods my veins, but I hardly get a moment to enjoy it as a door bursts open. Cameras pan to the soldiers that file in, their barrels pointing in my direction.

Shit. "See? One must ask—why are they ***so*** afraid of little ol' me?"

One heartbeat passes, then two, and on the third, I drop behind the lectern just as a shot rings out into the air.

Two shots follow before I realize that the security guards I used Sitri's magic on are returning fire on the soldiers, and I feel an arm wrap around me. My head snaps to see the security guard from the steps, and he ushers me toward the back wall. Lifting the curtain, he shoves a small panel open and pushes me first through the hidden exit.

We hardly get a few feet in when another shot whizzes past me, the security guard jerks, and I don't need to look to know he's been hit. Leaving the chaos behind, I dash further into the small tunnel and out of view from everyone in the conference room.

A modicum of guilt eats away at the back of my mind, but I shove it away.

They were all going to die here, anyway.

I sprint away from the madness with Sitri's fires erupting behind me to clear my escape, blocking the tunnel with a wall of flame. The tunnel finally ends with a dimly lit door, and I shove it open, hurling myself through it and into an empty hallway.

When shouting erupts to my left, I sprint in the opposite direction, my limbs burning as much as my lungs, and the adrenaline that had pumped through me in the conference room has made my legs jittery and unsteady.

Cardio was never my forte, and with so much exertion so fast, I desperately need a break.

I slow to a stop when I make it to the cafeteria, my chest heaving as the TVs lining the room play the piece from my flash drive, and my heart stutters.

Time to enact part two of this plan.

An alarm goes off as garbled voices from countless radios fill the air, and I know I'm out of time.

So I run.

Sprinting down the lesser traveled hallways I vaguely remember from my limited time here, my lungs burn and every muscle in my body aches until I finally push past the doors into the main concourse.

From here, the five primary buildings surround this entrance like points of a star, and I hurl myself to the center pavement.

When movement up ahead catches my attention, I slow to a stop. Gulping down desperate breaths, I turn in a circle, seeing soldiers with weapons drawn, appearing between each building. My gaze sweeps from one to the other, and through every window, even on the roof of each one, I see a barrel pointed at me. A bright red light blinds me as quick as it's gone, I glance down to see multiple lasers pointed at my chest.

I swallow against the lump in my throat.

This is it.

"Maris Sylvara, put your hands up." A voice far away yells out. Where it comes from, I'm not sure, nor do I really care.

Raising my hands in surrender, I turn in a full circle to see myself completely surrounded, with more uniformed soldiers pouring from the main barracks.

In some way, I'm surprised to see they still have so many numbers after Sitri had forced his way in to rescue me. Then again, I don't know that he hadn't spared as many as possible.

Sitri never struck me as someone who blames the hand for the will of the mind.

I have come to realize that I am not that considerate.

"Get on the ground, correspondent." Another voice yells, though they all seem hesitant to get anywhere near me.

Probably a smart move.

With so many weapons pointed in my direction, I resign myself to knowing that this might be my end, but I can only hope that my story will turn from just an ember to an uncontrollable wildfire that even these assholes can't control.

Just like Sitri said... though I doubt this was what he was wanting.

I would have been a fool to think it could have ended any other way, I suppose.

Not when I'm not bound by the same rules as Sitri.

As I gaze into the hard eyes of the masked soldiers, a tear rolls down my cheek when I realize the person I'm searching for is not here.

No, those golden amber irises won't be amongst the crowd because he's unconscious and under Anne's care right now.

The only person who needs or deserves saving right now is him, and I'm the only one who can give him a future free of war.

Even if it means I won't be in it.

That might be the hardest part to come to terms with, and I know I'm being entirely selfish by hoping for anything different.

Resolve weighs my stomach down like a cement block rooted to the core of the earth, and I sink down to my knees as the soldiers take a step closer.

Each second feels like an eternity, and I watch the line of armed men from my peripherals.

"Hands on the ground!" One soldier shouts, and I immediately comply, bracing myself on all fours as a tear slides down my nose.

My fingers curl into the concrete that melts beneath my touch, and I bury them into the earth. Footsteps grow closer, and it's not until they're right beside me that it happens.

The earth rumbles at first before it fractures in a line mere feet in front of me. Within seconds, the gaping crevice erupts with flame, and columns spiral into the air, coiling around each other like a tornado summoned from the depths of hell itself.

If I were religious, the sight of it might have made me think that Lucifer had sundered the earth to come to claim my soul himself.

The two torrents of fire dance together before more flames engulf the surrounding area, and screams fill the air in earnest as people get caught up in it.

Shots ring out in stuttered thunderous bursts, with a couple of bullets whizzing past me, but I don't let myself lose focus. I consciously urge Sitri's flames to go where my eyes can't see, feeling his power like an extra limb reaching further and further, like spinning torrents of destruction.

I hear the next series of shots before I feel them, still engrossed in consuming every living being in this God damned barracks and the surrounding pavilions. It's not until a sudden sharp punch hits my bicep like a sledgehammer, another slams into my thigh and my left hip, and that's when I realize I've been hit.

Before the pain can register, I shift my weight to my right side, and urge Sitri's flames to help me as more screams fill the air.

My body screams in pain, but I can't give in to it now.

Only death himself could stop me from finishing what I've started.

For him.

Tears pour from my eyes, mixing with the crimson pooled beneath me, but I push Sitri's magic further, urging it to cover every inch of the base.

But it's not enough.

It won't be enough until every base of this military operation is gone.

I can feel it now, the push and pull of my will to its response, like a whispered question and a breeze against my soul in answering. I don't need to look up to see the devastation it has brought to the barracks, but if it obeyed my will, it would be reduced to ash by now.

It's not long before the distant screams quiet, the random gunfire ceases, and my head's sagged against the ground with my breathing labored. My uninjured leg burns as I strain to keep my weight off the other, and with each passing second, I can feel the blood draining from my body.

Considering the scope of what I just did, something tells me this might be exhaustion from the overuse of magic more than just destroying everything around me.

Then again, I've never been shot multiple times, so it's very possible that could be what's causing me to feel like I could fall into an eternity of sleep.

Distantly, I can still feel the caress of his magic, like a ghost in my soul—the way Sitri's magic surged in response to my call, destroying not one, not two, not three, but all the enemy's encampments across Kharidia simultaneously.

In the beginning, I'd only intended to cut the head off the snake, but when Sitri's magic worked in the conference room, I knew I had to try.

Thank God that I did.

With no encampments left, and word having spread about the truth of their presence here, then maybe, just *maybe*, the civilians—and Sitri—will have a chance at a real life.

My chest squeezes painfully at the thought of him, and I choke back a sob as I shift to take the weight off my hip. My vision blurs from the pain as I stare at the bloodied, ash-covered ground.

There's a dulled note of panic as I don't see an end to the blood pouring from my body, but there's nothing I can do about it now—not when my body is broken, and Sitri's magic can't heal me.

Hurried footsteps approach to my right, and I jerk back onto my heel with a wince, ignoring the way my hips scream in protest.

A small column of flame hurtles toward the newcomer, they surge forward before colliding—and absorbing—into a bare chest.

My attention rises slowly to where two irises burning bright like sunlight gaze back at me.

If I wasn't already dying, I think my heart might stop beating, but the relief that floods me when I see him awake and unharmed is enough to keep me going at least a little longer.

The world spins and my muscles tremble beneath my weight as tears pour from my eyes. "Thank God." I whisper, collapsing as my strength gives out.

Before my head hits the ground, Sitri's caught me, hauling me into his arms with his brows furrowed. The mix of concern and panic etched into his features sends a pang of guilt through me as I reach for his face.

My numb fingertips just graze the stubble along his jaw before my strength wanes and my arm falls to my chest.

"I need to get the bullet out, Maris." He says in a hurry, and I follow his gaze to my thigh where crimson pours steadily. "If I don't, you'll just keep bleeding out."

His bright gaze meets mine, and I can tell he's pissed, even if he's relieved that I'm not dead yet.

I nod, and he presses his forehead to mine before I feel the pressure of his fingers digging into my thigh. The pain that follows makes me cry out before my voice cracks, and I suck in a desperate breath.

The pressure suddenly releases, and he pulls out a warped bullet as I pant, fighting the wave of nausea that's come over me.

The pain is a stark contrast to the numbness in my limbs from blood loss, so I still welcome it.

It's a sign that I'm alive, at the very least.

"That's it?" I whisper sarcastically between relieved breaths.

As if the universe is playing a cruel game, something in my hip cracks like it just popped into place, and my chest heaves. I clutch my side as Sitri presses his lips to my hair.

"What the hell were you thinking, Maris?" He whispers, glancing over my body once more before a searing pain radiates from each of the bullet wounds.

"I had a plan." I whisper between pained breaths, and his eyes flash in warning.

"You nearly died. What if I hadn't woken up? What if I couldn't reach you in time? What if they had caught you?" He searches my face, and emotions constrict my throat. "You think you can just show up in my life, change everything and then disappear?"

My lips part, but he just shakes his head. "Caass gave me your message while I was still unconscious, Maris. That was enough to wake me from the edge of death to come find you. Now, I'll be damned three times over if I don't hear it from your lips."

The name doesn't sound familiar, and I frown. "Caass?"

His brow tugs up before his lips twitch. "Lennard."

"Oh." I whisper, and my last words to Lennard–Caass–come flooding back as my cheeks burn.

Sitri must notice as he leans in, pressing his forehead to mine. "Say it, Maris." He whispers, sending a shiver down my spine.

Feeling his breath skate over my skin, my chest flutters. "I love you."

His head rolls to the side, but he keeps his forehead pressed to mine as his grip tightens on me. "Again."

"I lo—" His lips crash against mine, and he hauls me further into him, clutching me against his chest. My limbs are still too weak to do much, but I dig my nails into his chest as he nips at my bottom lip.

I inhale a sharp breath as he deepens our kiss, and if I didn't know better, I'd have thought that maybe I did die, and this is my own personal heaven.

In five minutes I've gone from thinking it's my time—that this was the end for me—to being in Sitri's arms, and inarguably there's nowhere else I'd rather be.

Somehow, in all of this chaos, we ended up with one of the very few best-case scenarios. I don't know who to thank for this, but some odd part of me wonders if God had anything to do with it.

When Sitri breaks our kiss, my lips are swollen, I'm out of breath and the feeling in my limbs has blissfully returned as desire pulses through me.

Even when they bury my corpse six feet underground, I don't think I'll stop wanting him.

"We should get you to Anne." Sitri whispers, and I lean in to press my lips to his.

Sitri's ability to heal fast, and his flame has already stopped the bleeding and closed the bullet wound in my bicep, leaving me to believe it's the same for the other two.

I don't care enough to look, though.

So I protest leaving this spot by wrapping my hand around the back of his neck, and deepening our kiss.

A low sound rumbles from his chest, and whatever arguments he had dies on his lips as he shifts to lie me on my back. Ignoring the dulled pain in my thigh, I lean toward him as hovers on top of me.

The desperate need to be close, driven by the fear of what we almost lost, makes my desperation for him a beast that I don't want to tame.

He must feel it too, the sudden shift from being grateful, to wanton claiming, because his hips dip to meet mine as I dig my nails into his skin.

He skillfully unbuttons and tugs my pants down before doing the same with his. He only breaks our kiss for a moment before he leans his delicious weight against my hips.

Whether because of my near-death experience or thinking I'd never see him again, I feel especially needy, like I may very well die if I don't feel him inside me in the next minute.

"Never scare me like that again, Maris." He growls against my lips, and I nod as his dick pulsates. Sitri's teeth graze my lip and I gasp as the tip of his dick notches against my pussy.

"Sitri, I swear to God if you don't fuck me—" I whisper against his lips, and without warning, he pushes in hard.

Wincing, he doesn't give me a moment of reprieve to accommodate his size, and even with how wet I already am, he still needs to pull out an inch, only to push in harder.

The raw, desperate need I feel echoes in the way he pushes in rough, animalistic movements until he's buried deep. That's when he finally pauses, searching my face as we both breathe each other's air. "Say it again, Maris." He whispers, easing himself out to the tip.

"I love you—" I breathe, my voice cracking as he slams into me, and my eyes roll back. He fucks me in a way that has his soul bared, with our bodies an aching, unspoken language. Digging my heels into him, he swallows my throaty pleas, and snaps his hips to mine.

He slams into me hard and fast as I lose myself in him. His taste, his scent, his hard body. The way he fucks me into the rigid, unforgiving ground feels more primal than the tenderness I'd felt before, but I revel in it all the same.

Because I know we were so close to losing this.

The ground bites against my bare skin as he picks up his pace, wrapping his arm around my shoulders for leverage, and the angle of his dick hits that delicious spot that brings me to the edge of my orgasm with each thrust.

He slams in once more before he comes, pushing me over the edge, and my entire body goes taut as waves of euphoria crash over me. Sitri kisses me senseless as I ride each aftershock of pleasure, and we both come down from our climax.

By the time he pauses for breath, I'm not sure that I know what day it is, my name or anything else for that matter.

"Did I hurt you?" His sunlight irises search my eyes with a hint of concern, as if anything he could do would cause me pain.

I shake my head, releasing a small laugh. "No. The gunshots hurt me."

His lips twitch, and he wraps his free hand around the small of my back as my eyes flutter shut. "Good thing you heal fast then, but better to get Anne to take a look."

He hauls me upright into his chest, keeping himself buried inside me as my legs tighten around his hips. The wind around us picks up, and I don't need to open my eyes to know he's transported us to our room in Anne's house.

There's still something that's unsettling me, and I pull back to look at him. "Sitri, why did you share your power with me? How did you know we'd need them?"

He searches my face for a long moment before pushing to his feet and carrying me to the bed. "I didn't know it was going to be needed. I just did it as a precaution, and thank fuck I did."

Countless possibilities I never want to consider almost surface, but I shove those thoughts away with force as he lays us both down and presses tender kisses to my collar.

Still buried deep inside of me, he throbs, and I release a contented sigh as he continues to kiss his way up my neck to my jaw.

Reflecting on what he said about God throwing them a lifeline, my eyes slide shut, and I silently offer a thank you into the void of nothing in my mind, hoping God might be listening.

Chapter 36

Two weeks later...

"Looks like that's the last of them." Sitri pats his hand twice on the box of supplies, backing away as two civilians close the tailgate. They give us a wave before walking to the front of the truck.

The engine rumbles to life as my phone rings, and I glance at the random number before answering. "Hello?"

The line is choppy with static but thankfully clears when a voice comes through the speaker. "Hi, Ms. Sylvara. My name is Dylan Greene, and I'm your former manager, Ben Thornton's replacement. I'm calling to reconnect with you, considering everything that's happened."

My heart sinks into my stomach.

I knew this day was coming. I just hoped it wasn't happening so soon.

My salary, along with the revenue generated from the livestream, has been our primary source of income to help get the civilians what they need to rebuild.

Well, along with Sitri's, of course, but I demanded for days that he let me try to do this with my income, only to protect his finance accounts and identity as much as possible.

With how deep the corruption runs, who knows what they'd try if they knew.

"Oh, uh, right. Nice to meet you, Mr. Greene."

Sitri's eyes narrow, but he stays quiet at my side and I feel like I'm going to be sick.

"Ms. Sylvara, it's my understanding that you submitted the viral piece and pushed it for publishing before going on national news to expose the countless war crimes and extermination of Kharidians that have since gone viral on media and news outlets?"

Shit.

The lump in my throat grows, and I lock eyes with Sitri. "Yeah, that was me." My voice wavers and I swallow hard as Sitri's arm wraps around my shoulders, pulling me into him. His chest crowds my vision as the wind picks up around us, and when he sinks to his knees in front of me, my eyes widen.

The familiar sight of our room at Anne's house makes my heart stutter, and I nearly forget there's someone on the phone when static echoes from the receiver and clears.

"Well, first off, on behalf of us all here at News Alliance, we wanted to say thank you for your continuous commitment to reporting news with integrity."

Sitri gazes up at me as he unbuttons my pants and tugs them down, before doing the same with my underwear. He drags the material off before lifting my bare leg over his shoulder.

His free hand grasps mine, he laces our fingers together, and I choke down a gasp when his mouth is on me.

God, this fucking demon.

"Ms. Sylvara?"

Oh, shit. "Yes, sorry. Uh, thank you."

Sitri does something that should be wholly illegal with his tongue, and I nearly lose my balance as my thighs twitch. If it weren't for his grip on my hand, I'd have already toppled over by now.

"Secondly, we at News Alliance wanted to inform you that—" *Here we go.* "—we were so moved by the piece, in addition to the heroic effort you made during the press conference, that we would like to offer you a fifteen percent bonus."

If Sitri wasn't already making my heart rate go a mile per minute, I'm nearly certain it would have stopped.

"I'm sorry, I think I may have misheard you," I breathe. "Did you just say I'm getting a bonus?"

Greene chuckles, and Sitri's fingers slide into me as I squeeze his other hand. "Ms. Sylvara, have you had *any* access to the news back home?"

My eyes threaten to roll back as Sitri adds another finger. "No." I breathe, biting my lip to stay silent after.

Greene chuckles, and I can hear the smile on his face as I struggle to maintain composure, which is proving more and more difficult as pleasure builds in my core.

"Ms. Sylvara, your influence over the last two weeks sparked protests all over the world. Every state in our country has had protests organized every day, stocks crashed from boycotts, international trade has been affected, investigations have been launched nationally and internationally... We even saw protests outside our headquarters from people calling on us to protect your employment."

My eyes widen, and I nearly drop my phone. *This can't be real life.*

"It's even sparked political movements, with polls shifting drastically based on whether candidates had spoken out about the conflict." Desire builds in my core, and my mind's a chaotic mess as I move to retract my leg from Sitri's shoulder.

I need to think, and I can't think when he's about to make me come.

The moment I gain a small amount of distance, he tightens his grip on me. He hits a spot that makes my entire body shudder. I gasp and my phone drops to the ground.

My eyes roll back as he continues to coax pleasure from my body, and by the time I'm spent, there's a metallic tang in my mouth from biting the inside of my cheek to remain quiet.

"Ms. Sylvara, are you there?"

Sitri pulls back to ease my leg to the ground and reaches over to pass my phone to me. I shakily bring it to my ear as he places each finger in his mouth, sucking my arousal off as he waits for me.

"Yes, sorry. I'm here, I'm just in shock." I say quietly, swallowing against my heartbeat that still rages in my ears as I come down from my orgasm.

"Well, I'm glad I was the one to give you the news. We'd like to have you continue to gather information for a piece that shows how things are going in the region as the civilians there recover from the oppression they faced. Would that be something you're interested in?"

Sitri stands to his full height and walks me backward until my legs hit the bed.

"Yes." I breathe, and Sitri crowds my space, using his arms to support me as he eases me back onto the bed.

"Great. I'll email you the details—" I click to end the call before he can continue, and Sitri crawls over me.

"It worked." I whisper, a flood of relief crashing over me as his bright eyes search my face. "They saw everything. Change is happening, Sitri."

"And you did that." He says proudly, his fingertips shifting the hair from my face.

I laugh quietly and shake my head. "Giving me your power is not me doing it."

He raises a brow. "I would still be imprisoned if you hadn't shown up and literally burned everything to the ground, so yes, you did it yourself."

I know he's giving me more credit than I deserve, but I won't argue with him on semantics. Not when he's looking at me like he wants to devour me again.

Sitri unbuttons his pants and slides them down his legs before leaning over me once more. "Now, if you don't mind, I plan to spend the next few days showing you my own personal form of appreciation." He presses his lips to mine, and I taste both of us on my tongue as his dick notches against my pussy.

Pushing in, he groans, and desire pools in my core as he throbs hungrily.

With the war over, I shouldn't be surprised that a demon of love would choose to spend his time like this.

Not that I'll ever complain.

But I suppose I'll have to get used to it... and maybe purchase lubricant.

Epilogue

"Are you sure about this?"

Sitri appears from the walk-in closet, and my core turns molten. His white dress shirt disappears beneath the leather belt holding his deliciously perfect fitting dress pants. He meets my gaze with a smirk and buttons his shirt up to his collar.

"It will be fine, Maris." He says gently, tugging his black vest over his shoulders and buttoning it. "Anyone would be a fool to attack either of us, especially there."

I chew the inside of my lip and clasp my hands together to keep myself from wringing them.

When we'd gotten invited to a banquet in California to be guests of honor among countless high profile celebrities and politicians, I'd originally wanted to decline.

Sitri thought it would be a good idea to go, especially considering it might be one of the few times he'd get to see his brother, Oro, without drawing too much attention. Besides, with our role in exposing the lies the public had been told, us attending is more of a statement than anything else.

"Promise me you'll stay close?" I whisper, and his features soften as he closes the distance between us. His hands glide across the smooth material of my silken dress, and he shifts a long stray curl of hair behind my shoulder.

"I'll stay by your side," he murmurs, pressing his lips to my temple as my eyes flutter shut. "Besides, you're the flight risk, not me."

I can't help the laugh that escapes me, and he lifts my chin with his knuckle to tilt my head toward his.

"My brother doesn't make special requests often, Maris, so if he asked us to be there..."

I nod in response. "Yes, yes, then we go. I'm allowed to be uncomfortable with the risk, though."

He just chuckles and presses his lips to mine. "It will be over before you know it."

My stomach twists as he moves to the dresser to get the car keys, offering his hand between us, and I step in close to slide my palm into his.

I nearly died destroying multiple military encampments.

I can live through a banquet filled with politicians.

... Hopefully.

Acknowledgements

I have to first, again, say a huge thank you to Amanda Dumky for the insanely gorgeous cover. I will forever appreciate your immense talent more than you will ever possibly know.

A huge thank you to my husband, who supports all my chaotic hobbies, endeavors and passions without a second thought. I love you to the moon and back. In all the romances I write, there's always so many layers of the devotion and undying love that you surround me with that inspires these connections, and I will never take that for granted.

Thank you to my street team for being so supportive, hyping me up even when I was lost in the sauce, and always bringing excitement to my life. You are all beautiful humans and I cannot tell you how thankful I am to have you all in my life.

Lastly, much like with my Unbroken series, thank you to all the readers who decided to give this new series a chance. I can't promise it's the most well written, or well written at all... but I, as with many authors, put a piece of myself into my work, and taking the time to read it... well that may be the best gift of all.

It's just my hope that you enjoyed it, even if only for a moment before you move on to your next adventure.

Other Works by Aella C Grey

The Unbroken Series
> Shadows of Dusk (Unbroken Book 1)
> Light of Dawn (Unbroken Book 2)

Prince of Hell Series
> Summoned (Prince of Hell Book 1)
> Barred (Prince of Hell Book 2)
> Convalesced (Prince of Hell Book 3)
> Syndicated (Prince of Hell Book 4)
> Classified (Prince of Hell Book 5)

Eclipsed Souls Series
> Wings of Doubt (Eclipsed Souls Book 1)
> Obsidian Flames (Eclipsed Souls Book 2)
> Ascent of the Fallen (Eclipsed Souls Book 3)